UNEASY ALLIANCE

"In return for my silence about your treachery, I wish to exact an oath—a firm and solemn Sword Oath—from you, my lord."

Byruhn frowned. "What sort of oath, Duke Bili? Beware, I do not take threats lightly."

"Nor, I would hope," replied Bili, "would my lord take his sworn Sword Oath lightly. What I want is your oath that you never again, *no matter what the circumstances*, will make of me and my squadron military slaves bound by mental fetters and set to prosecute the wars of your kingdom. Will my lord so swear?"

Byruhn smiled coldly. "If you so distrust me, feel me to be without honor, what makes you think that I will abide by any oath, even a Sword Oath?"

"Because, my prince, you are a noble Sword-Brother, an Initiate. You know as well as I that if you should break the oath, that oath will kill you. . . ."

Great Science Fiction by Robert Adams from SIGNET

Bili the Axe

A Horseclans Novel

by
Robert Adams

A SIGNET BOOK

NEW AMERICAN LIBRARY

NAL BOOKS ARE AVAILABLE AT QUANTITY DISCOUNTS WHEN USED
TO PROMOTE PRODUCTS OR SERVICES. FOR INFORMATION PLEASE
WRITE TO PREMIUM MARKETING DIVISION. NEW AMERICAN LIBRARY.
1633 BROADWAY. NEW YORK. NEW YORK 10019.

SIGNET TRADEMARK REG. U.S. PAT. OFF. AND FOREIGN COUNTRIES
REGISTERED TRADEMARK—MARCA REGISTRADA
HECHO EN CHICAGO. U.S.A.

SIGNET, SIGNET CLASSIC, MENTOR, PLUME, MERIDIAN AND NAL BOOKS
are published by New American Library,
1633 Broadway, New York, New York 10019

First Printing, January, 1983

4   5   6   7   8   9   10   11   12

PRINTED IN THE UNITED STATES OF AMERICA

For Dr. Jerry Pournelle, a dedicated and motivated man whom I admire and respect;

For Wilson Tucker and the *real* Bob Tucker, boozing buddies whom I do not see nearly often enough;

For Joe and Gay Haldeman;

For Scott Bizar,

and for all the fine folk of the Chattanooga Science Fiction Society.

PROLOGUE

Those who spoke did not think the dying old man could hear them, but he could. Despite the drugs and other arts which the Zahrtohgahn physicians had administered to him to eliminate the pain of his infected wounds, Prince Bili Morguhn of Karaleenos could still hear his overlord and the others who now were discussing his long, long life and his imminent demise.

"If only he had been as are we," said Bili's half brother, the Undying Lord Tim Sanderz. "As it was, I had hoped for long, as he got older and older and stayed fit and far more hale than many far younger men . . ." He sighed sadly.

"No more than I had hoped, Tim," said the Undying High Lord Milo of Morai, concern for his realm mingling with the sorrow in his eyes and tone. "Bili of Morguhn is a remarkable man in a multitude of ways, and he's going to be devilish hard to replace. I'm sure that you and Giliahna will give it your best shot, but even with your great natural gifts and abilities, you are going to find it damned hard to fill the shoes of Bili the Axe."

Now it was the High Lord who sighed and sadly shook his head. "And it's my fault, really. Long years ago I knew that I should start grooming a likely man—if such exists—to take over the Principality of Karaleenos when Bili died or became too ill or senile to longer handle it properly, but he just lived on and on and on, never becoming even marginally inefficient, the reins of all the affairs of the principality always tightly in hand. So it was so much easier for me to just leave it all to him, who did it so well, and apply my own efforts to other affairs in other places, rationalizing falsely, deluding myself with the thought that it was better not to give offense to this most valuable and valued vassal.''

He sighed again. ''And now it's too late to take more than stopgap measures. At least, you'll have old Lehzlee for a few more years, he has been Bili's right hand for the last twenty or so years. I'll send your great-grandnephew, Djaik Sanderz of Morguhn, down here from Theesispolis for a farspeaker. It's possible that you'll have widespread support from Bili's people, since you're related to him, but don't go wasting a lot of time trying to woo or win over any who seem hostile or uncooperative—replace them immediately they demonstrate an unwillingness to change their ways to suit the new regime. Your strength lies in the west, among your relatives, so recruit there, in the western duchies and the Ahrmehnee *stahn*—Morguhn, Sanderz-Vawn, Baikuh, Skaht, and Kamruhn—and you might farspeak Prince Roodee of Kuhmbuhluhn; perhaps he has some likely men he can send you. You two are related, aren't you?''

''Rather distantly,'' replied Tim. ''His grandmother . . . no, great-grandmother, I think . . . was my father's get by his second wife, Mehleena, the fat, treacherous sow. Princess Deeahna was the youngest of that brood, too young to have absorbed very much of her mother's madness, religious fanaticism and treason; Giliahna had promised the then prince, her stepson, a bride of her own blood, and when this Deeahna was old enough, she was sent to Kuhmbuhluhn.

''The Princess and young Speeros Sanderz-Vawn were the only two of that pack who didn't die in disgrace. As you know, Bili had Mehleena's eldest, that buggering swine Myron, impaled right after that rebellion . . . after suitable public torture and maiming, of course. And although I was roundly criticized and castigated for the deed, I saw the young bitch who slew my sergeant so treacherously atop a stake, too. The eldest daughter, Dohlohrehz, married an Ahrmehnee who beat her to death when he caught her in bed with another man.''

''And what of this brother, Speeros? Did he find a prince charming to marry, too?'' queried Milo a bit caustically.

Tim shook his head. ''For some reason, Speeros shared none of the insanity and perversions of his mother and elder brother. Except for his height and big-boned build, he didn't

2

even look Ehleen. He and his sisters were taken as wards by various Clan Sanderz kith and reared by them and Chief Tahm, although, you may recall, Gil had little Deeahna brought up to Theesispolis a couple of years before she sent her to wed Prince Gy of Kuhmbuhluhn. It was Chief Tahm found a husband for Dohlohrehz amongst his Ahrmehnee kin. But even before either of the girls were placed, Speeros had ridden up to Goohm and enlisted in a squadron of dragoons—*enlisted,* mind you, the third-eldest surviving son of a Kindred *thoheeks.*''

Milo's dark brows rose. "Oh, yes, I'm beginning to recall. I gave that man a Golden Cat, Third Class, and a commission, didn't I? But . . . but I seem to recall that he died a *thoheeks* himself, Tim.''

"Just so.'' The blond man nodded briskly. "By the time you sent me to take over the cavalry arm of the army, that boy had clawed his way to a senior sergeantcy in the *lamtha* troop of the *Kóhkeenos F'tehró* Squadron. They and two battalions of the Seventeenth Regiment of Heavy Infantry held the whole damned West Ahfut Tribe off for almost two weeks after the disaster at Bleak Meadow.''

Milo's lips tightened at the grim old memories. "Better than six regiments of my Regulars, wiped out to the last man! That idiotic swine of a *Strahteegos* Tohnyos of Kahvahpolis never knew how lucky he was to die with those men he so stupidly misled; if he'd come back alive, I'd have had the bastard impaled before the entire army . . . on a thick, blunt stake, at that!

"But that stand that was made at Maizuhn Gap was magnificent. There's no other word fit to describe it, Tim. Three battered, understrength units, plus a handful of packers and engineers and various other service-troop types, holding off in the neighborhood of ten thousand blood-mad mountain tribesmen for the time it took the westernmost settlements to prepare for trouble and relief columns to get within striking range.

"But if the stand was magnificent, how does one describe that fighting withdrawal from the Gap? It was this Speeros commanded the withdrawal, wasn't it?''

"Yes. By that time, he was the highest-ranking man left in any of the units who was capable of command; the only two

3

officers not then dead were too seriously wounded to matter. He had them retreat slowly and in excellent order, and he saw the mountaineers bleed well for every rod and mile of the way, too. He made it back to Thorohspolis with about a thousand foot and almost half the original strength of the squadron.

"I had ridden up with a strong advance party of the relief column, Milo, so I was there when those bloody, filthy, unshaven, ragamuffin heros marched into the city—and I'm here to tell you that they *marched* in, with their drums marking the pace and their tattered banners unfurled, and a stirring sight that was. I don't think there was a man or horse that wasn't wounded in some way or other, Milo, yet even some of them who were hobbling along on makeshift crutches did their pitiful damnedest to strut.

"Speeros formally turned over his assumed command to me, then dropped his well-nicked saber and tumbled from off his horse. My surgeon found no less than nine wounds on that man's body, Milo, two of them so serious and so long untended that it was for long doubtful he would even live."

"As I remember, now," said Milo, "he looked none too hale when I put the chain of that Cat over his head. He retired soon after that, didn't he?"

Tim shook his head. "Yes, he retired, but not on account of those wounds. He served on at least two more campaigns in his new rank of squadron commander, but then Tahm of Lion Mountain died without issue and Clan Sanderz of Vawn chose Speeros to replace him as chief."

"What sort of officer did he turn out to be, did you hear?" asked Milo. "As I recall, after all these years, it's damned seldom I've heard a man's Cat cheered as enthusiastically as was his that day at Goohm."

"Most spoke very highly of Colonel Speeros. Those few who did not were Academy officers who dislike and distrust a mustang and always show it," Tim replied, adding, "His last campaign before he retired and returned to become Chief of Sanderz-Vawn was directly under my command, and I can recall no slightest reason to complain of his or his squadron's performance; that was the year we finally crushed the Western Ahfut Tribe, when we took back those standards they'd taken at Bleak Meadow."

4

"Well," grumbled Milo, "if lose a good senior officer I must, I'd far liefer he become a noble administrator for the Confederation than a useless corpse. I assume he was a good *thoheeks?*"

"Those few who could recall our late father—his and mine—likened Speeros to him. They said that he was hard but unstintingly fair in his treatment of all. Before he died, even poor old Bili over there had forgiven Chief Speeros his treasonous maternal antecedents and begun to not only address him as cousin, but even have him up here on occasion for hunts and the like."

"He wed and bred, then, did he?" inquired Milo. "You said earlier that one of his descendants is now chief."

Tim nodded again. "Yes, one of his wives was a noblewoman of Getzburk, who had been a member of the entourage of his sister, the Princess Deeahna of Kuhmbuhluhn; another—he had three wives, two of whom survived him—was a girl of the Vrainyuhn Tribe, an Ahrmehnee relative of his predecessor, Chief Tahm; the third was a Kindred chit, daughter of a far-southwestern *thoheeks*, Chief Breht Kahrtuh of Kahrtuh—you know, Milo, the clan that breeds our war elephants."

"One of the clans," answered Milo. "Clan Djohnz was the first clan in that pursuit; Kahrtuh and Steevuhnz came down there two or three generations later. I know—I was with them."

They talked on, and old Bili would have enjoyed joining in their discussions and reminiscences, but death was very near now, and he could no longer speak aloud easily. He might have used his powerful mindspeak abilities, had not the drugs fuzzed his mind in that direction. So, as the two low voices droned on, he let his mind sink into memories of far happier days of the distant past.

CHAPTER I

Little Djef Morguhn's dark-blue eyes first saw the wan light of Sacred Sun three weeks after the midwinter Sun Birth Festival. The infant was big, too big and big-boned for his mother's narrow pelvis to accommodate, so he was perforce delivered by means of Pah-Elmuh's Kleesahk surgery, when two days of unproductive agony had shown that a natural birthing must result in at least one and possibly two deaths.

One of the narrow-hipped Moon Maidens had already died in her effort to give birth, and Lieutenant Kahndoot had remarked to Bili that this was one of the principal reasons the Maidens of the Moon Goddess had never increased their numbers any more than they had over the centuries—very difficult birthings resulting in the deaths of mothers, infants or both being not at all uncommon to their heritage.

Bili wished that Rahksahnah had been so frank with him, much earlier, when Pah-Elmuh might have easily aborted the babe with no danger to the mother, and he had bluntly said as much.

The Moon Maiden officer, Kahndoot, had just shaken her head and smiled. "No, Dook Bili, our Rahksahnah would have considered that an act of cowardice. Besides, she has come to love you deeply and she longs to be the woman who bears the son who will one day succeed you. Being who she is and what she is, she fears not death, if her death be the price of her victory."

Not that these frank words mollified or in any way brought Bili comfort during the two long days and nights of his woman's torture, while he paced and swore and tried to stop his ears to the moans and groans and strangled-off screams. Finally, after he had entered the prince-chamber by very brute force and seen for himself just how weak Rahksahnah was now become with strain and blood loss and unceasing pain, he had frantically mindcalled Pah-Elmuh.

The midwives, who had so stubbornly resisted his, Bili's, entrance to the room, willingly and gladly surrendered this difficult birthing over to the renowned Kleesahk healer; for, were the truth known, they were frankly despairing. They all watched the huge humanoid's procedures with fascination. So, too, did Bili . . . and Rahksahnah.

Bili was familiar with pain-easing drugs and with the esoteric hypnotism practiced in lieu of drug anesthesia by the black physicians of Zahrtohgah, but use of either of these methods left the patient bereft of consciousness or so near to it that it did not matter greatly. Yet, although still very weak, almost swooning with the long, protracted agonies and substantial losses of blood, Rahksahnah was clearly conscious, her tooth-torn lips trying to form a smile as she looked up at him and the hulking Kleesahks who were readying the instruments Pah-Elmuh would soon use.

Sensing the concern of the young *thoheeks*, the senior Kleesahk chose to use his powerful mindspeak, beaming into Bili's mind a reassurance. "Lord Champion, my way is far better than those of which you think. Yes, I too know of many plants, infusions of various portions of which often serve to ease pain, but most of those plants also are poisonous in large doses, and enough of any of them to ease the pain of birthing would necessarily be very close to a fatal dosage, for the pain of birthing—even of an easy, normal birthing, which this is assuredly not—has few peers in agony of man or Kleesahk or beast.

"However, after the Wise Old Eyeless One taught my father the ways in which he could use his mind to help other beings to heal themselves, my father discovered that both the human and the Teenéhdjook brains, if properly stimulated, can cause the release into the body of certain natural substances which are better at blocking out awareness of pain than even the strongest plant infusions I would dare to use.

"My father passed this arcane knowledge on to me before he died, and you have seen me use it to relieve the sufferings of wounded folk and beasts since the very first day we two met. This is the same art I have just practiced upon your

8

battle companion Rahksahnah. Like the poor female who died before I could be summoned, Rahksahnah's body is ill suited for easy childbirthing. Her hips are as narrow as a male's, and the opening in her pelvis is too small.''

Bili gritted his teeth and beamed his grim question on a restricted, personal level, lest Rahksahnah—also a mind-speaker—overhear. "Then what will you do, Master Elmuh? Slay the babe and remove the body in manageable pieces? If such must be, it must be, for her life is dear to me and this world abounds with broad-hipped human brood stock on whom I can get babes aplenty.''

Pah-Elmuh smiled, showing a mouthful of yellow teeth as large as those of a warhorse, though shaped and arranged much like those of a human. He beamed. "Be not so pessi-mistic, Lord Champion. I have the knowledge and the skill to save both. I shall open the womb and remove the babe, then close up the body again; I have done such before.''

Bili frowned. "But it is very dangerous, is it not? I have heard of such a thing being done, though only rarely, in the lands to the east, whence I came. Often the babe lives, true, but the woman usually dies, soon or late.''

Pah-Elmuh smiled again, admonishing, "Lord Champion, all living things must die, soon or late. But both Rahksahnah and this babe will live. Those of whom you speak, those men of the east, have not a way to bid the patient's body to mend itself of the effects of their surgery, while I do. That it is that removes the deadly danger, here. Watch—you will see.''

And Bili watched, and Rahksahnah watched and the cluster of wise women and midwives all watched the seemingly impossible nimbleness of the Kleesahk's thick, black-nailed, eight-inch fingers. Long, sure strokes of his bronze knives opened one layer after another of skin and flesh and hard, dense muscles to finally expose the near-bursting uterus. But the most amazing thing to all of the human watchers was the almost total lack of blood flow from the incisions.

Bili beamed a question at Pah-Elmuh but was answered just as silently by the surgeon's Kleesahk assistant. "Your pardon, Lord Champion, but Pah-Elmuh's mind is as busy as are his hands, just now. Indeed, his mind it is that is prevent-ing the female's body from bleeding, for he feels that she already has lost more blood than is good for her.''

9

When once the uterus was opened, the babe lay exposed, though enclosed in a sack of tissue. Pah-Elmuh carefully lifted it out, sack and all, severed the umbilicus, then waited while his assistant tied off the cord near to the babe with a short length of strong thread.

When the Kleesahk had stripped off the tissue sac, the midwives and wise women all exclaimed at the size and fair shape of the boy babe and waited for the huge humanoid to impart the slap that would shock the infant into breathing in his first breath of air.

But Pah-Elmuh did no such thing; rather he simply regarded the tiny morsel of human flesh resting upon his broad, hairy hand, while his mind instructed the mind of the babe. Drawing in a deep, deep breath, little Djef Morguhn roared out his rage and indignation. Then the Kleesahk gave this newest member of the squadron of Bili, Chief of Morguhn, to the waiting women, while his huge hands went about the task of closing the deep incision in Rahksahnah's body, that incision still having bled no more than a few drops.

On Djef Morguhn's eighth day of life, Prince Byruhn rode in from the north, with two of his noblemen and a dozen dragoons. All without exception were bundled to the very ears in furs and woolens against the frigid weather, both the men and their mounts showing the effects of their long, hard journey through the deep snows from King's Rest Mountain. Nor, Bili, was quick to note, was that all, for both the prince and the tall, slender nobleman showed new scars, while the short, broad and powerful-looking nobleman walked with a decided limp to which he was clearly not yet accustomed.

While the dragoons proceeded on to the ancient tower keep and Count Steev's servants bore in the baggage of the noble guests and the prince, those three huddled dangerously close to the blazing hearth, sipping at large containers of hot brandied cider, while clouds of steam rose up from their sodden woolens and ice-crusted furs.

Having been early alerted telepathically by Lieutenant Kahndoot, whose Moon Maidens manned the outer works and the ponderous gate, Bili had immediately set the servants assigned to him and Rahksahnah to moving mother, babe and all effects to another room, thus freeing the prince suite for Byruhn. He himself had first alerted Count Sandee, then descended to the first floor to greet his employer and temporary overlord.

Draining off the rest of his brandied cider, Prince Byruhn whuffed twice, then began to unwind from about his thick neck a lengthy, silk-lined woolen muffler, remarking with a twinkle in his blue-green eyes, "Come you not too near us three ere we've bathed and changed clothing, Cousin Bili, for I trow I've as many fleas as my horse has hairs. But wait, come you with us to the bathhouse. I'd know more of your fine campaign, and I'm certain you'd know of mine own."

"They are a singular people, most singular." The prince addressed Bili from the huge, sunken, tile-lined tub now full of steaming, herb-scented water. "They are not Ohyohers originally. Their legends say that they came from somewhere beyond the Great Inland Sea, to the north of Ohyoh, and for the last two or three score years they have been slowly moving south through the Ohyoh country, conquering and looting or at least disrupting every demesne through which they passed, but never trying to settle or occupy their conquests for any long period of time.

"Then, some few years back, a very strong leader arose amongst the native Ohyohers. He organized almost all of the small statelets under his banner and has since been pushing these Skohshuns—as the enemy call themselves—hard, endeavoring to hurry them across the river and out of Ohyoh entirely. He is succeeding, to my detriment, alas."

Bili wrinkled his brow in thought, then interjected, "My lord Byruhn, on my first campaign, in Harzburk, King Gilbuht's army faced a unit of Freefighters who called themselves by the name of Skohshuns or something very like to it. They were all infantry, as I recall, armed with poleaxes and spears, and lightly armored."

The prince nodded, flinging droplets of water from beard and mustache. "Then these afflicting our kingdom are likely of the same ilk, young cousin. Precious few of them go or fight as proper horsemen. The bulk of the ones to the north are armed with overlong pikes, poleaxes, long, spiked maces and a few warhammers; only the sparse cavalrymen carry true swords; the only edge weapon of most is an oversize dirk, three fingers in width and some foot and a half in length, but without a guard of any description.

"The horsemen go in panoplies of decent-quality armor—a mixture of mail and plate, mostly—and their steeds are protected with plate, mail, horn and leather. But the only protection afforded the foot is a brimmed cap of steel, a skimpy breastplate, a pair of leather-and-mail gauntlets and, sometimes, a pair of elbow cops."

The short, broad nobleman, he of the recent leg wound, snorted from his own watery place. "Scant need those bastards have of more armor, Cousin Byruhn, since it's damned seldom any blade or point can get near enough to them to matter. I trow, I can still see those hedges of steel points in my mind's eye, waking or sleeping."

The taller, more slender man, he of the new facial scar, sighed. "Aye, it was a near thing, that sad day. Had our good Kleesahks not clouded the minds of the Skohshuns when they did, all three of us and full many another were dead meat."

"As you may surmise, Cousin Bili," said Prince Byruhn grimly, "Ehlyuht and Pehrsee here are referring to the first, last and, to date, only full-scale battle against the invaders. Because the Skohshuns withdrew to the north after the battle, our New Kuhmbuhluhn folk have been hailing it as a victory, but I and all else who lived through that shambles know better. Full half of the Kuhmbuhluhn forces committed to that field were either killed or wounded."

Bili felt a sinking feeling deep in his gut, knowing without knowing that none of his squadron would be seeing home this year. "Then . . . my lord prince means that half the warriors of the Kingdom of New Kuhmbuhluhn are dead or incapacitated?"

"No, Steel be thanked." Byruhn shook his massive head. "Unseasonal heavy rains had delayed most of the eastern contingents and I was compelled to march and fight without them. With what I have left—with the eastern force of Count Wenlahk, my survivors, such force as Count Sandee can raise—and with, I hope, your fine squadron, dear cousin . . . ?"

Bili arose from his seat and spoke firmly. "My lord prince,

12

we two gentlemen have an agreement between us. I and my folk have fulfilled our end of that agreement to its fullest extent; all of the Ganiks have been slain or driven out of your lands. Now is the time for fulfillment of my lord's part of the agreement; I and mine, most of us, are not mere vagrant mercenaries—we have homes and lands from which we have been long away and to which we desire to return."

The young *thoheeks* thought it politic not to add that with the eastern areas cleared of the last of the outlaw Ganiks, he and his so-called squadron might have ridden east into the Ahrmehnee mountains at any time, with or without Prince Byruhn's leave. Indeed, it had been his thought to order that very thing when winter had suddenly and early clamped down its hard and merciless grip on Sandee's Cot and all lands about. He should have marched east months ago, winter or no winter, he belatedly realized, while this devious royal personage was still licking his wounds in the north.

"Sit down!" the prince ordered without thinking, then added in a softer, friendlier, and familiar tone, "Please resume your place, young cousin, and hear me out. Lest your mind be filled with thoughts of the inconstancy and ingratitude of princes, bear you this in mind: In normal times, my word has never been questioned, nor had need to be. But these be far from normal times; we of New Kuhmbuhluhn have been driven to very bay; already we show blood and the hounds are snapping all around us.

"Now, you are a man much like to me, Bili of Morguhn. I knew that for fact early on. Were your domain as severely threatened as is mine own, I know that you would seek, would demand, aid wherever and from whomever you could find it. I am come south to do just that. But in view of the splendid service you and yours already have rendered me and New Kuhmbuhluhn, I shall not demand, as I might; rather I shall address our assembled squadron at sometime after the nooning tomorrow, allow them to sleep upon it and give me their firm answer on the morning following. Perhaps not all will wish to stay another year and fight another campaign, but I am to the wall. I will take whatever force I can fairly get. The remainder may ride east with my blessing and sincere thanks for last summer's service.

13

"There is a chest of gold among my baggage to pay those who decide to return east. You and I will have to decide upon a fair rate of pay for them, cousin."

Some lingering presentiment nudged still at Bili, telling him that this conversation was a waste of breath, that this prince had no slightest intention of allowing even one of the eastern warriors out of his grasp until his ends were fully achieved. Nonetheless, he said, "My lord prince, while a bit of hard specie will assuredly please the Confederation nobility—both Kindred and Ehleen—I think that the Maidens and the Ahrmehnee would consider their service paid for by the old plate I took from the royal armory here and had adapted to them, that and the horses they now ride, which came from the Sandee's Cot herd or from the Ganiks."

"And those are just the things I cannot afford to let them take out of the kingdom," said Byruhn bluntly. "Am I to properly outfit replacements for those men lost in the fight against the Skohshuns, the armories of the several safe-glens must perforce be stripped to the bare walls.

"The loss of horses, too, was very heavy in that battle. Mountain ponies run half wild in profusion, as you know, but in my present straits I cannot allow any full horse that was not ridden into New Kuhmbuhluhn by your folk to depart the kingdom. Indeed, I hereby offer far better weight of gold for troop horses or, especially, full-trained destriers than they could bring in any other domain."

The prince looked down briefly at his big, chapped hands clasped together on the edge of the bathing pool, then he glanced back up at Bili from beneath his thick red-gray brows. "You must know, of course, young cousin, that I intend to hire away from you—for gold or lands and, may-hap, a title—every sword arm that may succumb to my blandishments? Aye, you have served me fully and well and our original agreement is fulfilled and done and right many would aver that that which I am come here to do is dishonorable and duplicitous—double dealing and ingratitude of a stripe to stink to the very tip-tops of the highest mountains. But know you that I can do no other, at this fell juncture in the affairs of the Kingdom of New Kuhmbuhluhn, so sorely pressed are my house and our folk by these invaders from the north, these Skohshuns."

14

The nobles and officers heard it first from Prince Byruhn at dinner on the day of his arrival. He was completely candid, taking the bulk of the blame for the military disaster squarely on his own hulking shoulders.

"Due to the predominance of unmounted men, I rashly assumed that when once we had driven the smattering of heavy horse from the field, the sketchily armored foot might be routed and dispatched at our leisure.

"Please understand, however, those Skohshuns with whom our arms have been sparring for the past few years have been almost all either heavy horse or pony-mounted foot used as dragoons. But large numbers of Skohshuns have crossed over the river from Ohyoh since their vanguard managed to hack out a base of sorts around and in what once was one of our safe-glens. Although these massed ranks of lightly armored foot were a new form of opponent to us, they apparently are a well-established mode of warfare for the Skohshuns, for a long period of drill and training was certainly required to make scarcely supported infantry stand so firm in the face of an assault of heavy-armed horse . . . drill and training and a long experience of victories over mounted men.

"The heavy horse of the Skohshuns would not stand and fight on that fell day; rather did they disperse before ever we reached them and take up positions on both flanks of the formation of pikemen. I should have suspected something at that juncture, for never before have Skohshun horsemen seemed craven when faced with battle, but I did not, alas, which presaged the death or grievous injury of full many a brave man, that day."

The prince sighed, then took a draft from his goblet and went on. "It may possibly be that things might have been different had I awaited the arrival of my own infantry . . . but I rather doubt it. If the New Kuhmbuhluhn gentry could not hack through that damnable pike hedge, I find it hard to believe that any number of lighter-armed foot could do so.

"But we tried, that we did! We charged them again and again. Even after most of the horses were dead or too badly hurt to bear our weight, we threw ourselves at those goddam dripping pikepoints and the bastards behind them . . . to no avail.

"Whilst we still were hacking at them ahorse, footmen armed with huge poleaxes came out from their flanks to harass our own flanks and rear. Once most of us were afoot, that damned Skohshun cavalry made to ride us all down. Would've, too, save for the timely arrival of our own foot and the heavy horse who had served as a rearguard on the march.

"Then, to add insult to injury"—the lips of the prince became a tight line and frustrated rage glittered in the depths of his blue-green eyes—"the dirty swine just sat or stood there while we withdrew, not even offering to attack or pursue!"

After another deep draft from the goblet, an even deeper breath, he added, "And, for all I know, that cursed line of pikemen—five men deep—stood on that field until the damned sun set, not one of the lowborn scum even so much as nicked, and with the best, the finest, the richest blood of New Kuhmbuhluhn clotting on the points of their overlong pikes and peculiar poleaxes.

"Methinks that the only thing that saved the kingdom from being overrun in the wake of my disaster was the abnormally heavy rains of last autumn. Like most men, these Skohshuns give over campaigning in winter; indeed, they haven't even mounted any raids since the disastrous battle. But my father, the king, and I are only too cognizant of what must surely happen in New Kuhmbuhluhn when once the snows be melted and the time for campaigning arrives in these mountains.

"With a good third of my gentry slain last autumn and another third, at the least, either permanently crippled or still recovering from wounds, our straits would seem severe enough, but there is more and worse, yet. So many destriers did we lose to my folly that I cannot even properly mount such effectives as I have left, not on trained and steady beasts, big and tall enough to bear the weight of full-armed men.

"For this reason, I must not only strip every man of an age to fight from this and the other safe-glens, but every trained horse as well, and this must include all of those horses from the Sandee herd and those taken from the Ganiks that you and your force have been using. I also must have back those arms

16

and equipments that originally came from the armory in the tower keep.

"To those of you who own your horses, I stand ready and eager to pay you your asking price for them—within reason, of course—in gold. Nor will any go east afoot, for each horse will be replaced with a couple of large ponies, which really are better suited to mountain travel than are full horses, anyway.

"To those of you who are professionals, I hereby offer employment at top wages, and, are our arms finally victorious, those of you Freefighters who chance to be noble-born might bear in mind that New Kuhmbuhluhn is just now rife with new widows and other bereaved kin of the gentry slain at the Battle of the Long Pikes. Moreover, with these lands now purged at last of those manbeasts the Ganiks, my father will be in need of loyal men to invest with new fiefs."

Lieutenant Kahndoot contacted Bili silently, telepathically, "My lord, may I address a question to Prince Byruhn?"

While the prince paused for another draft, Bili said, "Lord prince, one of my officers, Lieutenant Kahndoot of the Moon Maidens, would have of you an answer to a question, if it be your will."

Setting down the goblet, the royal personage showed strong, yellow teeth and nodded. "Ask away, lieutenant."

The tall, broad-shouldered, powerful-looking young woman paced to the open space before the high table, to a creaking of leather and a clanking of armor which she alone in this hall was wearing, having but just come from wall duty to this special conference.

Having served nearly a year beside the easterners, she and most of the other Maidens had of necessity become far more adept at speaking Mehrikan of one dialect or another, so her question was only slightly stilted.

"Spoke my lord of lands which might be given to men of proven loyalty, men who had chosen to fight these Skohshuns for my lord and his royal father. What of women who so fought? Might they, too, receive lands, perhaps a large glen?"

Byruhn nodded brusquely. "If these women of whom you now speak be the justly famous and renowned Moon Maidens, lieutenant, why I say that a warrior be a warrior, to my way of reckoning, and I'd be right glad to know that you and your sisters rode under my banner. My gratitude will be equal to all my warriors, and, yes, there is a fine, large, once-rich glen in the north, needing only to be purged of trespasser Skohshuns to be once again ours to give in fief."

The steel-clad woman nodded and bowed stiffly. "I thank my lord. I now must bear his words to my sisters."

The prince nodded himself, then addressed his audience, "If any others of you would question, do so now."

A tall, slender whipcord of a man took two steps forward from the knot of Bili's officers. His eyes were the yellow-green of some great cat, and his movements no less feline, all easy grace and controlled power. Like Bili and all the other men from the Middle Kingdoms, his scalp was shaven and that scalp was furrowed with old scars. His melodious tenor voice bore the nasal accent of a native Pitzburker.

"Lord prince, Freefighter Captain Fil Tyluh respectfully prays your indulgence."

Byruhn smiled warmly. "Now there speaks old-fashioned courtesy, personified! There's no doubting your wellborn and noble antecedents, young sir. Say on, Captain Tyluh. What would you of me?"

"This, lord prince. As a professional, I would as lief swing steel for your gold as for Duke Bili's, and so, I think, would most others of the Freefighters here; but I and they have a peculiar problem, to whit: Many of us wear and ride borrowed gear and horses. When we all rode west across the Ahrmehnee *stahn*, Duke Bili . . . ahhh, persuaded certain of the lowlander nobles of the Confederation to part with their fine-grade panoplies and well-trained destriers that all of his squadron might be better armed and mounted.

"Now, though I know not how the others might feel, I would consider myself less than honorable were I to take leave of Duke Bili's service and enter into that of another while riding and wearing property not truly mine own."

"There can be no doubting the depth and breadth of your honor, my good captain," said Byruhn solemnly. "Indeed, it will be honor to me and to my House to number such a man as you amongst my officers. As for your mount and plate, fear not; I shall see to it that the owners receive full value in gold."

He turned then back to the rest. "If none else has a question of me, then retire to your tower quarters and relay my recent words to your companions and troopers, for I would know who will and who will not join under my banner by the coming morn. All have my leave to now depart my presence."

When all save Bili, Count Steev Sandee and the huge Kleesahk, Pah-Elmuh, had filed out into the frigid night, the prince said, "Cousin Bili, I have kept you from your wife and new son long enough this night, so you may retire also; the next matters I have to discuss are with Steev and Elmuh. On the morrow, we'll breakfast together, eh?"

With Bili departed abovestairs, Prince Byruhn quickly closeted himself with the grizzled old count and the hirsute hominid within a small, thick-walled study, the door of which was not only closed and heavily barred, but now guarded with bared and shining blades by the two northern noblemen.

His blue-green eyes gazing fixedly at his goblet, the silver stem of which he was rolling back and forth between his thick, callused fingers, the prince said resignedly, "I had hoped, when I rode down here, that this would not again be necessary, that affairs could be handled openly, honestly, completely aboveboard, this time . . . but it seems that such is not to be, after all.

"I know that you don't like it, Steev, that you didn't like the way I . . . ahhh, *recruited* Duke Bili's squadron last year, that you will like even less a repetition of that delusive manner of persuasion after having campaigned with these lowlanders for so long, but, man, I have no choice.

"Every ounce of gold that his majesty and I could scrape up is in my chest. There is barely enough to pay retaining fees for the Freefighters and purchase prices for such trained destriers as I had expected to be able to buy. But if, as the captain averred, the horses *and* the armor of most of the Freefighters I had expected to hire on is going to have to be paid for before they can sign on with me, the situation is flatly impossible; New Kuhmbuhluhn is rich enough in land, but hard specie—gold or even silver—is something else again.

"And Steev, Elmuh, we *must* have the help of Duke Bili's

19

squadron! Even with them, there is a good chance that our arms will go down to eventual defeat. Without them, it's a sure certainty.''

The huge, hairy Kleesahk spoke then. Gravely he spoke, but slowly, for his nonhuman vocal apparatus was ill suited to reproduce the speech sounds of mankind. "It is foreordained that victory shall be ours under the leadership of the Lord Champion, this Bili of Morguhn; such was prophesied long years before any of us was born, my lord prince, and the prophesies of the Old Wise One never have erred. This is why I have done your bidding before and will do it again—putting into the sleeping minds of these lowlanders the desire to fight for New Kuhmbuhluhn—though I like such underhandedness no better than does Count Steev, especially when it be imposed upon men and women who have already done so much for us in cleansing these lands of the detestable Ganiks.

"But if they remain not in New Kuhmbuhluhn, then our Lord Champion will not remain. Yet he is predestined to stay beside us and bring us victory at the last battle, so Fate must already have decided that I and the other Kleesahks do whatall my lord bids us do.''

Having said his say, the hominid departed for the tower, wherein he and the other Kleesahks would mesh their powerful minds and, for a second time, do the bidding of Prince Byruhn.

When he had refilled the prince's goblet and his own, old Count Steev wrinkled up his scarred forehead and remarked, "You'll not be getting the full squadron, you know, my lord, no matter what arcane stratagems Pah-Elmuh and his Kleesahks wreak for you this night.''

Byruhn gave over playing with the goblet and devoted his full attention to his elderly vassal, one side of his single red eyebrow arching up. "Riddle me not this night, Steev. The ride down here was exceeding wearisome and my body craves a long, warm sleep. The Kleesahks did well enough when last they cozened the lowlanders into fighting for us, so why should they be less successful this time around?''

The old nobleman shrugged. "Oh, I doubt not that the minds of all those brave men and women will be convinced that they must again risk lives and health for New Kuhmbuhluhn,

20

my lord, but the bodies of not a few will be unable to follow the dictates of their minds."

"That many are wounded, then?" queried the prince. "I had understood that Cousin Bili sustained relatively few casualties in the course of his campaign."

The count showed crooked, yellow teeth and shook his gray head. "There are a few cripples, yes, but I speak not of them, my lord. It's the Moon Maidens. Many of them are gravid—so big in the belly that they cannot even don their armor, much less mount a horse or ride north in the dead of a bad winter."

The prince relaxed and shrugged, recommencing his toying with the stem of the goblet. "A bad winter, yes, and all of the portents promise that it will be late in departing into spring, which will likely give most of these former Maiden warriors time to foal, I doubt me not. If these Skohshuns adhere to the same tactics they've followed before, they'll not even begin to raid until the spring rains are done, so there will be a plentitude of time for Cousin Bili and the squadron, with you and your men, to get up to King's Rest Mountain, where I'll be marshaling my forces."

Old Steev shook his head. "A warcamp be no place for babes at suck, lord."

Byruhn nodded once, forcefully. "Agreed. Nor do I want superfluous mouths to feed in New Kuhmbuhluhnburk, either the city or the citadel, not when the possibility of a siege be looming. Therefore, it were best that some few of the Maidens remain here with the spawn of themselves and their sisters. Even as poorly manned as it will, perforce, have to be, I can see no possibility of Sandee's Cot falling to these Skohshuns. Besides, the knowledge that their children are down here, in the south, will give the squadron an additional reason to see to it that the invaders are stopped, defeated, driven back, in the north. Eh?"

The old man sighed, turning his hands palms upward in a gesture of surrender. "What you have ordered wrought this night and these future things you plan, here, may well be necessary to your mind, lord prince, but still are they one and all dishonorable and I fear me that no good can come of such devious infamies. But they are your royal will, and I am your sworn man."

CHAPTER II

Brigadier Sir Ahrthur Maklarin, after easing his healing but still aching leg to a more comfortable position on the padded stool before his chair, took a swig from his jack of beer, then brushed the foam off his thick, drooping, gray mustache with a gnarled, callused and very hairy hand.

Showing worn teeth in a grimace of pain, he remarked, "Call it a great victory if you want to, Earl Devernee, but another such 'victory' could well be our ruination. Have you any idea how close, how damnably close, those feisty bastards came to hacking through, breaking our pike hedge? It just may be that we've finally met our match in these Kuhmbuhluhners. Perhaps it would be better to parley in the spring, rather than to go on fighting; they seem to be civilized and basically decent folk. Were the old earl, your father, still alive, I think that's what he'd do."

The young man to whom he had addressed his remarks did not answer; rather did he turn to the three other men, saying, "We've heard one opinion. Are there others?" He arched his thick brows and looked expectantly around. When a movement indicated a desire to speak, he nodded and said, "Colonel Sir Djaimz, what is your feeling on this matter?"

The man who nodded and began to speak looked to be a good ten years younger than the injured brigadier, but in all else they appeared as alike as two peas in a pod—average height, solid and powerful bodies with thick and rolling muscles covering big bones. Though only beginning to stipple with errant strands of silver, the colonel's mustache was no less thick and worn in the same, drooping fashion. "Earl Devernee, I cannot but agree with much of what our wise and experienced brigadier has here said. It is long since our

22

Skohshun pikes have been pressed so hard or stung so bitterly by so small a force of riders. Are we confronted, come spring, with anything approaching the size or composition of that stout band of warriors who stung us so badly in the most recent engagement, my voice will be unequivocally added to that of the brigadier.

"However, Earl Devernee, there is this additional matter to consider: Badly as they hurt us, I'm of the considered opinion that they were hurt worse . . . far and away worse. And such as I have squeezed out of the prisoners taken on that field tends to bear out my assumptions. These Kuhmbuhluhners have been here but a few generations; they were not very many who arrived and they are not many more now. Almost all of their nobility were among the heavy-armed horse who fought us so tenaciously, so splendidly, last autumn, and we all know how few of that force rode or hobbled or crawled off that bloody field.

"Therefore, I seriously doubt that we need even think of facing another such battle, for, brave and daring and stubborn and altogether worthy as these foemen have proved themselves to be, I surmise that their strength now is so sapped that they no longer can offer any dangerous sort of open battle."

The old brigadier cleared his throat explosively. *"Haarrmph!"*

The colonel immediately fell silent and, after a moment, the earl nodded his permission for the senior officer to speak.

"I have seen more than sixty springs, and I have been on campaign for nearly fifty of those war seasons, and I am here to tell you all that no formation, no tactic, no folk are ever unbeatable, least of all us Skohshuns; we've been routed in the past—although no one of you is old enough to remember it—and in just such a situation as this. The folk who broke the hedge that time were much like our present opponents— stark, brave warriors whom we had sapped and bled and pushed to the very wall over a period of years just as we have done here with these Kuhmbuhluhners."

The young earl nodded. "Yes, brigadier, I think I recall my late father speaking of that disaster. Kleetuhners, weren't they, those who routed us?"

The old officer had another swig of beer, then shook his head. "No, Earl Devernee . . . but yes, too. Yes, we were

23

defeated once by the Kleetuhners, but that was many years ere even I was born and they are not the folk of whom I'm here talking; it was subsequent to our eventual merger with the Kleetuhners that our current tactics were developed and perfected.

"No, it was over forty years ago, this time of which I speak. I was then an ensign of foot and I came damned bloody close to dying that day, so I remember it full well. There was never a merger with those valiant folk possible. So long and hard and unstintingly did they oppose us that, in the end, we found it necessary to slay every adult male and female and many of the young'uns, even. The empty lands and a very few children was all we secured in the end.

"Those admirable folk called themselves Sinsnatyers, and almost every one of the couple of score boy children we adopted of them has become a fighter of note in Skohshun ranks. I greatly fear that if we push these Kuhmbuhluhners too hard, too far, we may well end with a similar situation or a worse one, mayhap. We now know their mettle and they ours, so should we now offer to treat . . . ?"

All of the other officers made to speak, but Earl Devernee forestalled them, raising his hand and saying, "Allright, brigadier, nothing can be lost by trying your idea; we can't fight for some months, yet, anyway. You choose three heralds, send them to me, and I'll draw up a set of demands and concessions—a great many of the former and a very few of the latter, of course."

But the brigadier frowned. "I had been thinking along lines more of negotiation between more or less equals, Earl Devernee, but we can try it your way, to start. Don't any of you be surprised, however, if these feisty bastards send back both heralds and list with detailed instructions as to where we can insert said list!"

General James Hiram Corbett, U.S.A., returned the saber flourish with a hand salute and acknowledged the crisp report of his subordinate, Major Gumpner, with a nod of the head. Then he smiled. "Okay, Gump, let's get this show on the road. I'll join the column after I've had a few last words with Dr. Sternheimer."

As the major trotted off toward the formation of men and

their beasts, Corbett reined his big riding mule around and toed it over to the communications building. There he dismounted, hitched the mule and strode inside. After returning the salute and greeting of the duty sergeant, he said, "Get the Center for me, please. Dr. Sternheimer, of course."

The young radio operator seated himself at his console, threw several switches, turned some knobs, then began to intone, "Broomtown Base calling J&R Kennedy Research Center."

"Center, here," the reply presently came. "Who are you calling?"

The general strode over to the console and picked up a mike. "This is General Corbett. Get me Dr. Sternheimer, stat!"

"I'm already here, Jay," a smooth, deep voice replied. "I had an idea that you'd call just before you left. Have you thought of something else we can supply?"

"No, David, we're as well equipped as it's possible for us to be, now. Barring unforeseen circumstances, I'll be in contact with you or the Broomtown Base once every day, most likely when we halt for the night. Is that a suitable arrangement?"

"Of course it is, Jay—whatever is easiest for you and your party. Your mission is vital to us, here at the Center, so you'll get all the cooperation we can afford you. How soon do you think you'll need the copters?"

Wrinkling his forehead, the officer answered, "We'd best just play that one by ear, David. At this stage, I simply am incapable of estimating a date. My intel sources lead me to believe that there is a great deal of movement up north, so much that it sounds like a migration of some people or other. Since they're said to be heading west and south and east, we are certain to come face to face with them no matter where we angle our route of march, which most likely means fighting at least part of our way."

"Then perhaps you should have more troops, Jay—and I think there are some machine guns in the Center armory, too."

Corbett sighed. "David, David, you mean so well, I know, but you simply don't understand the logistics here. If these four troops of dragoons can't do the job, then a damned full-strength regiment couldn't accomplish it. And supplying more than the two hundred and fifty-odd now in this force would be a real nightmare; the preparations alone would probably keep us from starting before this time next year, if that early."

"Well, then, Jay, how about those machine guns? I can have them up there in only a few hours . . . ?"

Another sigh from Corbett. "David, thank you; most sincerely, I thank you for your obvious concern, but no thank you on the machine guns. For one thing, only I and a very few of my current officers have ever fired one. For another, I've no faintest idea where I'd be able to round up the additional pack mules I'd need to carry God alone knows how many more thousands of rounds of ammo for the damned things. Besides, we're well enough armed, in my considered judgment, without any fully automatic weapons.

"Each trooper has a rifle and fifty-five rounds of ammo for it, plus four grenades, a bayonet, a saber and a dirk. Each of the officers and senior noncoms has a carbine, pistol, saber and dirk, plus grenades if they want them; they carry fifty-five rounds for their carbines and at least fourteen for their pistols. I've also seen to it that every one of my packers is armed with and qualified with a carbine or rifle. The ammo carried by the men plus the spare ammo in the mule packs gives us something over thirty-two *thousand* rounds for the shoulder weapons, alone. I am convinced that we cannot possibly need more than we have."

"Allright, Jay, allright," said Sternheimer. "I make no pretense of knowing the best ways of handling a military situation, never having had any training or experience along those lines. I simply wish no stone unturned in seeing to it that we at the Center provide you everything and anything you need or might need to accomplish your ends, up there. We lost poor Erica, last time, we certainly don't want to lose you, too."

Corbett noted silently that the Director made no mention of Dr. Harry Braun, Dr. Erica Arenstein's former husband and her murderer. Because he had been suffering from a severe infection in a broken leg, Braun had been sent ahead along with an escort of three men when a sudden and unexplained malady had struck down most of Corbett's then command.

But instead of proceeding as ordered and then sending back aid from Broomtown Base, Braun had coldly murdered again, then informed all at Broomtown and the Center that he was the only survivor of the party, that Corbett and all of the others were long since dead.

Of course, when Corbett and his reduced party arrived to put the lie to Braun's fanciful tales, the murderer's rising star had abruptly plunged to absolute nadir. Unwilling to kill one of his peers—one of the few twentieth-century scientists and specialists who made up the hierarchy of the Center—Sternheimer had given some thought to the murders, misdeeds and assorted lies of Harry Braun, then arrived at a truly fiendish punishment just short of a richly deserved execution.

After being openly stripped of all his offices and the privileges he had had, he was assigned to a demeaning and most tedious job. But that had not been the extent of Sternheimer's savage retribution, and Jay Corbett could not repress a cold shudder when he thought of what else had been done to Braun.

Braun had been drugged, and taken to the transfer laboratories and his mind had been transferred from its young, healthy body into another one—an older one, which was slowly dying of an exceedingly painful and very unpleasant variety of cancer. Each time Corbett had visited the Center since then and had chanced to see the bent, shuffling, unwell body in which Braun was now imprisoned, he had been nauseated, wishing that he had shot Braun when he had had the opportunity, for any death would have been far more merciful than this form of lingering torture.

When he had finally bidden the director goodbye and gone back out to where his mule was patiently waiting at the hitchbar, he could see that Major Gumpner had already started the long column moving out of the town precincts, headed due north, up the trail that wound through the mountains toward the centuries-old treasure they were seeking to reclaim.

Here, in the southerly reaches, where the northbound track was almost as wide as a road, the column could proceed four to six abreast and thus make better time, but the general knew that all too soon they would be out of Broomtown lands and the trail would narrow till no more than two or, right often,

27

only one rider at a time could travel it; then the column would string out.

There would be no danger in this—he hoped—for the first few days or weeks, perhaps, of travel, for the mountain folk hereabouts knew the Broomtown men of old and respected them. Rather, they respected the rifles and pistols that the Broomtowners carried and used to deadly effect, when such proved necessary.

But farther north, in the long, broad stretch of mountains which were home to the savage, marauding Ganiks, the column might very well need every rifle, carbine, pistol and edge weapon, every last grenade and round of ammunition to accomplish its mission and return safely to Broomtown Base. Corbett had had to fight large packs of the degenerate aborigines twice on his previous, disastrous expedition, and he was not anxious to repeat the experience this time around.

But, he thought, what will be, will be. At least this time we'll be closer to full-strength, I hope, without a damned earthquake or forest fires to contend with. Then, too, we'll have Old Johnny on our side from the beginning, and, in his element, he's worth at least another full troop of men. He chuckled to himself. It was a damned lucky day for me and for quite a few others when I smashed Johnny's shoulder and then took him prisoner instead of killing him the way we did the rest of those wounded Ganiks.

As a platoon of dragoons approached, their officer called them to attention in their saddles and then, as they came closer, drew his gleaming saber and saluted Corbett with a practiced flourish, while, on the command of a brazen-voiced noncom, the troopers executed an eyes left.

Corbett drew himself erect and uncased his own saber to return the courtesy. Recognizing the face of the young officer, he thought, Vance Cabell, if he lives long enough, will be as good a leader as was his uncle.

Corbett still experienced a twinge of guilt whenever he thought of the elder, now-deceased Cabell and of how it had been his orders that had sent the Broomtown noncom off to his death at the hands of the murderous Dr. Harry Braun. He was ruminating on his guilt, his eyes following the young officer and his platoon, when a familiar voice nearby gave him a start.

"The younker do put a body t' mind of ol' Sarge Cabell, don't he, generl—way he moves an' sets his mule?"

Corbett turned in his saddle to behold the speaker—a bald but bushy-bearded man, wrinkled and graying with late middle age, but still erect of carriage, muscular and clearly strong. Skinhead Johnny Kilgore forked his mount of preference—one of the small horses the Broomtowners had bred up from the wild mountain ponies—and he had so schooled the little equine that it now could move almost as silently as the woods-wise man himself.

Mock-seriously, Corbett demanded, "What the hell is my chief scout doing back here? You should be up ahead of the column, by rights."

The old cannibal's wide grin caused his bushy eyebrows to hump up like a pair of fuzzy caterpillars. "Aw, generl, hain't no need fer Ol' Johnny up ther yet awhile. Them Purvis Tribe fellers'll do yawl jest fine till we comes to git inta Ganik ter'tory. And I'd a heap rather ride lowng of you an Gump an' fellers whut I knows."

Corbett could see the man's point, and, even had he not, he would have found it difficult to be truly angry at Johnny, who had saved his life and those of many other Broomtown men for all that he had been—technically—a prisoner-of-war at the time.

Responding to the gapped grin of the sometime-Ganik with a smile of his own, the officer said, "You're more than welcome, Johnny. I can think of no man I'd rather have beside me on a dangerous trail." His grin widening and a note of banter entering his voice, he then added, "But only so long as you continue bathing and washing your clothes."

The Ganik barbarians never bathed or washed their rags and often went clothed in green, uncured hides and pelts. The stench of Old Johnny when first he had been captured had—as Corbett recalled—been enough to turn a hog's stomach; moreover, he had been crawling with fat lice and had harbored more fleas than a sick dog.

But his months with the Broomtowners had altered his overall appearance and personal habits drastically. He was now clothed decently in a mixture of military and civilian garb—dragoon boots and leather-faced trousers, a dark-green cotton shirt with flaring sleeves, a snakehide waistbelt with a

29

buckle of chiseled silver and a broad-brimmed dragoon hat bouncing on his back by its cord.

Corbett noted that both his shirt and the scarf occasionally visible through the beard showed the precise and highly decorative embroidery of Old Johnny's new woman—Sergeant Cabell's widow, already gravid of Johnny Kilgore's seed.

As the rearguard platoon departed the marshaling area, General Jay Corbett set his big mule to a ground-eating canter toward the head of the column, with Old Johnny in his wake. As they went, Corbett gave quick but careful visual inspection to each man, each animal, each packload they passed, silently acknowledging the formal greetings of officers and the less formal ones of civilian packers with an abbreviated cavalry hand salute.

When at last he and Kilgore joined the head of the column, the squat, powerful, thick-limbed Major Gumpner smilingly saluted. "Is it the general's opinion that the column is in proper order, sir?"

Frowning, Corbett grunted, "As proper as it's ever going to be, Gump. I just pray God we've foreseen and provided against every possible contingency, this time out. I don't want the blood of any more Broomtown men on my hands."

The major shrugged. "The general ought to know better. He's been soldiering for what, a thousand years? Even if through some freak or miracle we don't have to fight going up or coming back, we'll still lose men—accidents, disease, snakebite, maybe drownings, things that are or will be nobody's fault. The general taught me that himself, more than twenty years ago, when I was just a younker."

"I know, I know." Corbett sighed. "I'm being irrational, unrealistic, but that tragedy up north, when the train was mashed to death under that landslide, still haunts me. I think that after this mission is completed, I'm going to turn all field operations over to you and your staff and hie me back to the Center."

Gumpner smiled once more and shook his head chidingly. "The general knows he will never do anything of the sort. He is just not the type to willingly trade his saddle for a chair."

Jay Corbett chuckled, his good humor restored. "You know me well, don't you, Gump? Know me better, probably, than I know myself. Your father knew me that well, too, though, and you're almost him all over again."

Gumpner's tone became one of deep humility. "Thank you, sir, thank you sincerely. That was the highest compliment I could have been paid."

"If'n yawl two lovebirds be done a-billin' and a-cooin'," remarked Old Johnny, who had kneed his mount up on Corbett's right side, "yawl might remark thet one them Purvis boys is a-comin' back hell fer leather."

Rahksahnah's warm, moist, even breath bathed Bili's shoulder as she slept, snuggled against him in the deep, warm feather bed, walled in by the thick woolen curtains from the damp, chilly drafts of the night. With the arm that held her, he could feel the hard muscles underlying her warm, soft skin; no tender, fluttery maid was this woman of Bili the Axe, Chief and *Thoheeks* of Clan Morguhn, but as stark and proven a warrior as one might find, capable of taking hard blows and returning buffets no less hard. And Bili could have asked no better mate.

But although his body was utterly spent with lovemaking, he did not sleep this night. For all his solemn words to the contrary, Prince Byruhn had no slightest intention of allowing a single one of Bili's squadron to depart eastward, of this Bili was certain. The young war leader was certain, too, that the crafty royal personage was even now weaving some arcane plot to ensnare them all in his service until these Skohshuns were either driven back whence they had come or extirpated.

Bili felt the need to counsel with some other officer, but Rahksahnah would, he knew, have to arise all too soon in order to give suck to their son, so he sent his questing mind out in search of Lieutenant Kahndoot, whose keen intellect he respected every bit as much as he did her personal battle prowess and her tactical abilities.

The woman's mind was sleeping, however, and try as he might, he could not enter it or rouse her. So he cast out for the equally familiar mind of Captain Fil Tyluh . . . only to meet with an identical situation. Nor, it developed, could he reach Lieutenant Frehd Brakit or any one of the mindspeaking noblemen of the Confederation. He knew the impossibility of

31

all of his officers and nobles being in sleep so deep at one and the same moment of any night. Not natural sleep, at least.

A drunken revel in the tower, perhaps? He thought not; in Kahndoot's case, certainly not, for she had been on duty until moonrise. Some drug introduced into the food? Not likely, for united as his force seemed, still were they of several disparate elements with differing cuisines and messes when in garrison here. That left only some form of mental control, and control by an exceedingly powerful mind. But whose?

He knew of experience that there was no point in probing at the mind of the prince, for, although not himself a mindspeaker, that personage had been taught how to erect and maintain an impervious mindshield by the Kleesahk, Pah-Elmuh.

Pah-Elmuh! Of course! What other creature in all this glen or in any of the surrounding lands could boast so powerful a mind? But could even the accomplished Kleesahk cozen so many minds at once? Probably not, but Bili knew that the Kleesahks could and often did mesh their minds with others of their species in order to increase or enhance their mental abilities. And all of the Kleesahks slept tonight in the tower keep.

Bili thought hard. It seemed vital that he know what was going on this night, whether or not his suspicions of Prince Byruhn and his motives were justified. But he could not penetrate the shield of the prince, and he was totally unfamiliar with the minds of the two gentlemen who had ridden in with his temporary overlord. However, there was another Kuhmbuhluhner mind with which he had, during the recent campaigning against the Ganiks, become most familiar.

Old Count Steev Sandee had never so much as suspected himself to possess mindspeak ability until Bili had, in a battlefield emergency, attempted to mindspeak the Kuhmbuhluhn nobleman . . . and succeeded, after a fashion. At the very best, Count Steev's mindspeak was marginal, and his mindshield was correspondingly weak, but this would make the task to which Bili had set himself that much easier of accomplishment. Not that the young *thoheeks* did not feel a twinge of conscience in the contemplation of thus violating the sleeping mind of a fine old man he had come to consider a friend—to the exceedingly talented mind of Bili, such a thing smacked much of a variety of mental rape—but he managed to set conscience at a distance in this instance through the rationalization that this praying was, after all, for the good of those men and women who depended upon him and whose very lives would be the forfeit should he fail them or make an erroneous decision.

Therefore, he sent his mental beam out again into the night, seeking, questing after the well-known mind of Count Steev. Found, the shield of that mind was no barrier to him and he was able to slip into the old nobleman's mind without awakening his victim, as easily as a sleek otter slips into water. And, in that terribly troubled mind, he found the answers to most of his questions, a full confirmation of his long-standing suspicions of Prince Byruhn's motives and methods.

Bili of Morguhn had thought it deuced odd when, last year, all of the members of his mixed group—even the Confederation nobles, who had never before been known to easily agree upon anything amongst themselves—had bespoken him of their unanimous decision to serve the needs of Prince Byruhn for as long as it took to rid Southern New Kuhmbuhluhn of the foul Ganiks. Now he knew that that had been no miracle but an example of Kleesahk mind manipulation done at the behest of the prince. And this night another such mass cozening was being perpetrated against or upon all who lay in their unnaturally deep slumber in the massive tower keep.

"Allright," he silently told himself, "now I know; it's no longer mere possibly unwarranted suspicion of Byruhn. But, now that I do truly know, what is there for me to do? How can I undo this infamy, free my folk from this bondage into which a dishonorable man has had them cozened, tricked, deluded?"

He made a wry face in the darkness. More likely than not, there was nothing he could do, not really. By morning, the now sleeping Kindred, Ehleenee, Freefighters, Maidens and Ahrmehnee would all be fully cozened into the firm belief that their unanimous decision to help fight yet another of Byruhn's wars was assuredly their own decision, arrived at rationally and individually. Now was the time to put a stop to the insidious trickery being wrought by the Kleesahks at Byruhn's command, but before even so strong and adaptable a mind as Bili's could wreak or attempt to wreak such, he would have to know far more than he now did about the methods of the Kleesahks.

And such was very unlikely, only possible if Pah-Elmuh or another of the hominids should suddenly make him privy to the secret; and maybe not even then, for the minds of the Kleesahks were extremely different from the minds of men, being capable of powers, feats, abilities which no human mind could match or copy.

So, what then? Openly accuse Prince Byruhn of treachery? Bili lacked any scintilla of real proof, and he could, moreover, be certain that the slavishly loyal Count Sandee's conscious mind would never permit him to reveal aught that might compromise his overlord. Nor was it to be conceived that Pah-Elmuh or any other Kleesahk would betray the very dishonorable secret of their prince.

Bili simply had to absorb and digest the unpalatable fact that, in this instance, he was helpless. On the morrow, when his folk announced to him their group decision, his only options were to either take Rahksahnah and his new little son, Djef, and ride east into the Ahrmehnee lands and, thence, into Vawn and Morguhn, or to resume command and leadership of the squadron he had led for the past year.

Young as he was—not yet twenty summers—Bili knew himself and he knew that he never could coldly turn his back on his people, his proven battle comrades, thus leaving them to the caprice of this cold and calculating prince. And surely, too, the serpent-shrewd Byruhn had well known that fact himself, had included that sure and certain knowledge of the character of Bili of Morguhn in his schemings.

And the young war leader felt dirty, used, violated, though he reflected that he never truly had trusted this Prince Byruhn or his motives, had always sensed without really knowing that the dark waters ran far deeper than Byruhn's outward demeanor indicated.

"Yes, Lord Champion, you are right." The immensely strong mindspeak crashed into Bili's consciousness, not *through* his shield, but . . . somehow, someway, around or over or under it. "Prince Byruhn's treatment of you and yours has been less than what you—and he—would consider honorable from the very start. What he has done, has charged me and

34

the other Kleesahks to do to the minds of your followers, is neither fair nor just. But, please, Lord Champion, try to not judge us or him too harshly, for he feels that he could do no other.''

"I would not have used him so deceitfully, Pah-Elmuh, as he has used me and mine,'' Bili beamed silently to the mind of the senior Kleesahk, where he lay with his fellows in the tower keep.

"Ah, Lord Champion, say not such until you have worn for a while Prince Byruhn's crown, borne the weight of his cares and troubles. Long years ago, a faulty judgment on the part of a man of his house lost one kingdom; now recent events have rendered him frantic that he will be responsible for the loss of yet another kingdom, this land of New Kuhmbuhluhn. It has been my unhappy experience in my long life that desperate men—true men, that is, not Kleesahks or Teenéhdjooks—will often do devious, dastardly, despicable deeds in defense of their own. We Kleesahks do not value mere lands and material things so highly.''

"Then why," demanded Bili, "did you, do you, lend yourselves and your talents to such dishonorable purposes, Pah-Elmuh?''

"That I would do such was decided long long ago, before first my eyes saw light, Lord Champion. I have told you of the Prophecy, told you of the Last Battle of which you will be Champion and final victor. That battle looms ever nearer to us now, and it were necessary that I did and do the bidding of the prince; otherwise, you might have departed this Kingdom of New Kuhmbuhluhn and all might have then been lost, nor would your own illustrious deeds have been done. Can you not see, Lord Champion?''

"No," Bili replied bluntly, "I cannot. I see naught but treachery by wizardry, or its near counterpart. Over the last year, you have done many good deeds for me and my folk and I had reckoned you friend. Will you not now reverse the evil you have wrought this night, erase from the minds of my warriors there the counterfeit wishes and aspirations you and the other Kleesahks have implanted therein? A true friend could do, would do no less, Pah-Elmuh.''

Bili could almost hear a deep sigh from the Kleesahk. "I could wish now that my father had seen fit to get me upon a

35

Teenéhdjook, so that I were pure, with nothing of your race within me, Lord Champion. For I find it increasingly hard to behave as a true-man, where duty must be placed above friends and friendship, where necessities of the moment must take precedence to the rightness of actions.

"No, Bili of Morguhn, for all that you have been, are now and will be in time to come, despite the deep affection I bear for you, your brave mate and your fine cub, what has been done will remain done so that what has been foretold will take place when and as foretold. That this must be so, I deeply regret, but so it must be."

CHAPTER III

Ahrszin Behdrozyuhn, newly chosen *dehrehbeh* and war-leader of the Behdrozyuhn Tribe of the Ahrmehnee *stahn,* lay in the snow just below the brow of a hill. On his right lay two of the leaders of the lowlander force which had been engaged in helping his tribe stem the tide of Muhkohee that had begun to attempt invasions from the west some months before; on his left lay a brawny Moon Maiden and, beyond her, his cousin, Hyk Behdrozyuhn.

Down the slope of snow-covered shale and frozen rocks, some quarter-mile distant, an elongated mob of shaggy, pony-mounted Muhkohee were moving up the valley along both sides of the frozen brook. The savages were proceeding directly into the wind that whipped down the twisting, narrowing valley laden with flecks of ice and the firm promise of more snow yet to come. The cannibal war party rode hunched and miserable-looking, huddled into their furs and ill-cured hides, but with most of their primitive armament clearly in evidence to even the most casual eye.

Then the lowlander farthest right, the one known as Raikuh, spoke in a low tone, for all that the distant foes could not have heard him easily unless he had shouted, and probably not even then.

"There're a lot of the stinking swine, aren't there, Son-Geros? Five, six hundred, anyway. They're no better armed and mounted than any of the others were, but still our numbers are just too small to throw against them openly. So, what do we do? Pull the helpless villagers trick again?"

The man to whom Raikuh spoke might, Ahrszin thought, have been an Ahrmehnee himself, what with his wavy, blue-black hair, dark eyes, deep-olive skin tone and reckless courage in battle, save that his nose was too small and his body was not hairy enough. Nonetheless, despite his alienness, Sir Geros Lahvoheetos had won the respect and admiration of all the Behdrozyuhn Tribe many months ago and was accorded the deference that Ahrszin himself received; and the fact that he continued to be modest, unassuming and self-effacing only added to their deep respect and near love for him. The new young *dehrehbeh* reflected, a bit ruefully, that did this born-lowlander desire it—and he had several times made it clear that he did not—the elders of the tribe would depose him, Ahrszin, in a twinkling and name Sir Geros *dehrehbeh* in his stead; and Ahrszin was honest enough to admit to himself that such a move would be good for the tribe.

And the tribe needed some good luck. Hardly had they been able to reorganize themselves after the twin disasters of the invasion and pillage by first lowlanders, then a monstrous raiding party of Muhkohee, when earthquake and forest fires wreaked destruction all over the mountains. Then wave after wave of Muhkohee—both family groups and savage war parties—had begun to surge across the western border.

Ahrszin's father, his uncle Tahk—then the *dehrehbeh*—and many another brave Ahrmehnee warrior had fallen while defending the tribal lands against the inroads of these stinking savages. The Soormehlyuhn Tribe had sent some early aid, but when their border, too, was threatened by the Muhkohee, it had had to be withdrawn, precipitately.

The truly hard times had started at that juncture. Some of the less-defendable villages had had to be abandoned. Livestock that could not be driven or carted in quickly had had to be butchered and the meat left to rot. Standing crops had had to be burned. And despite these painful sacrifices, the tribe had still been hard pressed by the seemingly numberless Muhkohee.

Then, on a day of happy memory, Sir Geros and his column had come riding down from the north. A heterogeneous lot they had been—some two score Moon Maidens and a handful of Ahrmehnee warriors from far-northern tribes, mostly Taishyuhns, but with most of the near ten score total consisting of those very same scale-shirted mercenaries who had so savaged and ravaged and raped and burned their gory, charred path through Ahrmehnee lands not very long ago.

The distinctive armor and the nasal dialects of Mehrikan had set Behdrozyuhn teeth edge to edge, and Ahrszin's eldest cousin, Knahtcho, had to exercise extreme force to prevent incidents of retribution until the bulk of the tribesfolk learned just how great a blessing these grim, steel-sheathed lowlanders were for Behdrozyuhn interests.

Sir Geros and his lowlanders had come seeking some trace of a great lowlander *dehrehbeh*, who had been separated from the others during the period of earthquakes and forest fires and, in company with a similarly mixed lot of Ahrmehnee, Moon Maidens, mercenaries and Confederation nobility, had disappeared in the mountainous area south of what had once been the Tongue of Soormehlyuhn; with him had been the hereditary war leader of the Moon Maidens, the *brahbehrnuh* and at least two Ahrmehnee headmen.

Those Soormehlyuhns who had come south to help the tribe before their own lands were threatened had, of course, told the tale of the force of lowlanders that had miraculously appeared when all seemed irrevocably lost to save a mixed force of Ahrmehnee and Moon Maidens from a thousands-strong mob of Muhkohee raiders. They had then joined with those they had saved to drive the surviving Muhkohee off the Tongue of Soormehlyuhn, only to be themselves scattered if not killed when the massive shifting of the earth had shaken down the Tongue and altered the very shape of the land. Upon learning that these newcome lowlanders were mostly of that party and that those they had ridden so far to seek were also, they became much more acceptable to the previously hostile tribesmen.

The campaign which had followed had been hard-striking and brutal, with no quarter asked or given by either side, but no sooner had the victorious Behdrozyuhns and their new, stark allies seen the backs of one batch of Muhkohee invaders, it seemed, than did yet another come trotting or plodding over the western horizon.

Had all of the encroaching barbarians been in large parties or had significant numbers of them been armed fighters, not even Sir Geros and his force would have been of much help to the beleaguered Behdrozyuhns, save perhaps to cover the tribe's evacuation of their homelands. But most of these Muhkohee seemed to be spiritless aggregations of less than a dozen to perhaps a score of men, women and children—some on foot, some in carts or wagons along with pigs and chickens or a few sheep or goats, with an occasional milk cow hitched behind. It was the rare one of these who bore anything even vaguely like a weapon, and those who did not immediately turn tail at the mere sight of a party of the steel-sheathed men on the big, lowland-bred horses were absurdly easy to direct back south and west, though some were heard to grumble that they wished the Plooshuhn-damned Kuhmbuhluhners would make up their minds. Such grumblings made no sense to the defenders, for there was not among Sir Geros' force a single man from the Principality of Kuhmbuhluhn!

The savage bands of pony-mounted Muhkohee were, of course, another thing entirely, few wearing any sort of armor, but each and every one of them armed to the teeth with a wide variety of weapons—most homemade and primitive, but there were a few rusty captured swords, spears, axes and dirks or knives.

Had it not been for the fact that the sole defensive items these tatterdemalions wore or bore were the occasional old and battered helmet, leathern caps sewn with bone or horn and crude shields of woven wicker and rawhide, Sir Geros and his force might have sustained far heavier losses than they had. But he and his well-armored and -armed veterans had been able to ride into the smaller mobs of Muhkohee and slay virtually at will the vicious but untrained, undisciplined, unarmored and ill-armed barbarians.

Nor was Sir Geros slow to take note of the reason for the bulk of such casualties as he did sustain; even if a fighter was not pinned or injured when his big horse went down, he had lost a part of his edge over his numerous opponents. Therefore, he had set every available hand to stitching padding between double thicknesses of strong cloth or leather, then sewing or riveting the resultant makeshift horse armor with disks of metal or horn, with scraps of Ahrmehnee chainmail or spare steel scales from the gear of his Freefighters—anything which might turn a blade or help to absorb and spread out the shock of a club or a dull-bladed axe. Furthermore, he saw lighter versions of this makeshift armor fitted to the mounts of the Ahrmehnee as well, and since then there had been fewer battle hurts and fewer still combat deaths, despite the quantity of heavy fighting in which he and the Behdrozyuhns had, perforce, engaged.

The Muhkohee survivors of these frays, however, seemed only to flee as far as they felt was necessary to continued survival; then, as soon as their depleted ranks had been somewhat filled back out by new arrivals trickling in from the north and northwest, they would launch another bloody incursion into Behdrozyuhn lands and the hard-fighting little composite force would find itself once more campaigning in that same once-fertile, now-barren and fought-over area in which they—the leaders—lay this very day, spying out the influx of another and even larger mob of Muhkohee.

In reply to Captain Raikuh, Sir Geros began to slide carefully backward, down from the crest, still upon his belly, muttering, "No, Pawl, some of those stinking bastards down there look very familiar, so I don't think that the village routine will work a third time—for all they're savage barbarians, the leaders at least don't seem to be stupid; they catch on fast, I've found.

"Anyhow, I'd liefer discuss these matters when I'm not wet and freezing and hungry, and I'd imagine that most of you are of a like mind, eh?"

On the long, circuitous ride back to the large village that was the base of the force, the sky to the northeast rapidly became an even darker gray, and, with the wind now almost a live and fiercely biting thing, only a fool would have failed to guess that one of the fearsome midwinter blizzards was charging down upon the lands of Behdrozyuhn at full gallop.

Huddled like his companions into the voluminous, thick, hooded cloak which, being of bleached wool, had been camouflage as well as protection from the elements back there on the hillcrest, Captain-of-Freefighters Pawl Raikuh rode deep in thoughts of the last year or so.

"Who would've thought it two years ago, that I, Pawl Raikuh, trained to arms since my seventh year and soldiering for close to thirty-five years, would be cheerfully taking orders from a man half my age who had spent the best part of his life as a servant to noblemen—a mere valet and minstrel? Yet I foresaw some of all this . . . when? . . . sometime back during the siege of Vawnpolis, I think. Or was it earlier than that, on the march into Vawn? Hell, I can't recall! Damn this chancy second sight, anyway.

"Oh, yes, our Geros has come far indeed from his humble beginnings, for all that he fights against and complains of advancement every step of the way. He's going to make a great captain, if he decides to go that way. This past year's campaigning has been proof of that if nothing else.

"Not that he'll ever have the real need to swing steel for a living, what with holding rich lands in two duchies of the Confederation, with powerful noblemen his friends and debtors and practically falling over each other to heap more honors upon him. And for holding that Silver Cat the damned Confederation will pay him thirty ounces of silver a year for as long as he lives; no measly annual income, that, even for a belted knight.

"And he's a rare way of winning people over, that Geros. When first we rode down here, the Ahrmehnee hatred of us was so thick in the air you could've spread it on ice with a cold knifeblade, yet now they all love him like a brother." Raikuh chuckled softly to himself. "And from the looks they give him, not a few of those fine, high-breasted Ahrmehnee wenches would love him as anything but a brother, had they the chance. Hell, for all I know some of them already have. Geros can be damned secretive, comes to his personal life, and he's got the rank now to make it stick.

"And it's not just that Geros is a good warrior and very adaptable to new peoples and situations that will stand to make him a superlative Freefighter captain. He's the ability to quickly see both problems and solutions to those problems at one and the same time whether those problems be of a strategic or tactical or logistic nature. For all his soft voice and disarming manner—or, maybe, because of them—he is damnably adept at getting his own way, at winning sometime opponents over to his side. Turn a man of his talents loose in the Middle Kingdoms with a decent company at his back and he'd likely finish his life as a duke or, at least, a royal count.

"But for all his undeniable genius at it, I fear me that our Geros really detests wars and fighting, as he has right often claimed. When and if we ever find Duke Bili or at least find out what happened to him and the others, Geros is far more

42

likely to hie him back to Vawn or Morguhn or Lehzlee and plump him down on a patch of land to set about siring a family and raising livestock and crops, and a criminal waste of a good captain that will be, too, for all that he'll likely be far happier at such than he would have been at marshaling troops and laying the groundwork for great, crashing battles for some grand duke or king or other. But such a waste, such a pure and unadulterated waste of a soldier.''

And while old Pawl Raikuh rode on into the gathering storm mumbling and grumbling to himself, the man who was the hub of his thoughts was himself thinking.

"It is beginning to seem that these Muhkohee will never stop coming. I know that the Lady Nahrda and her Moon Maidens are as anxious to push on and try to find some trace of her *brahbehrnuh* as am I to find *Thoheeks* Bili, but we can't just desert these brave Behdrozyuhns; without the weight of our arms, they'd stand no chance at all against so many. They never were one of the larger, more powerful tribes, apparently, and over the last two years their numbers and strength have been even further reduced . . . and it doesn't add to my own peace of mind to recall that I and most of these good men who are down here with me had a bloody hand in the decimation of these Behdrozyuhns, albeit under orders of our suzerain, Milo, the High Lord.

"Therefore, I feel strongly that both Lord Milo and *Thoheeks* Bili would be the first to agree that we owe far more to these poor, valiant folk than ever we can repay and that the small service we render this one, weakened tribe will possibly go far to strengthen the alliance that the High Lord and the *nahkhahrah*, Kogh Taishyuhn, are hoping to effect.

"Not that I enjoyed frightening away those poor, peaceable families of farmers, but it is clear that they are of the very same race as these savage raiders, so I can understand why the Behdrozyuhns insist that they, too, be driven hence.

"This latest mob of shaggies is the largest we've ever had to face down here, the largest aggregation of them I've seen since those thousands that *Thoheeks* Bili led us against just before the earthquake and the fires separated us. . . . Was it only a year agone, and not quite that? It seems like several years.

"Of course, *Thoheeks* Bili may be long dead, gone to
43

Wind in the fiery aftermath of that volcanic eruption that caused the earthquake, but Pawl doesn't think so and everyone knows that Pawl has second sight. And the *nahkhahrah*'s new wife, the witch woman, Mother Zehpoor, averred before we left the lands of the Taishyuhn Tribe that both *Thoheeks* Bili and the *brahbehrnuh* still lived and that I would find them, though the way would be long and dangerous.

"Well, it's assuredly been long and these damned Muhkohee have made it dangerous enough, true. But withal, it has been good to experience these Ahrmehnee as friends and allies after having known them for so long a time as victims or as enemies.

"These Behdrozyuhns are a remarkable folk—hardworking, but jolly and caring and generous to a fault with their own or with those they call friends, even former enemies like me. I'm not any part Ahrmehnee, yet the elders keep hinting that when once I find *Thoheeks* Bili, nothing would please them more than that I return here and become their *dehrehbeh*. And, oddly enough, I think I could be very happy here, among them.

"But, of course, I'd be happy anywhere that I didn't have to swing steel—to hurt and maim and kill, to shed the blood of other men day in and day out.

"Yet that is just what Pawl wants me to do, expects me to do for a good part of the rest of my life. He's already hard at the planning of a condotta for me to captain with him as my principal lieutenant, when once *Thoheeks* Bili is found and our commitment to him and the Confederation is at an end. Old Pawl has done much for me these last years, and I would hate to disappoint him, but . . .

"Oh, dammit! I just don't enjoy my life anymore. Why couldn't they just have left me the servant that I was? Why did they have to start ruining my prospects for happiness? After all, I did nothing that any other man of the Morguhn Troop wouldn't have done in like circumstances. If they had to foist titles and lands off on someone, why not Pawl instead of me? He's nobleborn and a professional soldier, to boot; he'd have taken to these added burdens like a stoat kit to fresh blood. When I was just a sergeant, I could have easily slipped back into my servant's life after the rebels were scotched and the duchy was again at peace. *Komees* Hari Daiviz of Morguhn would've hired me; he said so, once.

"But now, even if I don't feel constrained to give in to Pawl and become a Freefighter captain, even if I don't come back here to the Behdrozyuhns and let them make me a chief, still will there be little peace and quiet for me in Morguhn. Holding title to lands in two widely separated duchies, as I do, Sir Geros Lahvoheetos of Morguhn and of Lehzlee will most likely spend half of every year in a saddle rather than a chair, even if the Confederation doesn't exercise its option to force me to serve a few years as an officer in the western armies.

"And even if I sold the damned baronetcies, both of them, no nobleman would hire on a belted knight as anything but the one I'm trying to avoid—a soldier or bodyguard or castellan. So what am I to do? Perhaps, when once I've found him, *Thoheeks* Bili will have an answer to my problem."

Then he wrinkled his brows over the more immediate, more pressing problem—that large band of Muhkohee raiders. "Hmmm. There're two hundred and twelve of us, at least there were as of this dawning, but twenty-nine are recovering from wounds or are too sick to sit a horse in this abominable weather, which leaves me with a total of one hundred and eighty-three. The Behdrozyuhns number one hundred and thirty-four prime warriors, and if I could take all of mine *and* all of theirs, there'd be no question of making a quick bloodpudding of those raiders.

"But, unfortunately, we can't be sure that that mob is all of the buggers; they're prone to splitting off smaller groups for any reason or none, and we've had a few near things when we were unexpectedly flanked by returning units. And so, young Ahrszin will insist—and I will concur; I'd order it even if he didn't, in fact—that at least a good third of our effectives be left behind to guard the village.

"Consequently, any way you hack it, we'll be riding against at least three times our numbers, and likely in snow of such a depth as will slow down our mounts and largely nullify the shock value of a full-blown charge. Of course, one saving factor is that those shorter-legged ponies of theirs will be more hampered by deep snow than our taller mounts. The same might be said for the ponies of the Ahrmehnee, except that these Ahrmehnee warriors prefer to fight on foot and usually use their ponies only to get them to where the fighting will take place."

The dusk came early, and it was full dark before the five riders came within sight of the stockade with the lights of the watchfires glinting between the interstices of the tall, perpendicular logs. Keenly aware of the numerical insufficiency of his force even when combined with the Behdrozyuhn warriors, Sir Geros had had the village perimeter ditched and palisaded last summer, adding refinements to the defenses as time and manpower presented themselves.

At first, the Behdrozyuhns' response to his plans had been at best scathing—stout Ahrmehnee fighters needed no walls to hide behind like womanish lowlanders, thank you! But after the dawn attack of a large band of Muhkohee was beaten off, in large part because of the ditch, mound and uncompleted palisade, the village elders had changed their minds and had set the entire, refugee-swollen community to helping Sir Geros' followers at the task.

Now, this winter evening, there was a wallwalk of sorts a few feet below the irregular top of the palisade and a fine defensive platform beside the main gate as well as at each of the corners, with yet another not yet completed beside the smaller gate. The defenses were nowhere near as strong and complete as Sir Geros would have preferred and, being all perforce of wood, were terribly vulnerable to the threat of fire—either accidental or deliberate—but he still could not resist a sense of pride whenever he looked upon his new accomplishment, and the existence of even this much wooden security served to free a significant number of warriors for inclusion in his field force.

Immediately a keen-eyed gate guard sighted the five riders emerging from the forest two hundred yards away, a Freefighter hornman began to wind his bugle, while a file of archers hastily uncased and strung their hornbows, then took their assigned places, arrows at the nock.

Proceeding at a fast walk, Sir Geros, Raikuh and the others threw off the cloak hoods, peeled back mail coifs or removed helmets that their faces might be more clearly visible to the tense watchers atop the gatehouse—hungry as they all were, none of them wished to try digesting a steel arrowhead this night.

The keen wind quickly sucked all trace of warmth from their exposed noses, cheeks and ears, so that every one of the five was more than happy to hear the raspy voice of Lieutenant Bohreegahd Hohguhn exasperatedly ordering, "Opun the plaguey gate, dammitawl! Cain't you nitwits see it's Sir Geros' party out thar? Unstring them damn bows and git 'em back inside afore they's ruint, heanh, and lemme git back to mah damn suppuh afore the fuckin' mutton gits col'!"

As the ponderous bar was raised, Geros shook his head in silence. Bohreegahd should not berate the watch for doing their duty by the book for all that it took him from his meal. But he would wait a few days, then find a distant, quiet place to tell the lieutenant his thoughts privately, so as to not shame him before his peers or undermine his authority over his subordinates.

Bohreegahd Hohguhn, old Djim Bohluh and the bulk of the two Morguhn Troops of Freefighters had been absent from the huge Confederation camp when Sir Geros and Captain Raikuh had decided to desert that camp and ride west in search of their missing employer, *Thoheeks* Bili of Morguhn. But when Hohguhn returned and learned of the desertions, he and the others had remained only long enough to properly outfit themselves before setting out on Sir Geros' trail. Ostensibly, Hohguhn and the rest were riding "in pursuit," to bring the "miscreants" back; but everyone—from the High Lord on down—knew that these pursuers were actually reinforcements and that none of either party would be back until they found Bili the Axe or proof of his death.

Initially, over one hundred and fifty riders had followed westward behind Sir Geros' banneret—twoscore Freefighters, four and thirty Moon Maidens and in excess of fourscore Ahrmehnee warriors, mostly of the Soormehlyuhn Tribe. But most of the Soormehlyuhns, upon arriving in their lands to find their kinfolk hard pressed by invading Muhkohee, had left with Geros' regretful blessing and a promise to rejoin him whenever they could feel their lands and folk once more safe from the encroachments of the cannibals.

With the departure of the black-haired, big-nosed warriors

47

he had come to respect, Geros and his reduced following had ridden on, feeling most vulnerable. Therefore, it had been a distinct and pleasurable relief to be reinforced by Hohguhn, and his more than fivescore Freefighters.

The few Ahrmehnee still riding with him when at last he had entered the territory of the Behdrozyuhns, most southerly of the Ahrmehnee tribes, had been mostly Panosyuhns with a sprinkling of Taishyuhns and two lone Soormehlyuhns.

And thank Sun and Wind and Steel for all twenty-five of them, too! Behdrozyuhn lands had been thoroughly ravaged by Freefighter reavers early in the short but brutal Ahrmehnee campaign, and Geros was certain that had he and his force ridden in without representatives of neighboring tribes in their midst, he and the Freefighters might have found it the price of simple survival to have extirpated the few sound warriors that the beleaguered little tribe had remaining then.

Not that the sensitive young knight would have blamed the Behdrozyuhn men a bit for a violent reaction. For all that the deeds had been ordered and then thought necessary for the good of the Confederation, his soul still cringed at thought of some of the outrages which had been perpetrated upon the near-defenseless Ahrmehnee villagers by the huge force of Confederation nobility, their retainers and their hired mercenaries, the Freefighters.

But he was, nonetheless, vastly relieved that a further confrontation with the combat and massacre that would surely have ensued had not been necessary. It suited both his aims and those of the distant Confederation far better that he and his force were fighting beside these Ahrmehnee against a common foe. And from what he had seen of them, Geros felt secure in his belief that these ruthless, savage, barbaric Muhkohee raiders were the implacable foemen of any civilized race.

Despite the overcrowding within the expanded confines of the village, the elders had insisted that Sir Geros take for his use a snug two-room stone house. It was before this structure that he dismounted. After relinquishing the reins of his mare, Ahnah, to a brace of his retainers, he trudged wearily and carefully up the icy steps onto the covered stoop, where he

48

shed his sodden cloak and kicked the worst of the ice from
off his jackboots before entering the large main room of his
home.

But within, a surprise awaited him.

CHAPTER IV

Bili of Morguhn awoke early, despite the late hour at which he had sought his bed and the long period of sleeplessness thereafter. Immediately the prince and his two gentlemen had broken their fast, Bili approached him.

"My lord prince, I would have words with you in private, if it be your pleasure."

The prince smiled jovially and boomed, "Why so solemn, young cousin? Sit you down and break your fast, ere we all hie us down to the tower keep to ascertain how many of your folk will fight for me in the north."

Bili did not answer the prince's smile in kind, and his speech was utterly flat, emotionless. "Thank you, no, my lord. I hunger not, this morn. As for the temper of the men and women of my squadron, I already know the gist of what they all will say, having mindspoken Pah-Elmuh in the night just past. *Now* will my lord deign to receive me in private audience?"

In Count Sandee's narrow, windowless little office, with the thick oaken door shut and bolted securely, Bili and the prince faced each other across the width of the age-darkened table. Prince Byruhn strove to proffer the impression of utter relaxation, but Bili could sense that the huge, hulking royal personage was every bit as tense as was he.

Byruhn shoved his ever-present goblet across the board, and Bili obligingly filled it from the ewer, then returned it before half-filling one of the other goblets. But although the prince quickly quaffed a large measure from his own vessel, Bili barely sipped the sweet honey-wine.

Then, without preamble, he said, "My lord prince, you have dealt neither honestly nor honorably with me and my folk, a fact that I had suspected for most of the year that we have served you. There is nothing that I can do to thwart your designs upon us, your ideas cunningly planted in the minds of my squadron so that they think them their own desires and aspirations, for the one individual who could help me in that regard, Pah-Elmuh, is your sworn liegeman and will not defy you, for all he knows that it was dishonest, dishonorable and immoral to do your bidding in this regard."

Byruhn raised one side of his bushy eyebrow and asked in a solicitous tone, "Are you quite well, young cousin? Mayhap you're feverish. What on earth are you rambling on about?"

But Bili just regarded the prince levelly. "My lord prince, while I no longer feel that I can trust you, I still hold a modicum of respect for you, for your obvious valor, for your proven intelligence; please credit me, too, with some reasoning ability and perception. We two are alone in this chamber and I already have admitted to you that I am helpless to do aught to nullify the treachery which you had the Kleesahks wreak upon my followers. Can you not, therefore, be truthful with me in private if not in public?"

The prince drained his goblet and shoved it across for a refill. "Hmmph! You've never been aught save blunt, young cousin. So, yes, I have twice had the Kleesahks put all your folk lodged in the tower keep to sleep and then becloud their minds, giving them sensible, believable reasons to wish to fight for the Kingdom of New Kuhmbuhluhn—once last spring and again last night.

"That I did not do the same to you—as I could easily have had Pah-Elmuh do—was partially out of my respect for you and partially out of the fact that I recognized your sense of loyalty to your subordinates, recognized that you would not willingly desert them but would continue to lead them until you and they were again east of the mountains.

"But you aver that you have known, or at least suspected, since spring. Tell me, what bred such suspicions, cousin?"

Bili shrugged. "To begin, just a gut feeling that you thought yourself and your house sufficiently hard pressed to lead you to have your will of us by fair means or foul. Then, that morning at the foot of the tower keep when every one of the Confederation nobles with me agreed that we should war on the Ganiks for you, I knew full well that they had been in some manner cozened by you or your agents, my lord."

Byruhn regarded him quizzically. "But how, young cousin?"

Bili showed his teeth briefly, though his eyes remained cool and alert. "Simply that I never before that had seen or experienced the agreement of Kindred nobility on anything, any point, without endless, maddening discussion, often ending in personal insults if not near bloodletting. It just was not natural for all those Kindred to so easily agree with each other, much less to be in full agreement with the Ehleenee, the Freefighters, the Ahrmehnee and even the Moon Maidens."

"And last night . . . ?" the prince probed on.

Again, Bili shrugged. "I tried to mindspeak some of my officers and my hornman, but I found all to be in very deep sleep. There again, it was unnatural for all of them to have been so soundly asleep at the same time without some form of soporific having been administered them.

"I knew better than to try to glean the truth from your mind, lord prince, for mindspeaker or no, you have an exceedingly powerful shield—Pah-Elmuh or whoever schooled you well in that regard. Therefore, in the best interests of those who depend upon me, I did that which I knew to be wrong and did delve into the sleeping mind of a man I deem friend. And that is yet another thing for which I deem you culpable, my lord, that your misdeeds made it necessary for me to do so loathsome a thing to a friend.

"Then, later, whilst I mused upon the truths now confirming all which I had formerly only suspected of you, Pah-Elmuh mindspoke me. When he admitted all that he and the other Kleesahks had wrought on the sleeping minds of my folk for you, I begged him to reverse his cozenings, but he sadly refused me, citing his allegiance to you and your house."

His elbows set on the tabletop, Byruhn steepled his fingers and regarded Bili over their summits, his square chin resting on his thumbs. "So, now that you are privy to this knowledge, young cousin, what intend you to do with it? I warn you, I have good and, to me, sufficient reasons for all that I have done—or, rather, have ordered done—and so I would never admit in public that which I have admitted in private."

Bili nodded curtly. "Which is why I bearded you in private, my lord prince, to get solid answers for my own mind,

52

not an open admission of guilt. I lack the power to elicit such as that and I know it full well.

"No, as I told my lord in the beginning, I know what has been done to my squadron and, through them, to me in the past; I also know that under present circumstances, I am helpless to do aught with the secrets I now hold. But I wish my lord to be fully aware that I do know what I know. In return for my continued silence on these matters, I wish to exact an oath—a firm and solemn Sword Oath—from my lord."

Byruhn frowned. "What sort of oath, sir duke? Beware—I do not take threats lightly."

"Nor, I would hope," replied Bili, "would my lord take his sworn Sword Oath lightly. What I want is your oath that you never again, *no matter what the circumstances*, will make of me and my squadron military slaves bound by mental fetters and set to prosecute the wars of your kingdom. Will my lord so swear?"

Byruhn smiled coldly, briefly. "Words are cheap; they are only air, after all. If you so distrust me and my motives, feel me to be without honor, what makes you think that I will abide by any oath, even a Sword Oath?"

"You are without doubt a noble Sword Brother, my lord prince, an Initiate. You know and I know that no outside compunction is necessary to keep an Initiate of the Sword faithful to a solemnly sworn Sword Oath; for, if you should break the oath, that oath will kill you—the honor of pure Steel is not lightly cast aside, not by any Initiate, reasons or rank notwithstanding."

The gaze of the blue-green eyes wavered momentarily and the prince shifted in his armchair, appearing suddenly a bit uncomfortable. "You and all your followers are within New Kuhmbuhluhn, within one of the strongest strongholds of New Kuhmbuhluhn, sir duke. All of you are within my power. Only a bare word from me would see all of you slain, while you I, myself, could kill within this very chamber, and none to upbraid me for that act. So how, then, do you think to bring to bear such pressure upon me as to compel me to an oath which might be my death should I decide its terms to be contradictory to the good of the kingdom?"

Bili replied, "Yes, we all are in New Kuhmbuhluhn, but

we did not enter into your lands by choice, and you have but just admitted to having held us here, far beyond the time we would otherwise have departed, by way of a dishonorable strategem. Oh, aye, we're in your power, right enough, but you'll not have any of my squadron murdered, not when you need them to help you fight these Skohshuns of whom you speak.

"As for your veiled threat against me personally, my lord prince, you are surely aware that I do not fear you as a man, as a warrior. I will be happy to meet you either for a blood match or to the death, here in this chamber or at any other time or place, with any weapons or with none. Yes, you are a bit bigger and, mayhap, somewhat stronger, but I am both younger and faster, probably more agile, and of a certainty possess other talents of which you could not be aware.

"But, at one and the same time, my lord prince, I know full well that I have nothing of that nature to fear from you or any of your liegemen, not so long as you have need of the Kleesahks, who one and all hail me as their Champion of the Last Battle—whatever that really means. You and I both know that your killing of me—whether done or ordered, whether forthright and open or made to appear a 'regrettable accident'—would be the one certain way to alienate the Kleesahks from you, your house, your kingdom and your schemes.

"So let us two cease to tensely stalk about one another, hackles erect, snarling through our bared fangs like a brace of strange hounds. I'll unbar the door and have one of your gentlemen fetch down your sword when you speak the word. You can then swear your oath upon your Sacred Steel. That done, we two can proceed down to witness that farce at the tower keep, then you and Count Steev together with me and my officers can get down to the serious business of planning this next campaign against these Skohshuns."

For long minutes, Prince Byruhn spoke no word. He simply sat, glaring at Bili from beneath his white-flecked red eyebrow. One at a time, he cracked the scarred knuckles of his big hands. Next, he brought up his goblet and drained it, his throat working rapidly.

At last, he rasped out, "By my steel, your impertinences are hard to swallow passively, young cousin! But you're correct, of course, in your assumption that I'd fear to kill you even did I feel it necessary for New Kuhmbuhluhn. And I suppose that if I refuse to swear your wretched Sword Oath, you'll hotfoot it down to the tower keep and set about the partial wrecking of the Kleesahks' night's work on your men and women. Am I right?''

Bili just nodded.

"To stop you, for sure, I would have to kill you or have others do it, and that takes us back to the sorry fact that I dare not bring about your death . . . yet.''

The prince gusted a long, exasperated sigh, stood up with a crackling of joints, leaned to reach across the table and secure the ewer, the dregs of which he emptied into his goblet.

"Allright, sir duke, you may have my sword fetched back to me, here; I'll swear your oath on it. But whilst you're about that matter out there, find you one of the Sandee servants and tell the oaf to refill that ewer and bring it to me . . . and tell him that it damned well better be *full*, this time round!"

A voracious flea biting hard into a very sensitive portion of her body awakened Dr. Erica Arenstein. Grumbling curses and wishing for the umpteenth time that the nearby brook would thaw so that she might have herself a thorough wash and chide Merle Bowley and the other surviving Ganik bullies into doing likewise, she clawed at her crotch. Finally managing to dislodge the pesky parasite, she drew her legs up tight once more, snuggled against Bowley's warm back and sought the sleep from which the pain of the fleabite had torn her.

As the wind howled around the rocks of the mountain, she reflected that she and the small party of survivors of the once-huge main bunch of Ganiks had been lucky as sin to chance across this smallish, low-ceilinged cave; although even the shortest of them could only enter and proceed about it at a crouch, while most of them were required to do so on all fours, those same circumstances made it—the fore part of it, anyway—possible to heat to somewhere barely above freezing with a trench fire and slate reflectors. With a higher roof and consequently more space to absorb the heat, they all would likely have long since frozen to death of a frigid night, despite huddling together like a litter of puppies under the blankets and the ill-cured, smelly bearskins.

Their escape itself had been a very close thing, with the vanguard of the Kuhmbuhluhn force to be heard entering the outer section of the caverns even as she and the twenty-odd men clambered up the makeshift ladder in the narrow airshaft which those ancients who had enlarged and improved upon the natural caverns had bored through the living rock. They had emerged from their climb upon the north face of the mountain, well enough armed and supplied, but all afoot in a country that was now the undisputed domain of their enemies.

But the resourceful woods- and mountain-wise Ganiks had not stayed long afoot. By the time Erica had slyly guided them to the westernmost edge of the ruin of shattered rocks, splintered trees and shifted earth that once had been a plateau called the Tongue of Soormehlyuhn—a period of some four days and nights—all were mounted bareback on small mountain ponies.

Although the body that Erica inhabited was that of an Ahrmehnee woman in the mid-twenties—shapely, vibrant and rather toothsome—it was not the body in which her consciousness had been first born. Erica had often had to think very hard to recall just what that first husk that had contained her had looked like, for it had been dust for almost a millennium now.

She was one of a group of scientists which had, a bare two years before the man-made catastrophe which almost exterminated mankind and plunged most of the survivors back into barbarism and savagery, developed and perfected a device for the transference of minds between bodies. While radiation and plagues extirpated whole populations and races of mankind, while roving mobs of maddened, starving people scoured the face of the earth, Erica and the others had sealed themselves within the main complex of the J&R Kennedy Memorial Research Center—a large proportion of which had been built underground anyway—situated between Gainesville and Tallahassee, Florida, and carried on their various projects.

Via powerful transceivers, the group had kept abreast of the rampant insanities afoot across the rest of the continent and world as long as anyone continued to transmit. Blindly, the men and women listened to the destruction and death of city after city, country after country, as hunger and violence and disease brought civilization first to its knees, then to its death. After a short while, the steadily dwindling number of broadcasters were widely scattered and were located mostly in out-of-the-way places.

The majority of the residents of the Center were multilingual, and this fact was of great help in communication, for signals sometimes came, toward the last, in obscure languages and dialects.

For a few weeks, they were in daily contact with the captain of a Russian trawler in the North Atlantic, until lack of fuel and supplies and a near mutiny of his crew forced him to seek his home port; then they never heard from him again. Another Russian station, this one somewhere in the Caucasus region, stayed on the air sporadically for almost a year, broadcasting in Russ, Armenian, Farsi, Turkish and Georgian; from the natures of the final transmissions, the Center personnel assumed that one or more of the plagues had finally wiped out the distant facility.

This was what assuredly happened at their last U.S. contact—a military installation of so hush-hush a nature that they never knew its exact location. The last North American contact was with a field biologist in far-northern Canada; that one ceased suddenly in the midst of a sentence and could never again be raised.

Another such contact—a Japanese whaler and its factory ship, cruising in Antarctic waters—announced its intention of essaying a passage of the Straits of Magellan and never again broadcasted or acknowledged a transmission.

At the end of the second year, only three stations were still broadcasting on any sort of regular schedule—one in Uppington, Union of South Africa, one in southeastern Siberia and one in Queensland, Australia. By the end of the third year after the Center had been sealed, even these few were becoming unrelievedly silent.

After five years, the director, Dr. David Sternheimer, had unsealed the Center and sent out well-armed patrols into the surrounding areas. Their mission was not only to reconnoiter but, if possible, to bring back prisoners—young, healthy men and women, boys and girls, who had survived the plagues. The teams had met with notable success, and it was into these plague-proof younger bodies that Sternheimer and the rest had transferred their minds, driving out and away from the Center all of the confused or insane consciousnesses now in occupancy of much older bodies which mostly were dying of one or more of the plagues.

As time bore on, Center patrols brought in more and more of the scattered pockets of survivors to settle around the Center, engaging in farming and stock-breeding and unaware that they were, themselves, breeding stock of a sort . . . not at first, not in the beginning.

Slowly, as their strength of numbers waxed, as their shops and small manufactories repaired or refurbished garnered fire-arms, fabricated ammunition and explosives, the folk of the Center were able to vastly expand their holdings of land and to bring many more subjects under their suzerainty. Within less than two hundred years, Sternheimer and his fellows felt that they were strong enough to push on northward and eastward into the rich agricultural lands of what had been the state of Georgia.

And they had done so, not moving as rapidly as they might have done with their disciplined troops and superior arms and the coordination of long-distance communications, preferring rather to consolidate their gains as they advanced, which was the method proved through their earlier, Florida conquests.

Their way took time, a great deal of time. Cities, towns, hamlets, even the larger farms, when once conquered or taken over had to be carefully searched for still-usable arti-facts, for books of any description, for the thousands of minutiae for want of which the Center industries might one day grind to a halt. Once found, these items must be sifted by experts, packed and sent back south along with the hostages. For their hostages, they took as first choices skilled craftsmen and/or persons capable of reading and writing. Sometimes they removed entire populations to Florida, replacing them with an equal number of folk whose preceding generations had all lived and died under the sway of the Center.

For this reason, they had not advanced far when the invaders—thousands of them—landed at points all along the Atlantic Seaboard, established strong beachheads and began to fight their way inland. Where possible, the aliens proceeded up rivers, supported and supplied by their shallow-draft ships and boats.

Although the invaders were no better armed than their indigenous opponents and, in the beginning, suffered from a complete dearth of mounted troops, they were all veteran warriors, well organized and with a firm, mutual purpose. Moreover, they often benefited from the more than willing help of certain of their erstwhile opponents.

This last factor—the fact that many of the Americans hated and despised their own American kin with far more venom and vehemence than they did the foreign invaders—was what gave victory after victory to the aliens, as well as adding to their numbers. Forces which had consisted of no more than two or three thousand warriors upon landing often had tripled or quadrupled or even quintupled their strength by the time they were compelled to leave their boats at the fall line and move out of the tidewater lands and into the rich piedmont.

It was also another facet of this situation that defeated the forces of the Center when finally they came face to face with a sizable number of the invaders and their indigenous allies. Thanks to their firepower, the battalion-sized force wreaked bloody havoc in the initial stages of the contest, but then the ammunition ran low and radio contact with the bases within the newly conquered areas ceased to exist.

Not until the tattered, battered survivors of that doomed battalion had fought their way back to the environs of the very Center itself did they become fully aware of just how great a calamity had occurred in the areas to their immediate rear. Not until then had anyone realized just how deep and strong ran the hatred of the conquered for the Center conquerors.

In town after town, village and hamlet and farm, the people rose up to butcher Center personnel and the native satraps, smashing into ruin anything that smacked of the Center, burning buildings and vehicles. Nor had the risings been confined solely to the new-conquered, for Georgian areas now populated principally by folk brought from Florida had joined in the rising as wholeheartedly as their new neighbors. And these former Floridians it was who had coined the hate-filled battle-cry of the risen people—"Witchmen!"

Within bare weeks of the first contact between Center forces and the oncoming invaders, risings within Florida had shrunken the holdings of the Center to a mere shadow of its former glory; and these few remaining square miles were under constant and heavy siege by former subjects now allied with the invaders. But that siege never succeeded, and eventually the besiegers gave it up as a useless waste of time and wandered back home to fight among themselves.

More time rolled on. Generations were born and lived and died. The horrifying stories of the Witchmen to the south devolved from memory to legend to mere myth, believed by the few—the very young or the very superstitious—but doubted by most. Few adults would have believed that these deathless creatures, these Witchmen, moved among them . . . but they did.

The processes of mind transference had been vastly refined over the centuries, so that machinery, equipment, even a laboratory environment no longer were necessary to a man or woman experienced in the techniques. Witchmen and Witchwomen inhabiting the bodies of well-known locals made the very best, the least detectable spies, and within a century or so their slender network stretched out north and east and west throughout almost all of what had once been the eastern half of the United States of America.

The Greek-speaking invaders had interbred with the native Americans and had slowly coalesced into a good-sized state comprising most of what had once been New England and parts of eastern Canada, in the north. To their immediate south lay the sprawling ruins of New York City, virtually deserted, but a veritable treasure trove of metals and other valuable loot and therefore hotly and frequently fought over by the invaders. Then there were several small but exceedingly aggressive black states scattered along the banks of the Hudson, and the huge and acquisitive Kingdom of Pennsylvania—which comprised all of Pennsylvania, New Jersey and Maryland along with parts of West Virginia, Virginia, Delaware, Ohio and New York State.

And the only thing which had checked the southerly expansion of the mighty kingdom was an even larger and more populous kingdom, this one another Greek-speaking state, the Kingdom of Kehnooryos Ehlas—or, in English, New Greece. This kingdom stretched from coast through tidewater and piedmont and highlands and, in places, into the mountains of what had been the states of Virginia, North and South Carolina, Georgia, Alabama, Mississippi and part of Louisiana, plus a generous scoop of northern and eastern Florida, along with almost all of the northwestern panhandle of that former state.

But years and generations of comparative peace and relatively easy living had served to dull the cutting edges of the former invaders, to dim their martial fires. They were no longer expanding their territories in most places, and many of their borders were held by hired mercenaries who, quite naturally for their ilk, fought as little as possible and then only when forced to it.

Then came another catastrophe, this one natural but no less awe-inspiring. Tremendous earthquakes rocked and racked and wrecked the entirety of the known regions. In the mountains, volcanos dormant for millions of years spewed forth suddenly, rivers changed their courses overnight, lakes tilted and emptied and became dry land, while other lands subsided to become lakes or swamps or, on the seacoasts, dank salt fens. Then, before any could barely recover from the slackening quakes, a series of mammoth tsunamis smashed onto the length of the Atlantic Seaboard—highest and most destructive in the south, less so toward the north—drowning cities already half ruined, ripping up forests and crops, fouling with salt the rich soil it did not strip away. No one was ever able to accurately enumerate the total loss of human life due to the quakes and tidal waves, but none disputed that it had been tremendous.

When at last the land ceased to tremble and began to dry out, it became clear that the entire shape of this section of the continent was forever changed. The changes had been especially traumatic in and around the Center, for almost all of the peninsula of Florida had sunk to almost or below sea level, leaving the Center itself now surrounded by a single vast swamp.

Few of the Center buildings had suffered damage, luckily, but long months and years of unremitting toil were required to boat in rocks and gravel and soil to raise the area above the encroaching swamp, and even after this herculean task was accomplished, it was readily apparent to all that the complex and its man-made island could only house and support an

61

absolute minimum of personnel and that, consequently, higher ground somewhere to the north or west must quickly be found and settled.

Fortunately, this last was not at all difficult during the chaotic years that immediately succeeded the seismic disturbances, for all order had broken down over vast stretches of the mainland, roads and bridges and even mountain passes had been obliterated, armies and fleets destroyed, and large cities were become mere rubble where traces of them existed at all above the lapping, muddy waters of the sunken coasts.

On a sizable island in the shallow inland gulf now covering portions of southwestern Alabama and southeastern Mississippi with its brackish waters, the first of what was to eventually be a series of "advance bases" was set up. But Base One proved tenable for only about fifty years, then steadily rising waters forced movement onto the true mainland.

Base Two was established near the overgrown ruins of the area known centuries before as Birmingham, and that one lasted for over a century and a half. Then a mysterious and almost always deadly epidemic took off eight or nine out of every ten inhabitants, and the few survivors owed their lives to the last-minute discovery of a vaccine by the feverishly working Center medical laboratories.

At that juncture, Dr. Sternheimer ordered the inland base completely stripped and abandoned, withdrawing all surviving folk to the main Center complex or to another base on the much-shrunken and almost uninhabited island of Cuba, to the south.

Not for two centuries did they try to establish another base to the north, and when at last they did, it was in a very different way. Choosing a particular small tribe of the distant descendants of Americans in an isolated area of the Southern Mountains, they sent in a cadre to teach these illiterate near savages, who were scratching a bare subsistence out of the rocky soil while fighting off attacks by wild beasts and stronger neighbors. Within a couple of generations, thanks to more and better foods, carefully monitored and controlled reproduction, improved housing, sanitation and medical care, and the subsequent decline in deaths and impairment due to disease, the stunted, brutish primitives became a tribe of tall, strong, well-proportioned men and women, most of them clearly possessed of a high degree of native intelligence.

It had been then that Dr. Sternheimer had had schools begun to teach young and old alike elementary subjects, advancing those who seemed to own the potential into more involved education. When he felt the time to be ripe, the Director brought in Major Jay Corbett—one of the original, many-times-transferred minds—from his previous assignment and set him to molding the men and boys of Broomtown into a body of well-trained, disciplined soldiers. For Sternheimer knew that sooner or later he would likely have real need of a corps of dependable troops, units capable of moving fast and striking hard. For the Center and its plans were now faced by several minor threats and a single major one.

The seismic disturbances of centuries past had not only shaken and reformed lands and lakes and seas, but they had shaken apart and destroyed states and governments and all existing order.

Of what had been before, only Kehnooryos Mahkedohnya— the northernmost Greek-speaking state was still more or less the same, with few of its high, rocky coasts submerged and its people still ruled by an aristocracy.

The neighboring Black Kingdoms had mostly ceased to exist; almost all had been swallowed up by the present Caliphate of Zahrtohgah, which occupied almost all of New York State not now underwater. The handful of smaller, weaker Black Kingdoms that were still extant were so only by the sufferance of the Caliphate.

The vast Middle Kingdom, with large areas of its eastern lands now submerged or, at best, become salt fens, now consisted of three large states and scores of smaller ones, constantly shifting alliances and consequently constantly warring.

The even vaster kingdom of the southern Greek-speakers had likewise sundered, though not so thoroughly as had the Middle Kingdom. Despite multitudinous rebellions, invasions by the indigenous mountaineers and war bands from the southerly portions of the Middle Kingdom, and the simultaneous outbreak of a hot, deadly and involved dynastic squabble, the ruling house of the Southern Greek-speakers had managed to hold on to something over a sixth of their former lands, all just south of the Middle Kingdom lands.

Of the rest of the former kingdom, the northeastern portion had become the Kingdom of Karaleenos, while the southeast and southwest had called themselves by the name of the formerly united state, the Kingdom of Kehnooryos Ehlahs, briefly. Then they decided upon the Kingdom of the South, though they were not truly a kingdom under any name, merely a loose confederation of powerful noblemen—*thoheeksee,* or dukes—who customarily chose one of themselves to be king for life, or until he displeased enough of them to be violently deposed and replaced. David Sternheimer had slowly, over the years, decades and centuries, worked his agents—each always in a body of whatever race and class was appropriate—into sensitive positions and had been gradually jockeying the internal and external relations of the various states toward a position or alignment that might eventually be favorable to a takeover by the Center of the entire Eastern Seaboard, either covertly or overtly.

Then his painstakingly constructed house of cards had been dramatically tumbled. The wild card that effected this destruction was a human mutant, Milo Morai, who had led a horde of horse nomads on a two-decade trek from the high plains of the west to the east coast, where they quickly conquered both of the south-central Greek-speaking states—Kehnooryos Ehlahs and Karaleenos. Fifty-odd years later, this Morai and his forces had halted—if not actually defeated—a huge army of Southern Greeks led, supposedly, by their king, Zastros, but actually led by Dr. Lillian Landor, from the Center.

Dr. Landor had been killed, but not by Morai; however, he had slain several of Sternheimer's agents—colleagues and friends—torturing most of them to death or near death. On the single occasion when the two had spoken—on a transceiver captured from Dr. Landor—Morai had flatly refused to cooperate in any way with the Center or its patriotic aims and had served notice that he would kill any Center personnel who entered lands ruled by him and his fellow mutants.

Not that this threat had stopped Sternheimer from implanting his agents in Morai's Confederation or from continuing his attempts to disrupt and weaken the newer and the older states and principalities. When, a few years after the death of Dr. Landor, Morai had commenced a campaign which ended in generally discrediting the Greek church and weakening its hold on its former adherents, the Director thought that he had seen a way to strike this Confederation hard enough to possibly fragment it.

Gradually, over a period of years, Center agents had worked their way up in the hierarchy of the weakened, impoverished and much-demoralized church. From the still-faithful laity, they had carefully earmarked the fanatics, the perpetual malcontents, the manageable lunatics, rabble-rousers, incurable romantics and violence-prone elements.

From this societal flotsam and jetsam, agent-clerics in certain carefully chosen areas had formed sinister and highly secret societies, the announced purpose of which was to kill, drive out or bring to the True Faith all men and women of the Confederation, as well as to return ownership of all land to the descendants of the original Greek-speakers. Once sworn by terrible oaths, the members were sent out to prostelytize amongst all classes.

In most places they had been highly successful in their efforts, and the plan might well have created considerable havoc had it been carried out as planned, but it was not. A single small city in southern Karaleenos had, for reasons unknown and now forever unknowable, risen and butchered most of the ruling nobility, but then had fallen to Confederation forces, with most of its leaders—including the Center's agent—taken alive. Apparently, this agent had been tortured into revealing most of the plot, for when the two western Karaleenos duchies arose more or less on schedule—their successes were to trigger all other risings—Confederation troops were ready and waiting within easy marching distance to crush the second before it had well started and to then march against and so bottle up the first that those waiting elsewhere for the word never received it at all.

Two more Center agents were captured and carted off to the Confederation capital to have additional details of the Center's plans agonizingly wrung from their suffering bodies by Morai's skillful and dedicated torturers. One of the nuggets of information had been a second facet of Sternheimer's plan.

One of the largest and fiercest tribes in the mountains to the west of Karaleenos was the Ahrmehnee—descendants of Americans of Armenian extraction. Formerly resident in the foothills rather than the mountains, they had conducted bloody and productive raids against the Greeks for hundreds of years. When the Greeks were mostly displaced by the horse nomads, the like was practiced upon them until Morai came with his armies and drove them off their ancestral hills and up into the mountains. Though they still raided after that, they suffered much for those raids, finding the Horseclansmen and their get as tough and feisty as any Ahrmehnee.

With the Confederation armies spread out, fragmented, in the process of putting down a score of rebellions in distant, isolated areas, Sternheimer had thought that a full-scale invasion of blood-hungry mountaineers might very well be just the thing to utterly dismember this troublesome Confederation.

To effect this, he had had Drs. Erica Arenstein and Harry Braun and Major Jay Corbett transfer into the bodies of captured Ahrmehnee, after having been hypno-taped in the oral and written language of the tribesmen, their religious practices, superstitions and folk ways. Then they three and a few Broomtown men had established a camp just south of Ahrmehnee territory where the Broomtowners stayed while the three agents rode on in search of the *nahkhahrah*, the paramount chief of the Ahrmehnee *stahn*, with most of the functions of a priest-king.

When found, the old man—at least eighty, though still strong, erect, active and appearing twenty years younger—showed himself to be shrewd, intelligent and anything but ingenuous. However, his hatred of all lowlanders ran deep, and these People of Powers, as he soon came to call them, were saying things that he had prayed to one day hear.

He sent out word for all warriors of the *stahn* to gather around the village that he called his home, then sent Erica, a wise woman from his tribe and an honor guard of warriors to the Hold of the Maidens of the Moon—fierce, man-hating amazons who were distantly related to the Ahrmehnee and who sometimes allied with them on larger raids.

Within the sprawling, natural fortress of the Moon Maidens, Erica discovered not only a few hundred of the hard-muscled, lithe and savage female warriors ready to join with the Ahrmehnee against the western marches of the Confederation, but a true treasure trove of artifacts and printed matter from the long-vanished twentieth-century world. Such had been her elation that she had hardly been able to wait to get back to the *nahkhahrah's* village to confer with Corbett and Braun.

Their task of arousing the fierce Ahrmehnee accomplished, the three agents had ridden south, but only as far as their base camp and its long-range, battery-powered transceiver. Sternheimer's response to notification of the find—the books and manuals, the various well-preserved machines and devices, the spare parts and rare metals and, most especially, the vast assortment of transistors—had been prompt and lavish.

The Director had personally supervised the immediate assembly of every pack animal upon which his people could quickly lay hands at Broomtown, loaded a few of them with the special supplies requested by Dr. Arenstein and Major Corbett, then dispatched them north escorted by a troop and a half of Broomtown dragoons under the command of Sergeant Major Vance, an experienced and highly respected Broomtown Regular.

Fast as Vance had marched his column—and in view of the general conditions, he had marched them fast indeed—by the time he and the column had reached the camp of the waiting agents, conferred with them, and trailed them at a discreet distance back up to the Hold of the Maidens, the marshaling of the Ahrmehnee host was well underway. No men of fighting age remained in the Ahrmehnee villages through which they rode, and all three hundred-odd of the young Moon Maidens had ridden forth behind their hereditary war leader, the *brahbehrnuh,* leaving the near-impregnable hold guarded by girls and women under fifteen and over thirty; the men of the hold were not allowed to bear weapons or know the proper use of them.

With the Broomtown riflemen hidden within range of her small, personal transceiver, Erica reentered the Hold of the Moon Maidens, trailed by a couple of laden pack mules and her two male "slaves"—Dr. Braun and Major Corbett. Despite the frigidity of the mountain winter outside the hold, within lay a warmth that was almost oppressive in its intensity. But it was this continuous warmth that enabled the folk of the hold to grow two and three crops per year and thereby become wealthy through trading their constant surplus.

None of the women paid much attention to the curious pokings about of a brace of unarmed men, slaves at that, and so Dr. Braun was not long in confirming Erica's estimate of the great value of her finds within the warren of natural and man-made caves honeycombing the mountain. He also confirmed her other assumption.

The hot, sometimes boiling, mineral springs which fed the shallow lakes and helped to heat the hold, the unnatural warmth of the very rocks and soil of the place, and in particular a crescent-shaped crack near the entrance to the caverns—called by the inhabitants the Sacred Hoofprint of the Lady's Steed—all indicated that the hold was sitting squarely atop a barely quiescent volcano.

Judging by its frequent forcible ejections of fumes and searing jets of gases, Braun and Corbett agreed that the Hoofprint was a large vent for the indescribable pressures beneath the hold and that were that vent to be plugged in some way, enough of an eruption might be triggered to cover any traces of their looting of the hold caverns after they had gassed most of the folk to sleep and slain the rest.

So it was decided, and, riding widely and seemingly aimlessly, Braun and Corbett emplaced their gas bombs, all set to be triggered by a single radio signal. Broomtown snipers were signaled to infiltrate closely enough to pick off the women manning the watchtowers and the single entry tunnel. When Erica felt the time was ripe, she coolly poisoned her hostesses, then she and the other two agents donned their masks, set off the gas bombs and radioed the snipers to begin their deadly task.

While the troopers and packers, all masked against the gas, bore manload after manload of the ancient artifacts and metals up from the labyrinthine caverns, across the central valley and through the tunnel to be loaded onto the pack animals waiting in the chill, clear air beyond, Dr. Braun, Major Corbett and a few selected Broomtown men fashioned an explosive device and positioned it on a ledge just below the lip of the Sacred Hoofprint, its timer set to give them all enough of a lead to be well away when its explosion sealed the vent.

Those few men and women of the hold who were not fully overcome by the gas were coldly shot, that there might be no living witnesses to the rape of the hold. When the last loads and last men were clear of the entry tunnel, it too was sealed by explosives. Then the agents, troopers and pack train began the long journey back south to Broomtown.

But, as Fate would have it, the agents and their Broomtowners had truly been hoisted by their own petard. The eruption, when at length it came, had affected far more than the area of the Hold of the Moon Maidens. The eruption had spawned and been preceded by terrific earthquakes, and one of the most intense of these had shaken down a plateau at the very time that the bulk of the pack train was passing down the section of trail that skirted it. Now, the corpses of the Broomtowners, their animals and the precious loads they had borne lay buried beneath the resultant rockslides.

None of the three agents had been killed, although Dr. Braun had suffered a badly broken leg when his big mule fell and pinned him against the rocky ground. Then, however, had come the actual eruption with rains of cinders and ash and white-hot rocks which had fired square miles of mountain forests and brush. But under the leadership of Jay Corbett and Erica, the survivors of the rockslides had survived the fiery holocaust, as well.

Because the large, long-range transceiver and almost all of their supplies lay buried with the rest of their original party under tons of rock, they had had no option but to press on southward as rapidly as possible, once Erica had used her surgical skills on Dr. Harry Braun.

During their first day's march, another Broomtown noncom and a few troopers rejoined them after having been separated from the main column in the aftermath of the quakes and the fires. They brought with them a bound prisoner—a shaggy, unkempt and very filthy man who averred himself to be a "Ganik," a term unfamiliar to any of the agents or the troopers.

Thorough questioning after drug injections had established that these Ganiks were a most unprepossessing race and were better avoided, being aggressive, vicious in the extreme and numerous in this part of the mountains. Among their common, everyday practices were the savage torture of prisoners, incest of every variety, bestiality and cannibalism.

Because of the danger of running into a large group of these barbarians, Corbett moved due west, into the mountains, then angled south, marching by compass bearing. In order to effect this, Braun had to be removed from his horse litter and strapped into the saddle of a riding mule. He was injected with drugs at regular intervals to prevent the pain from driving him into shock. He began to hallucinate that Erica was deliberately, sadistically torturing him, and nothing could then or later convince him of the baselessness of this charge.

Despite Corbett's painstaking precautions, the presence of his party was detected by a large group of the Ganiks, who trailed them for days, made one abortive dawn attack against the camp, picked off several troopers along the route of the march and, finally, confronted the reduced column—several hundred strong, though very ill armed—at one of the rare open areas, where the track crossed a small valley.

Having expected just such a confrontation, Corbett had already split his command, giving Sergeant Gumpner one full squad and the responsibility for Erica, Braun and all of the other wounded.

Therefore, the full column formed a wedge and charged the strung-out mob of Ganiks, commencing a deadly fire at twenty-five yards, then continuing at full gallop up the farther slope to the high, narrow, rock-walled defile that split the mountain. Here they divided, with Gumpner's people speeding on southward, while Corbett and the larger group prepared to hold back pursuit as long as possible.

The narrowness of the pass forced Gumpner's group to string out in ones and twos, soon to be separated by the twists and turns and the difficult, rock-strewn footing. Erica found herself behind Braun. When she caught up to him, he begged her to check his girths, saying he feared that they were loosening. Against her better judgment, she had dismounted and done so, only to find them both tight and secure. But when she looked up to tell him so, it was to see a face twisted in hate, a wild look in his bloodshot eyes and the gaping black muzzle of his big pistol.

After raving for a few moments, he tried to shoot her but

70

failed, so he kicked her viciously with his good leg, then slammed the heavy steel weapon down on the back of her unprotected head and rode on southward, even as she crumpled to the rocky ground.

She had been found by a brace of Ganiks, her rifle still slung diagonally across her back, and possession of it along with the fact that her female body was young and attractive had saved her from the stewpots. The leader of that small group of Ganiks had taken her for his own, raping her whenever the mood struck him and also making her available to his lieutenants, these latter called "bullies" in the Ganik "bunches."

For many days, Erica's mind was confused; except for her name and title, her memory was a blank. Then another, less forceful buffet by the Ganik leader brought all of her memories back in a rush at almost the same time that her principal rapist managed to kill himself through mishandling her rifle.

Securing the rifle and a supply of loaded magazines for it, she shot the cruel, slatternly Ganik woman who had been her jailer, then proceeded to shoot each of the bullies who had accepted the leader's offer to abuse her, being aided and abetted by the only two bullies who had not raped her—a pair of incestuously homosexual brothers, Abner and Leeroy. After the executions, oddly enough, the remaining Ganiks of the bunch had freely accepted her as the new leader and the brothers had aided her in selecting new bullies to enforce her dictates.

Shortly after this, the new paramount leader of all the Ganik bunches had ridden in with his bullies and the man he had chosen to be their new leader. Erica had shot three of the newcomers dead and coldly offered the same to any others who tried to displace her from her new status. The surviving bullies of the dead paramount leader had conferred amongst themselves and elected Erica to replace him, so she and the rest of the small bunch had ridden back to the camp of the main bunch.

This had all taken place in early spring. Later that same spring, well-armed, well-mounted forces of the Kingdom of New Kuhmbuhluhn—a group of misplaced natives of the Middle Kingdoms, or rather their descendants—had commenced a serious and successful attempt to either drive the entire

Ganik race out of their kingdom or kill them all. And having lived with the Ganiks long enough to learn to really hate and despise the bulk of them, Erica had not been able to fault the Kuhmbuhluhners in their purpose.

As the summer was ending, the fortified camp of the main Ganik bunch fell to the Kuhmbuhluhners. Those of its defenders who had not deserted were butchered in a final battle. Then while the victorious Kuhmbuhluhners rode up into the empty camp, Erica and twenty-odd bullies made a narrow escape.

CHAPTER V

Erica's announced reason for guiding the twenty-six Ganik bullies from the site of their defeat by the Kuhmbuhluhners to the place where the pack train had been crushed and buried was that she wished to secure more rifles with which to arm them. Of course, she also had a private reason. She hoped to get at and use the big, long-range transceiver to summon help from the Center, not wishing to spend any longer than necessary among the Ganiks—even these relatively civilized specimens of that degenerate race.

Arrived at the site of the tragedy, the Ganiks set to with a will at the spots Erica's memory told her were the most likely locations and, during the first day, found two rifles, three sabers and a big pistol. The agent assumed that the collection of crushed, clean-picked and partially disjointed bones among which the handgun had been found were those of the late Sergeant Major Vance, for only senior noncoms and the three agents had originally carried the short-range, big-bore weapons.

Erica appropriated for herself the pistol and the three magazines of thick, stubby cartridges, awarding a rifle each to Merle Bowley and Counter Trimain, and leaving the finely balanced stainless-steel sabers to whoever fancied them.

Then she and the leaders set the rest again to the backbreaking job of shifting boulders and heaving at rocks. But long days went by without the uncovering of much more in the way of weapons or even equipment. There was a multitude of bones, all of them as cleanly picked as the first ones found, and Erica was puzzled as to how any predator or scavenger had managed to get between or under the rocks to strip off the rotted flesh and muscle tissue and even cartilage and tendon, leaving abundant toothmarks on the bones.

Nor were these toothmarks restricted solely to bones. Metal fittings and equipment too showed where businesslike attempts had been made to devour saddles, belts, slings, cartridge boxes, harness, anything made of leather. She found it all most odd and not a little sinister, for the waterproofing compound used on Center leather goods normally repelled vermin of all sorts.

They worked northward along the verges of the landslide, where the rocks and boulders were mostly smaller. Farther in, the chunks of the once-plateau were far too large for ten or twenty times her available force to handle without the use of explosives to fracture them.

Some usable items were garnered, including quite a bit of ammunition, but all of the rifles they came across were clearly damaged to one degree or another and Erica did not know enough about them to be certain that any repairs she might undertake were proper for safe operation, so she simply emptied them of magazines and ammunition and left them among the rocks. After those found on the first day, only one other undamaged rifle was found, and this one was presented to Horseface Charley.

It was while Erica was showing the huge, ugly man how to operate the weapon that she discovered him to be one of those rarities—a natural marksman. From his first shots until the day he died, she never saw him miss any stationary object on which he leveled his piece, usually firing one-handed, from the hip or waist, working the bolt left-handed for rapid fire. Not even the hellish recoil of the heavy-caliber arm seemed to bother him. He easily kept the rifle barrel level and steady.

When they arrived at the area that Erica figured to have been just beyond the tail of the train, she and her three lieutenants set the lower-ranking bullies to work higher up on the slide. This, of course, called for the shifting of far more stone and other debris before reaching whatever lay or did not lie beneath. It was backbreaking, frequently frustrating labor, and only the physical fear of Bowley, Horseface and Counter Trimain and the respect in which all held Erica kept them at it through three more days.

Then the horror began, violently.

Because more than a score of hardworking men required a goodly amount of food, the better hunters were out each day, and luck and skill had both been good to them for as long as they had been in this area, which apparently had not been hunted since parts of it were burned over last spring. On this particular day, Horseface had taken the hunters out, leaving Merle Bowley, Counter Trimain and Erica to supervise the groups of sweating, grimy, loudly cursing Ganiks at work up on the scree.

Erica was closest when it began, and what she saw that day haunted her nightmares for months. A party of five men with a few yards of rope and a couple of pry poles—which poor, inadequate equipment was all that they had been able to make up from existing materials—plus much groaning, cursing and cracking of muscles, had shifted enough stone to get down to what had been ground level before the landslide. There they discovered the shattered leg bones of a mule.

The woman had known the bones to be those of a mule, for they were too long and thick to be those of a pony. Therefore, she had set the crew to work again, clearing the area just east of the space already cleared. As she watched the labors of the near-naked men, she had to rub her forearms hard to lay the gooseflesh, for as she recalled the transceiver had been packed on a big mule.

The workers had already sent some half ton of rock into the area they had earlier cleared when it became crystal-clear that they could do no more in this area. Indeed, not even the near-score of men nearby could have budged the irregularly shaped hunk of rock which immediately overlay the remains of that mule—over two meters long, almost that in width and more than a meter in thickness, Erica reckoned sadly.

It was cruelly frustrating to be so near and yet never know whether the precious transceiver really lay beneath that massive, unmovable chunk of rock or not. And therefore, she quickly agreed when one of the Ganiks—a short, wiry man, with Ahrmehnee features and skintone, called Big-nose Sheldon—opined that he thought he could squeeze his body into the space under the huge rock, where it partially rested on some smaller stones.

Slowly, first pushing out troublesome rocks, then shoving them far enough back to be kicked out, Big-nose inched his way under the monstrous slab of stone, perforce feeling his way into the inky blackness. Suddenly, the watchers heard a muffled shriek, so another of the men flopped onto his belly and managed to get himself far enough into the low space to grasp an ankle of Big-nose's now-thrashing legs, but pull as hard as he might, he could not seem to budge the still-screaming little man. So he shouted back and the other three Ganiks laid hands to his own legs and heaved.

Gradually, by dint of much effort, the three drew the larger man—still clamping the ankle of the smaller in his crushing grip—from beneath the slab, then all four took the legs of Big-nose and heaved again. Once, twice, and his buttocks came into view. Three, four more pulls and whatever force was obstructing his removal was overcome and they were able to draw him out into the daylight.

Erica had assumed that the rocks within had shifted and injured the volunteer, but when the twitching body was out and turned onto its back, it was obvious that something else, something living and fearsome, had been the cause of the little man's injuries and his resultant cries of fear and agony.

The big nose of Big-nose had been torn off completely; so too had his lips and portions of both cheeks. The remaining flesh of his face and forehead was in tatters, with white bone winking through the blood-dripping mess. One eye had been torn fully out and the other punctured; the lids were as shredded as what remained of the face.

Chunks of flesh and muscle were missing from shoulders and arms, and the hands and lower arms were coated with a slimy substance that looked to Erica like a thin mucus. But while all eyes were staring at the dying body of the mutilated Ganik, the real horror emerged to reclaim the meal so rudely torn from its jaws.

The other working parties of Ganiks, drawn by the disturbance and making their way over the uneven footing of the scree, saw the emerging monster before the preoccupied Erica and her reduced group.

"*Snake! Big ol' snake, Ehrkah!*" were the alarmed shouts that first drew her gaze to what had come from under the rock.

It was certainly no snake, she was certain of that, even as she stared in horrified fascination. For one thing, she knew that nowhere in these latitudes of the North American continent were there any snakes of this size—her trained mind said a length of about three meters and an almost uniform circumference of nearly forty centimeters. Nor had the agent in all her hundreds of years of life ever seen or read or even heard tales of a large, dirty-yellowish white snake that was annulated like a worm and left a slime trail like a snail or a slug. Nor did the creature's dentition look at all snakelike.

The four Ganiks who had drawn out Big-nose's body were backing in helpless horror from the arcane beast, having left all of their weapons along with most of their clothes in the camp. Erica, tired of carrying the heavy thing in the late-summer heat, had leaned her rifle against a rock some little distance down the slope of the scree, but the big pistol was tucked in her belt. She drew it, charged it and, after taking careful aim at the still-advancing creature, fired until she could be certain that she had hit the spine—if the monster had one—at least once.

Upon the first report of the pistol, Merle Bowley came running from the direction of the camp with rifle, sword and dirk. But even after two explosive rounds from the rifle, the successive impacts of the stones and small boulders flung by the assembled Ganiks and deep stabs in supposedly vital places by the blade of Bowley's longsword, the beast kept up its silent writhing and snapping at anything that came within proximity to its tooth-studded jaws, all the while exuding quantities of the thin mucuslike secretion from all parts of its elongated body.

"Dammitawl, Ehrkah!" Bowley finally snapped in clear exasperation. "What the hell kinda critter is thishere, enyhow?"

She shook her head. "How should I know? I thought you Ganiks were supposed to know every plant and animal in these mountains."

"Wal, I ain't never seed nuthin lak thisun, Ehrkah. Big ol' shitpile worm 'r snake 'r whutevuh, I jest wants to know how to kill it!" Bowley snapped back.

But at length, as they all watched, the serpentine thing's twitchings became more reflexive, weaker. Although the wicked jaws still snapped when the body was prodded with pry poles, they snapped at empty air, for the neckless head did not move. Nonetheless, when Horseface and his party of hunters rode back in with their day's bag some hour or more later, the long body still could be seen to ripple convulsively, the shudders running from end to end.

With closer examination now possible, Erica found the creature to possess a double row of sharp teeth in its upper jaw, though but a single row in the lower. After a moment, she took the magazine out of a rifle and was easily able to fit some of the teeth in the slack jaws exactly into the set of scratches in the metal.

Well, at least now she knew what creature had so easily gotten about under the rockslide to devour the corpses of both men and animals. But, big as the wormlike beast was, there had been a good fifty men and a third again as many pack animals, plus the ones the men had been riding, in the trapped and killed group, so how many of these wormlike horrors had it taken to consume all of that flesh? How many more of them were coiled under those rocks right now? Were they all this size? Bigger, maybe?

"Good God," she thought in horror. "Even with rifles and the pistol, twenty-seven—no, twenty-six, now—of us would be hard pressed to defend ourselves from one of these things, if it was larger, hard as they seem to be to kill. It might be best to move our camp a good bit farther out into the burned-over area. It's still fairly open out there, so we might at least be able to see the hellish thing coming."

But when she broached the idea, Bowley demurred. "Look, Ehrkah, iffen them thangs 'uz gonna come outen the rocks aftuh us in camp, they'd of done 'er by now. I reckon they lives in them rocks and don't come out lessen they's riled up.

"But tell y' what, we'll build us a big ol' watchfire come dark, an' me an' Horseface an' you an' Counter, we c'n take turns a-watchin' with the firesti—uh, rye-fulls, heahnh?"

After a subdued dinner of game and wild plants, the Ganiks flopped down around the cookfire, and soon most were snoring. Erica took first watch, being relieved by Bowley, he by Counter, and the last watch being that of Horseface. But there were no disturbances of any sort throughout the short summer night.

The next morning, however, all witnessed clear evidence that the loathy monsters had indeed been at work. Big-nose and the dead monster had been left where they had died. But the rising sun shone down upon only their well-picked bones, with several broad trails of slimy mucus issuing from rocky crevices and crisscrossing the new boneyard.

Accurately gauging the temper of the lesser bullies, Merle Bowley took Erica a little apart and said, "Looky here, Ehrkah, them mens, they ain' gonna work today, noway—lessen we kills two, three of 'em, they ain't. Sides, did you git you a good look at whatawl Horseface brought in yestiddy? Not one dang critter biggern a coon. We done jest 'bout hunted thesehere parts clean. I thanks it's time we moved awn. Mebbe nawth an' wes'; it's still some Ganiks up there."

Erica knew better than to protest the decision of her lover and principal supporter. For one thing, she could see the clear sense in what he was recommending. For another, she was not herself especially anxious to confront another of those crawling, wormlike, abundantly toothed horrors and so could easily empathize with the lesser bullies on that score. Lastly, she was becoming discouraged about ever finding the transceiver now entombed under tons upon tons of rock in who knew what area of the quarter-mile-long expanse of tumbled scree.

So she simply nodded agreement. "Allright, Merle, let's pack up and move on. I confess I'll feel much better about sleeping if we can put a few miles between us and this place before dark. We have between the four of us over five hundred rounds for the rifles, so we should be well enough off for a long while."

But Erica knew full well how very valuable the contents of the buried pack train were to the Center and so was dead certain that Sternheimer would eventually mount and dispatch an expedition to uncover and retrieve as much as still might be usable of the loot stripped from what had been the Hold of the Moon Maidens. Therefore, her last act before joining Merle Bowley to lead their followers away from the abode of the horrendous worms was to write a brief message with a stub of indelible pencil, enclose the missive in the flat case in which she had once carried her slender cigars and hang the case in an easily visible spot on the charred trunk of a dead tree near the former campsite. Not having found the transceiver, it was all she now could do.

Some century and more before, when the ancestors of the folk of New Kuhmbuhluhn had first ridden down from the northeast, the vast stretch of mountains, glens and valleys had been the sole preserve of scattered families of Ganiks and a single extended family of the hybrid Kleesahks. The newcome northerners had, however, proved to be most acquisitive and incredibly land-hungry, nor had they been at all tolerant of the customs and ancient religion of the Ganiks. Moreover, all of the male Kuhmbuhluhners were well armed and most were well versed in the use of said arms, and so their intolerance most often took the unpleasant form of armed harassment or open aggression.

Not that any of this was new or novel to the Ganik farmers, for almost from the beginning, their singular ways and outré practices had brought down upon the heads of their ancestors the scorn and downright enmity of all the neighbors they had ever had, wherever they had lived. So most of them—those who chose to continue to cleave to their ages-old behavior and values—had emulated all of their progenitors and moved on into still-untenanted lands to the south and west.

Some few dozen families, however, in the northeast of what had by then become New Kuhmbuhluhn, chose to forsake many aspects of both ingrained religion and traditional customs, becoming more akin to the Kuhmbuhluhners with every succeeding generation. But not all of these turncoat Ganiks had adapted as fully or as fast as had others to the new, sinful, sacrilegious siren song of the pagan northerners. Even down to the present day, there still were a few families of Ganiks of this northern group who were—or so Merle Bowley and the other surviviors were convinced—secret adherents to the old-time religion and therefore covert enemies of the Crown and the alien folk of Kuhmbuhluhn. Perhaps they would prove hospitable and willing to help these few remaining members of the main bunch of the once large and powerful force of Ganik outlaw-raiders.

If such atavistic Ganiks really existed in the northwest quadrant of the Kingdom of New Kuhmbuhluhn—and Bowley and the rest maintained to the very death that they did—they were exceedingly well hidden, for the small band of survivors never managed to locate a single one of them; the only way that they ever secured any food, supplies or the like from these northerly descendants of Ganiks was to take it either by stealth or by raw force. And immediately on the heels of their one and only raid, it seemed to the harried group that the entire countryside arose and mounted and rode against them under arms.

Relentlessly pursued by the vengeful farmers, tracked like wild game by packs of vicious hunting dogs, Erica and Bowley and the rest fled far and fast and by the easiest route available, which was how they had come to winter in a low-ceilinged cave in the side of a hill above a brook which, when it was not frozen, rushed down to join the large river some miles to the north. Erica thought that the river was probably the Ohio.

Hard as the winter had been, with the rifles and the uncanny marksmanship of Horseface Charley there had been precious few occasions when any of them had gone to bed hungry. And although the bodily filth and accompanying infestation of parasitic vermin still was distressing to Erica, she had learned to almost ignore the gagging stenches of the uncured hides and pelts, for at least they helped to alleviate the cold on the long nights in the cave.

She knew not what the spring would bring, only that there was patently no safety for her group here, in the north; she surmised that only the onset of the long, hard winter had prevented stronger forces from Kuhmbuhluhn hunting this last tiny bunch of outlaw Ganiks to death, an oversight that would most likely be rectified with the oncoming warmer weather.

Erica now realized that she had erred in so readily assenting to Bowley's suggestion that they ride northwest from the site of the landslide. They should have gone south, in the general direction of the Center. Not that she publicly disagreed with him, but she privately doubted that there were any of the old-fashioned Ganik lunatics still resident in any part of the Kingdom of New Kuhmbuhluhn—north, west, south or east. And now, thanks to her misjudgment, they were deep in hostile territory, with an aroused and pugnacious people between them and the direction of possible safety.

Had there been but herself and the three senior bullies, they would probably have been able to get through and out of the more densely populated northerly portions of New Kuhmbuhluhn fairly easily—going to ground in forests or wastes by day and riding hard along seldom-traveled ways by night. But such a solution to her dilemma would, were they to try it with their present numbers, most likely end in discovery by the New Kuhmbuhluhners and either a running harassment or pitched battles against forces so vastly outnumbering them that the possession of the firearms would, in the end, count for naught.

Nor, on the few occasions she had dared to broach the matter, would Bowley hear a single word in regard to deserting the lesser bullies and thereby reaching safety in the south.

"Ehrkah, these here boys is done stuck by us th'ough thick 'r thin, awl alowng. An' I aims fer to stick by them, naow, evun if it comes fer to mean dyin with 'em."

So, as she lay wakeful in the low, smoky cave, under the stinking bearskin, with the bloodsucking insects acrawl up and down the length of her unwashed body, Dr. Erica Arenstein was anything but optimistic. She thought, as she endeavored once more to find sleep, that the discovery of the cave was most likely the last piece of good fortune that she and her present companions would have. Actually, she mused glumly, it might have been better had they not found the cave; for had they tried to winter in the open, they would all most probably have frozen to death, which was, she had been told, one of the easier ways to die, if die one must.

Somewhere, far off in the forested hills and vales, she heard the bass bellow of some large animal. Possibly, she guessed, a shaggy-bull; they now had come far enough north to expect to begin meeting specimens of the outsize bovines. She wondered yet again as she had wondered for centuries just where and why and how these and certain other improbably fauna had first developed.

These shaggy-bulls, for instance, bore a slight resemblance to bison—the general shape of the skull, the huge hump of muscle set atop the shoulders, the long, shaggy coats of hair from which their name derived—but that resemblance was no more than slight. When mature, both bulls and cows bore great spreads of horn—thick at the bases and tapering out to a murderous needle tip sometimes more than a meter from those bases—and the shaggy-bulls were much larger than bison, tall at the shoulder as a moose, though thicker of leg and heavier of body than that far-northern ruminant.

They differed from bison in other ways, too. Where most

of the bison—which once almost-extinct species had increased vastly in many parts of the North American continent during the centuries since the near extirpation of the races of man— were herd animals of plain and prairie, their huge, shaggy cousins seemed to prefer forests and mountainous areas and often were found as solitary male specimens. When they did form groups, there was never more than one mature bull with one to three mature cows, possibly a calf or two, maybe one or two heifers not yet of breeding age and, rarely, an immature young bull, not yet driven off by his sire.

Because they were far more common west of the Mississippi River, Erica assumed that that most likely was where they had originated, but over the centuries, they had slowly spread until now they ranged as far east as that part of Kehnooryos Mahkedohnya which once had been known as Maine. And for all that they bred and matured slowly, their natural enemies were few. Despite their size and bulk, the monstrous bovines were incredibly fast and agile and, consequently, such deadly opponents that only the huge packs of winter wolves ever attacked adult specimens, and then only if starving and desperate.

Although the shaggy-bull hides were the basis for a fine and exceptionally tough type of leather, most humans tried to avoid the vicious, short-tempered brutes, which could outrun a full-size horse for short distances and absorb an appalling amount of punishment. Only the plains nomads and the gentry of portions of the Middle Kingdoms hunted shaggy-bulls with any regularity—the nomads for hides and meat, the burkers mostly for highly dangerous sport.

The distant bull bellowed yet again, but Erica did not hear him. Sleep had finally claimed her.

CHAPTER VI

With the skill and rapidity of long experience, Gy Ynstyn—
the "Furface" or bugler of the squadron as well as the senior
orderly of Duke Bili of Morguhn—packed his spare clothing
and meager personal effects into his saddlebags and blanket
roll. While doing so, he tried to pretend that he did not see
the glowering scowls cast in his direction by the other occu-
pant of the small tower chamber, who sat on a stool and
clumsily attempted to hone an even keener edge on her
already knife-sharp, crescent-bladed light axe.

The last storm of the long, hard winter was now but a
memory and its final, remaining traces were fast melting to
swell the icy streams cascading down the flanks of the mountains. The season of war was nearing; therefore, most of
Duke Bili's lowland squadron was preparing to take road
toward the north of the Kingdom of New Kuhmbuhluhn,
where Prince Byruhn and the Skohshuns—the foemen of this
new season's war—awaited them.

Earlier, Gy and his two assistant-orderlies had packed the
chests of the duke and his lady, snapped the locks in place,
then borne them belowstairs to the point at which the train of
pack ponies would be assembled. Now there remained only
his own gear to quickly pack or don, that he might speed to
the commander's side and be readily available to bugle orders
or changes to orders as the occasion might demand.

He had known full well for the two weeks since the
announcements of assignments that his war companion—the
sometime Moon Maiden, Meeree—had taken hard this matter
of being left behind in the Glen of Sandee while the bulk of
the squadron marched north to war. But he knew that she
knew why as surely as did he and the officers who had made

the decision, so he was hurt that she seemed to be blaming him—who had had no slightest choice or voice in the matter—and thus was making his leavetaking even more unpleasant.

Those being left behind fell into several categories: the farmer-stockmen of the glen, those under sixteen or over fifty, at least; the women and children of the glen; a skeleton force of sound warriors to help the young or old or crippled to adequately man the almost invulnerable defenses of the glen; those of the former Moon Maidens who chanced to be too far along in their pregnancies to be safely aborted by the skills of the Kleesahks, Pah-Elmuh and Ahszkuh; the handful of crippled warriors; and two of the Kleesahks.

There was one other category: some two dozen of the once Maidens of the Moon had given birth during the winter months, and those infants, each of them now fostered with a wet nurse from one of the resident farm families, were all being left in this, the safest spot in all of embattled New Kuhmbuhluhn, until the invading Skohshuns were defeated and their parents could return for them.

Meeree—former lover of the hereditary leader of the Moon Maidens, the Lady Rahksahnah, who now was Duke Bili's consort—had seldom lain with Gy and never conceived of him. That was not the reason she was to stay behind. Nor was she listed amongst the thin ranks of the warriors to man the formidable defenses of the glen; had that been the case, she might, just might, have been a bit less disagreeable. No, Meeree was on the short list of cripples, and she had alternately raged and sulked since first that list was published, for most of two full weeks, now.

"But, dammit, she *is* crippled!" Gy said under his breath, while securing his rolled blanket with lengths of thong, his frustration causing him to jerk so hard on one length that the tough rawhide snapped like rotten twine. "She has been for almost as long as we've been here, has been since that night that she first forced Lieutenant Kahndoot into a death-match duel, then attacked Duke Bili when he brought the duel to a halt."

The bearded man sighed, thinking, "She must have been mad, that night, to attack Duke Bili—and him in full armor and armed with his big axe. He could easily have killed her then. All of us expected him to do it . . . though I hoped

85

against hope that he wouldn't, of course. But it might have been better for poor Meeree if he had. Her arm has never been sound since the side of his great axe shattered it through the thicknesses of her target and armor, both. Nor has Pah-Elmuh's healing art been successful for Meeree, much as he has helped others.

"He claims that there is some something deep in her mind that negates his instructions to the other parts of her mind to properly heal the arm. That sort of thing is beyond my poor powers of understanding, of course, but I do know that as she is now become, it were suicide for her to attempt to ride into battle. Her left hand no longer seems to have strength; too weak and unsure it is to handle the reins or even to grasp the handle of a target.

"But she cannot or will not recognize this as the reason she is being left here. She insists that it is because Duke Bili distrusts her and Lieutenant Kahndoot hates her, and I know for fact that neither accusation is true. But she, she hates the two of them so fiercely that she will hear nothing good of them from me or anyone else, not even the Lady Rahksahnah."

Gy remembered he had borne Meeree's furious sulks and towering, screaming rages for more than a week before he had, in frustration that his efforts had been completely unavailing, humbly beseeched the aid of the Lady Rahksahnah. But if he had thought that her close relationship to Meeree in times now past would help, he had been wrong.

Almost immediately, taking time from her own many and most pressing duties, the hereditary war leader of the Moon Maidens had come to the lakeside tower keep, climbed the nine flights of winding, stone stairs, and called upon Meeree in friendship. But all had been for naught.

Every soul on that level and many on those levels above and below had heard the crippled woman's shrieking tirade—the verbal filth, abuse, insults and baseless accusations, the blasphemies of the Silver Goddess Herself. In the end, her movements stiff with the tight control of her grief and her anger, Rahksahnah had departed room and level and tower, speaking to no one. Back at Sandee's Cot—the palatial lodgelike residence of Count Sandee, wherein the lowlander nobles were lodged—she had taken Gy apart and spoken to

86

him gently, quietly, in her still-accented but more fluent Mehrikan.

"Man-Gy, know you that with you I, too, grieve, grieve for the Meeree that once was, not so very long ago. But I fear me that that Meeree who so loved and was loved by me inhabits no longer the fleshly husk that we still call by her name. Face that fact, we must, and also the harder one, that never again will she—the old Meeree—return to us who love her.

"I have mindspoken Ahszkuh the Kleesahk and opened my mind and recent memory to him. It is his opinion that this needless, pointless hate she has harbored has poisoned and infected her poor mind as bad, dirty blood will poison and infect a wound. He has promised me that while we all are gone on this season's campaign, he will spend as much time as he can by her, try to reach and cleanse of the infection those portions of her mind wherein it festers. But he also warns that he may be no more successful in the healing of her poor mind than was Pah-Elmuh in healing her arm."

"My lady . . . ?" breathed Gy hesitantly.

A smile flitted across her dark-red lips. "Fear you not to speak, to interrupt me if your words have bearing. Man-Gy. We, the Maidens of the Silver Lady, never knew or practiced very much of rank; all proven warriors were with us of equal standing, none inherently greater or lesser. Amongst the host of other differing newnesses, I have found such servility by stark fighters most difficult to understand and accept. But Dook Bili attests that such is necessary to the maintenance of discipline and order, so I give the appearance of adherence . . . in public, at least.

"But we two are not in public, now, Man-Gy. You are a well-proven warrior; I have seen you fight more than once. Too, we have much in common, so speak."

"My lady, Pah-Elmuh told me several times that something deep within Meeree's mind was . . . was nullifying the effects of his healing of her arm. Could . . . could hate do such a thing?"

Rahksahnah sighed. "Possibly, Man-Gy. No, probably. Hate can be very powerful, and it is a sword of two edges and no hilt—it cuts the wielder as deeply, often, as it wounds her at whom it is wielded, or so said the Wise Women of the

Hold. Yes, her soul-deep hate it probably was that obstructed the healing of Pah-Elmuh from poor Meeree's arm.

"Her hate is truly a sickness, for she hates not just Dook Bili and me, but every sound woman and man in the entire squadron, in the glen, in all this world. She hates even our Silver Lady, the Goddess, hurls terrible blasphemies against Her and Her sacred Will. She swears that the day will come when she will see Dook Bili's blood, and mine, and will impale our little babe on her spear before our dying eyes."

Gy shook his head forcefully. "No man or woman will harm you or the duke or your noble son, my lady, not even Meeree, not while still Gy Ynstyn lives and breathes! I do now forswear."

With his blanket roll firmly lashed and the ends tied for carrying down to the stables, Gy similarly rolled and secured his fine cloak, then slipped his padded jerkin over his head and rapidly did up the points along each side. They would all ride forth armed, but most of the armor for men, women and horses would remain on the pack saddles until and if it should be found needful to don the hot, uncomfortable stuff.

Around his slim waist he clasped his dagger belt, then slipped his sheathed dirk into the frog and shrugged into his wide baldric. When his saber was securely buckled on, slung high, for walking, he looped the braided, red-dyed lanyard of his bugle over his left shoulder so that the instrument hung within easy reach of his right hand.

Throughout all of his packing, Meeree had breathed not a single word to him, had grunted curses only when the chancy grip of her left hand had caused the honestone to slip and so interrupt the established rhythm of her task.

When Gy had shouldered his packed saddlebags and the rolls, he picked up his helmet from the strawtick mattress that had been his bed and, turning, spoke his first words of this day of departure to Meeree.

"I must leave now, Meeree. Soon it will be dawn. I wish . . . may you bide well until we meet again."

She dropped the stone from the fingers—now suddenly all aquiver—of her left hand, but clenched the haft of the axe so fiercely that the knuckles of her right hand stood out as white as virgin snow. The dark eyes that looked up at him were no longer dull with sullenness, but were become bright and sparkling with purest malice.

"You fear to tell me what you truly wish, eh, cowardly man-thing? Well, Meeree fears not any woman or man and so says as she wishes to say always. Meeree wishes you a slow and exceedingly painful death in the north, you and all of the rest . . . but, no, not all. Meeree wants the killing of your precious, woman-stealing Dook Bili and his new brood mare, that fickle sow Rahksahnah, all to herself.

"Now go, you stupid, sireless curdog! Get out of Meeree's sight before you feel the bite of her axe!"

With a deep sigh and a wordless shake of his head, Gy stepped through the doorway and closed the wooden portal behind him. But before he could lift his hand from the iron ring, the rough boards shuddered as if struck by a ram and, slicing its way completely through the tough, age-seasoned old oak, the bright, glittering edge of Meeree's crescent axe burst out to reflect the flames of the torch in the nearby wall sconce.

Below, in the stables that took up the entire ground floor of the massive old tower keep, Gy and the two assistant-orderlies—like him, both Middle Kingdoms Freefighters, Ooehl Abuht and Zanbehrn Kawluh—joined forces to rapidly saddle and equip their own mounts, then do the like for first the riding mounts, then the warhorses of Duke Bili and his lady.

While the mounted assistants held the bridles of the four saddled horses, Gy entered the area wherein the pack ponies were picketed, paced down the long rows with his torch held high and selected three of the larger, stronger-looking ones, then waited while hostlers removed his selections from the lines, bridled them and fitted on the special pack saddles used to transport armor and weapons. Then he, too, mounted and led the way up to Sandee's Cot, its environs now cluttered with traveling gear, carefully wrapped items of armor and spare weapons.

The sprawling residence blazed with light and a hubbub of voices emanated from the main hall, wherein the noblemen and officers were enjoying a predawn breakfast.

After setting his assistants to the job of packing the three big ponies, Gy entered the building to seek Duke Bili.

Even at this, the eleventh hour, Count Steev of Sandee still was fuming. Not that said fuming did or could accomplish anything other than to serve as a vent for his feelings, for such a man as he neither could nor would disobey a royal order, the will of his sovran.

"Now, dammit, Bili, if I'm truly the Count of Sandee, it's me should have the right to say who rides out of here for the north and who doesn't. Don't you possess that right on your own lands, back east?"

Having been hard by the old count for most of a year—riding knee to knee and often fighting beside him on the Ganik campaign of last year, as well as using his glen and his home as base and headquarters for the lowland squadron—Bili and all of his officers had come to like, admire and deeply respect the gruff, bluff, outspoken old warrior. Although he admitted to over sixty winters, he had campaigned as hard as any man or woman of a third his years. He knew the lay of the lands surrounding his glen as thoroughly as he knew the scar-seamed, liver-spotted backs of his hard, square hands, and that deep knowledge had right often been of immeasurable aid in flushing out the rabid packs of outlaw Ganik raiders.

But Bili and his officers all also knew and admitted to themselves and each other that which the elderly count either did not realize or, more likely, refused to admit to himself—his very age and the exceedingly hard life he had led for almost all of those sixty-odd years were at long last beginning to catch up to him, a fact which the keen-eyed and -eared Prince Byruhn had noted during his brief midwinter visit.

There had been many, many days during the winter just past when the old count's knee joints had been so stiff and swollen that he barely could hobble about, all the while grinding his worn, yellow teeth in agony. Even the simple act of mounting a horse had been an impossibility. It had been for this reason, principally, that the decree had come down from King's Rest Mountain that, in this time of dire crisis for the kingdom, the king felt that Count Steev could better serve him and the interests of the kingdom by remaining in his glen and holding it securely for the Crown of New Kuhmbuhluhn. Although the bearer of the message had been one of Prince Byruhn's noblemen, the beribboned document itself had been signed in the bold scrawl of his father, the king, and impressed with the royal cipher.

Nonetheless, old Count Steev had taken it hard. Like an aged warhorse, he heard the trumpet blare and he longed to gallop out to its brazen summons. But for all that he felt himself to be unjustly hobbled and penned, he was a loyal New Kuhmbuhluhner from top to bottom and the habit of firm obedience was too strong a fetter to break. He obeyed . . . but no one had ever called grumbling disloyalty.

The question he now put to Bili was the same that he had asked of every man of hereditary rank in the lowland squadron one or more times since the unsavory directive had first arrived, so Bili was just as glad, upon seeing Gy approach the dais from the direction of the outer door, to forestall the need to again carefully frame an answer.

"Your pardon, Sir Steev, but I needs must have immediate words with my hornman yonder."

Count Sandee nodded. "Name's Gy, isn't it? Yes, Gy. He's a singularly brave lad, as I recall. Were he one of mine own, his spurs would be gilt, long since. You're sure to take losses in the north, losses of all ranks and standings; yon's a fine replacement, say I."

As Bili pushed back his chair and arose from the board, the old man turned to one of the Ahrmehnee lieutenants, saying, "Vahk, good friend, you were there that day last summer when, with my good sword, I clove that Ganik bastard to the very teeth, right through his brass helm. So what say you—is a man who still can do such too old to ride to war?"

In her place beside Bili's now-empty chair, Rahksahnah was glad that Count Sandee had chosen Vahk Soormehlyuhn as his sounding board upon Bili's departure. Like the others, the warrior part of her respected the old man's ferocity in close combat, his sagacity in command, but there was more than this. There was the infant son, Djef Morguhn, she had borne to Bili and must so shortly leave behind in this glen for who knew how long.

Steev, Count Sandee, had been full with pride to entertain, to serve beside, a duke through the Ganik campaign; but his pride could only be described as fierce that that same duke's firstborn son had first seen light in Sandee's Cot. He had showered all sorts of valuable and sometimes ridiculous gifts upon the small morsel of humanity—everything from a bigboned colt out of his own destrier's get to a tiny but very sharp bejeweled dagger in a sheath of purest gold.

Therefore, although she grieved for and with him, the war leader of the Maidens of the Moon was at the same time very glad that Sir Steev would remain in command of the glen. Anyone or anything that threatened her little son would have first to pass the savage old warrior, and even she, at less than a third of his age, knew that she would think twice before she set herself against the old but still deadly fighting machine that was Sir Steev of Sandee.

Besides, she knew from personal experience that there was no answer to the posed questions really satisfactory to the old nobleman. When, some weeks back, the other Ahrmehnee lieutenant, Vahrtahn Panosyuhn—who was almost ten years the count's elder—remarked in answer to the perennial query that the king showed a distinct dearth of judgment to force an old and wise and valiant warrior into an unwanted and unwonted retirement from active campaigning, Sir Steev immediately rose to the defense of his sovran.

"*Der* Vahrtahn, had a New Kuhmbuhluhner or even one of the lowlanders so impugned the sagacity of my king, Steel be with him, that man would shortly be facing me at swords' points. But you, you are an Ahrmehnee; I know that your customs differ vastly and that you never have had a king or any real nobles.

"But know you now, it is the sworn—nay, the inborn—duty of an honest and honorable subject of whatever rank to obey the dictates of his sovran and of those placed in positions of authority by his sovran. While I do not feel my sovran to be right in this instance, right or wrong, he still is my liege lord and I will obey, will see to it that those under me obey his decrees so long as breath remains within me."

Rahksahnah had, that day, seen old Vahrtahn walk away shaking his white-haired head in bewilderment. Blind obedience to the will of any mortal man was not a survival trait and thus was utterly foreign to the nature of the Ahrmehnee, who individually and racially were nothing if not survivors.

* * *

The light drizzle which had commenced at about midnight continued on, and because of it dawn was very late in its appearance, though then it was only a bare lightening of the misty gray. And regardless of this natural respite, still was the column more than two more hours late in having the ponderous gate gapped enough for the vanguard to commence a negotiation of the narrow, twisting defile that led out of the safe-glen called Sandee's Cot.

The big man of twenty winters called Bili the Axe—Bili, *Thoheeks* and Chief of Clan Morguhn, Knight of the Blue Bear of Harzburk, commander of the two hundred-odd men and women making up the Lowlander Squadron of the Army of the King of New Kuhmbuhluhn—cursed and snarled and fretted at the delays—one or two of them major, but mostly minor and all completely unavoidable, in any case—even while he reflected that he had never in all his six or seven years of soldiering known or heard of a movement of a body of troops that proceeded on time and in the order preplanned, not that such rationalizations helped his temper.

Even ahead of the vanguards, the huge prairiecat Whitetip had leaped easily to the ground from the stone archway over the gates and now was at the place where the trailside fortifications ended, mindspeaking back to all of those whose minds could range him his personal reassurance that the way was clear, with no foemen to contest it.

Where two cats had served through the Ganik campaign, only the big male would accompany the march to the north. There were wet nurses in the glen for human babies, but none for kittens of such size as the litter that the female, Stealth, had so recently thrown. Therefore, she would stay behind to nurse and care for them through their weaning. But Bili had promised the bitterly disappointed young cat that should this present campaign spill over into another year, Stealth and her brood could certainly make their way north and join him and the rest of the squadron. He and Rahksahnah also had set the nursing queen a task within the glen—she was to guard the infant, Djef Morguhn, as zealously as she guarded her own get, being especially wary of the crippled Moon Maiden, Meeree.

Rahksahnah rode out with Bili's staff in the main column, but Bili himself stood beside Sir Steev until the last of the lengthy pack train had exited the glen and Lieutenant Kahndoot was beginning to mount her rearguard troops to follow. Then he turned to bid a last farewell to that doughty old nobleman who had for so long been his host, his friend and his ofttimes adviser.

"Sir Steev, thank you again for all your host of kindnesses to me and to mine. I hope that when next I stand here, it will be that we have come back for our babes and our companions that we may ride back eastward. But should this Skohshuns matter be too tough a nut to crack in one season, will you allow us yet another winter here with you in Sandee's Cot?"

The count showed every worn tooth in a warm smile. "Aye, Sir Bili, and right gladly. Unless I hear aught otherwise, I shall watch for your banner in the autumn. And fear you not, none of you, for the safety of your babes, for so long as I can draw breath and swing sharp steel, they are safe."

The boar bear burst from out a trailside copse and charged down the trail, moving as fast as a running man, his muzzle and bared teeth covered in bloody foam as red as his deep-sunk eyes. The point man's mule, however, did not need the snarls of mindless fury to give warning, for the wind brought the dilated nostrils the deadly scent and the animal first reared, screaming, then bolted, unseating its rider and leaving him, stunned and helpless, directly in the path of the oncoming ursine fury.

But the bear ignored the motionless man and charged on at the brace of riders behind. Had these soldiers—for such they were—been armed as primitively as were all other soldiers of this world and time, the maddened bear might well have had the satisfaction of fleshing claws and fangs before death. Instead a heavy-caliber rifle bullet smashed his spine and dropped him flopping in the weeds and dead leaves; the fierce snarls became a pitiful whimpering just before a second bullet blew out one side of his skull and ended his life.

A quarter mile back, with the main column, General Jay Corbett heard the closely spaced pair of gunshots and spurred forward, trailed by Major Gumpner and Old Johnny Kilgore, their pistols out and armed. Halfway up to the van, they met the runaway mule, its wide eyes rolling in fear, galloping flat out, but Old Johnny adroitly blocked the animal with his own mount and secured the loose reins.

By the time the old, bald Ganik caught up to the two officers, they had dismounted and joined the group in the vanguard who had alit to tend their semiconscious comrade and examine the dead bear. Passing the reins of the still highly agitated mule to one of the mounted troopers, the chief of scouts kneed his beast closer to the officers, then slipped his feet from his stirrups and slid down the off side to the ground to stride with a loose-limbed gait over to where lay the dusty-black carcass of the bear.

Wrinkling his pug nose, he remarked, "Suthin' shore do stink, Gen'rul Jay. Rackun some yore boys is a-trainin' fer to be Ganiks?"

A grin flitted across the senior officer's olive, Ahrmehnee countenance; most Ganiks never washed and often went clothed in poorly cured or raw skins and hides. "Not quite, Johnny, not quite. I think it's the bear we smell. Here, some of you men, let's get him turned on his other side. Christ, but he's big! If he was in full flesh, I'll bet he'd weigh in at six, seven hundred pounds, easy."

The dead bear's ribs and spine were clearly visible through his wrinkly skin and dull, lifeless coat. The reason for his insensate fury, starved condition and the gagging stench he emanated was clearly evident when the limp carcass was manhandled over onto its near side, however.

Most of the off side of the thick torso had been rubbed down to a nauseating mess of oozing flesh and crawling maggots. Heedless of the circle of men, a black cloud of flies descended to resume interrupted feedings immediately the bear was turned, and all of the men waved hands to keep strays from their sweaty dusty faces.

"Johnny," Corbett asked above the droning of the flies, "what in hell happened to this bear? Have you ever seen the like of this?"

The old man squatted beside the crawling carcass, lifted the stubby tail and considered the anus, then reached over the ham to poke about with a forefinger in the area between the short ribs and the pelvis. Slowly, he arose, wiping his finger on the leg of his trousers.

"Gen'rul Jay, it's boun' fer to be suthin' in that there bar's innards hurtid him plumb fierce. 'Pears he done been a-shittin' blood fer some time naow. I guesses a-rubbin' up 'ginst trees

95

and rocks musta eased him some, so he jest kep' at it till he'd wore awf awl the hair an' the skin, too. An' then th' dang flies went at 'im, o' course. It's suthin' in his belly, but ain' no way fer to tell whut, 'lest we's to cut 'im opuned an' look . . . ?''

Twenty minutes later, Corbett, Gumpner and Johnny Kilgore passed around and examined the object the old man had dug out and removed from the dead bear's terribly inflamed abdominal cavity—a deeply barbed bronze weapon point a good seven and a half centimeters long and five wide; socketed into the base of the crude point was a bit of hardwood dowel about two centimeters in diameter by a bit less than ten long, the unshod end being mashed and splintered.

Seeing Johnny first frown, then shake his head, Corbett snapped, "What is it, man? You recognize the origin? Is that it?''

Johnny nodded, the sunlight glinting on his bald head. "I shore Lawd does, Gen'rul Jay. Thet there be Ganik work. It useta be the end piece awf a Ahrm'nee sword sheath—they ushly makes up good p'ints fer darts an' they ain' so hard fer to work up as ir'n or steel is. Looks as how thet ol' bar, he bit awf the resta the shaf', then the p'int jest workted awn in futher.''

During his weeks with Erica and Braun in the Ahrmehnee *stahn*, Corbett could recall having seen many a wood-and-leather sword case with handsomely decorated throat, bands and chapes of cast bronze, and now, after Johnny's identification, he could detect the ghost of the one time art object in the hammered, defaced and sharp-honed point. But that was not what sent an icy chill coursing the length of his spine or set the hairs on his nape aprickle.

"Johnny," he said slowly, "I thought you said that Ganiks never, ever came this far south. How far could a bear travel, wounded that seriously? Ten miles? Maybe twenty, at the outside? But by your reckoning, we're still nearly a week's march away from the southernmost Ganik areas.''

The old man shrugged, palms outward. "Lawdy, Gen'rul Jay, I nevuh said I knowed everthin 'bout everthin, did I? The bunch I 'uz runnin' with whin you come to club me daown, it 'uz the futhes' south Ganik bunch that wuz. An' t'placet where yawl kilt everbody 'cept of me, that were as fer south as eny of us'd ever rode afore. That be awl I knows 'bout it."

He looked and sounded hurt, so Corbett forced a smile and a soothing tone. "All right, Johnny, all right—I'm not doubting you. I've never known you to lie about anything."

Then, turning to Gumpner, he said, "All right, Gump, we've got an iffy situation now, with a possibility of hostiles around the next turn. Two- or three-man points from now on, nobody to ride alone, in van, column or rearguard, for *any* reason; no one to break column for any purpose without the okay of his superior and without a couple of other men to accompany him.

"The van will maintain the same interval from the main column, but put a full squad halfway between the rear of the van and the head of the column; same thing for the rearguard, too. I want to know the very second a Ganik is sighted by anyone.

"Make certain that all those civilian packers have their weapons loaded and ready for action. And by tonight's halt, I want a damned good reason for why the leader of the van didn't at least try to contact the head of the column by transceiver to let us know precisely why those shots were fired."

He came erect, then added, "When we camp tonight, Johnny, we'll rig you up as planned, give you the worst-looking pony we can find, then let you start riding advance point, two or three kilometers ahead, anyhow. If you still want to, at least. I won't order you to—it could easily be your death."

Kilgore's head bobbed in a short nod of assent. "Shit, gen'rul, I ain' a-scairt of no livin' Ganiks. 'Sides, they awl knows me; I rid with the bunches fer a passel of years and them as ain' nevuh seed me has shore Lawd heerd of me. So shore I'll ride out termorrer, but afore we-awls leaves here, I wawnts me whut hide thet bar's got lef awn 'im, an' iffen a couple the boys wuz to help me, I c'n skin 'im a helluva lot quicker."

Foot to stirrup, Corbett turned and demanded, "In the name of God, man, why would you want *that* stinking, verminous thing, Johnny?"

The reformed cannibal showed gapped, yellowed teeth in a

97

broad grin. "Wal, Gen'rul Jay, suh, if I means fer to pass fer a wil', bunch Ganik, lahk I wuz, I'm way too clean, me an' my clo's too. Smelly as it be, I figgers thet bar skin'll be jes' the thang fer to cover up haow purty I smells."

Gulping down the bile raised at thought of actually wearing the rotting, maggoty hide, Corbett swung up onto his mount and told Old Johnny, "It certainly will do that, and you know best in that regard. Get any help you need, here. But just stay downwind of me, *please*."

CHAPTER VII

Sir Ahrthur Maklarin had had his work table arranged as close to the hot hearth fire as was possible without risking the setting alight of his clothing and the papers which now were piled high on the table. One would have thought that, as heavy as had been the winter's snows, the spring might have been decently dry, at least; but it was proving to be anything but, and his many necessary rides of inspection in the chill and wet had set every bone and joint and old wound in his body to aching as fiercely as a rotten tooth, and he knew of old that only heat would allay such pain.

Laying aside the quill pen for a moment, he first trimmed the lamps, then took from the hearth a copper loggerhead and, after he had carefully blown the fine ash from the glowing ingot, plunged it, hissing and spluttering, into his pewter tankard. After a tentative sip or two, he drained a deep draft from the now-heated mixture of beer and herbs, wiped off his drooping mustache with a characteristic wipe of his hirsute hand, then set down the tankard and returned to his figures and figurings.

The brigadier was a careful, planning officer. He worked his staff hard and himself ten times harder. He anticipated probabilities and possibilities, meticulously provided for and against each of them and calculated certain needs far in advance of the actualities. All of his immediate subordinates and his noble superiors—he had no real peers—were more or less in awe of the results he almost always achieved, for all their frequent and frustrated cursings of his slow, plodding preparations.

Under his generalship, Skohshun arms had suffered but a

single real defeat, and that one—which was the reason they had found it necessary to leave their fine lands in southerly Ohyoh, won at such cost by their forefathers, and cross the river to hack out a new homeland—could reflect only additional glory on the old war dog. His strategies and tactics had enabled his vastly outnumbered battalions to several times inflict such heavy losses upon the attacking hordes that their leaders at last had agreed to allow all of the inhabitants of the Skohshun Confederation to emigrate to the south, across the great river, bearing with them all that they wished and granting them five full years in which to leave Ohyoh.

Of course, there had been that close thing last year, in battle aganst the present holders of these new lands, these doughty Kuhmbuhluhners. But that had not been a defeat; the pike hedge had not been completely broken at any time; it had really been something of a draw—with both sides so severely stung as to willingly allow each other the opportunity to retire in good form.

The old officer again warmed his tankard's contents, then turned his chair half about and leaned back in it, thrusting his aching legs even closer to the source of the heat while he sipped and thought and muttered to himself.

"Not enough ash trees in this country. The lads of the battalions don't like the replacement pikeshafts one damned bit. Hummph—don't blame them, either. Oak's a damned sight heavier, foot for foot, and the stuff splinters easily, too. But we'll just have to make do with oak and maple until we hold and can explore more of these new lands."

He chuckled to himself. "If ever we get to. These New Kuhmbuhluhners seem damned confident, to have suffered such heavy losses last year. It could be all bravado, of course. I pray God that's all it truly is, else we may well be chin deep in the shit, for fair.

"No less than six battalions chewed up, *well* chewed up, and the earl hails it as a 'great victory,' simply because we were forced to allow what was left of their heavy horse to leave the field. We never even met their foot. Of course, it didn't look like much, that foot, what I could see of it. No organization to it, apparently, just the usual rabble of archers and slingers and dartmen with a few pole arms here and there. They might do a little damage to us at a distance, but they could never stand against an advance of our hedge.

"No, we have nothing to fear from the Kuhmbuhluhners this year . . . unless they manage to come up with more of that damned heavy horse. I wonder if they have. Is that why they're so damnably confident, why they rebuffed the earl's heralds with such scorn and contumely? It would help vastly in my plans and calculations if I had the advantage of some decent reconnaissance, but no matter how skillful and experienced the scouts I send out, they've never come back to me with anything of true value." He grimaced and then muttered regretfully, "Hell, most of the poor sods have never come back at all."

Major Wizwel Teague sat his shaggy pony at the forefront of the knot of the pony-mounted company officers at the edge of the field whereon the brazen-throated sergeants were engaged in putting his battalion of pikemen through the intricate maneuvers of close-order drill. From the distance, it appeared to him that the formations were shaping up well, despite the autumn and winter and early-planting season when most of these men had devoted their time exclusively to necessary civil, rather than military, pursuits.

He was tucking the oiled cloak more tightly around his throat in hopes of halting the drip of the cold drizzle from the cheekplate of his helm down his neck and under his gambeson when a sudden rattle of pikeshafts caused him to look up. From Number Two Company, some of whose ill-angled pikes could be seen to make X's against the gray, overcast sky behind them, emanated the screamed curses and verbal abuse of several enraged noncoms, punctuated shortly by the solid *thwacks* of the sergeants' sticks brought down with force upon the unarmored backs of the recalcitrant pikemen.

Teague simply went back to tucking in his cloak. Things were always so during the first few drills after the months of none, but he had chosen his sergeants carefully, and all were good, tough, experienced men. They soon would have the battalion moving in the certain and precise order demanded.

During the three weeks that it took to move his column up from Sandee's Cot to the more thickly populated country just south and west of New Kuhmbuhluhnburk, the capital and only walled city of the Kingdom of New Kuhmbuhluhn, the young commander was exceedingly glad that he had so stoutly resisted the well-meant advice of old Count Steev to convey his gear and baggage and supplies in wagons and wains.

Throughout the long years when the huge bunches of the outlaw Ganiks had ravaged and harassed the environs of the scattered safe-glens of the southeasterly portions of the kingdom, there had been a dearth of funds, manpower, peace or opportunity to maintain existing roads or to construct new ones, so Bili of Morguhn had more than sufficient delay and difficulty in establishing and continuing a decent rate of march for his squadron, pack trains and the unwieldy herd of horses, ponies and a few mules and asses.

But move northward they did, despite slippery, sucking mud as a constant deterrent, since every day on the journey saw either rain or at best a misty drizzle. It was hellish and miserable. Within the first half week, there was not a single square inch of dry cloth amongst them all, nor could clothing be dried, for there seldom was much sun and, since not even the Kleesahks could find much dry wood, many nights saw cold, cheerless camps. The cold, biting winds that scoured the heights and whipped through the vales might have served to at least dry some of the sodden woolens and linen and cotton cloth, had not each frigid gust borne upon it unneeded additional moisture.

Streams shown upon Count Steev's map as narrow, shallow valley rills proved often, under these adverse conditions of weather, to be ten or more yards across at the narrowest and belly-deep to a warhorse, where the Kleesahks found fords.

Horses and ponies fell on the slippery tracks, a few so badly injured that it was necessary to put them down. No men or women died or were seriously injured, but Bili at length ordered all to march dismounted until they had traversed that particular stretch of the journey.

Hardened veterans of war and campaigning though all the

men and women were, within a week everyone was sniffling, sneezing, hacking out lung-tearing coughs, feverish, and Bili would have halted for a while could he have found shelter and dry wood enough to last them long enough. But the map told the grim story—they must keep moving for at least a week more, did the weather not change for the better.

It did not. Pah-Elmuh did what little he could, but he freely admitted that head colds did not respond very well to his healing methods, though he could achieve success in clearing congestions from the lungs or binding loosenesses of the bowels.

Tempers became short in the squadron, and it often was all Bili and his officers could do to prevent fights, duels or outright murder. Amongst the suffering troops, animosities which had remained dormant during better times raised their venomous heads—racial, sexual or class distinctions. The Kleesahks proved invaluable in curbing these outbreaks of human violence.

Freefighter Sergeant Loo Haiguhn leaned to stir the stew just beginning to bubble in the pot hung over the tiny fire and, in so doing, chanced to slop a dollop out.

"Clumsy, stupid piece of male offal!" commented his war companion and mate, the Moon Maiden Klahra.

Haiguhn's head was pounding ferociously, it being a sudden and more agonizing stab of that pain which had caused him to spill the small bit from the pot. Straightening up, he snarled, "If you think you can do it better, you arrogant sow, do it! Cooking a man's meal is the proper job of a woman, anyhow!"

With an enraged hiss of "Impudent man-thing!" Klahra drove her fist in a short, hard punch square onto his dripping nose, which spurted bright blood beneath her hard knuckles.

But a backhanded buffet from the big, powerful sergeant hurled the slender, much lighter young woman to the squishy ground. Before she could even think of arising, Haiguhn had wiped the back of his hand across his nose, seen his blood and dropped upon her. His knees and weight pressed her shoulders into the sodden loam, and his big hands locked around her throat, tightening remorselessly, all reason fled from him.

Frantically, her whole being starved for air, Klahra's short-nailed fingers reached up past his muscle-bulging arms, tried in vain to find his eyes, clawing great, blood-welling gouges down his bristly cheeks.

Before Hohmuh the Kleesahk could reach them, even with the length of his strides and the rapidity of movement of his eight-foot stature, Klahra's face had become livid, her eyes and tongue protruding horribly. With a sigh of mingled sorrow and disgust at such senseless savagery as the two humans displayed, the massive humanoid picked up Haiguhn by his wide dagger belt and ungently shook him until he opened his hands and let go of the swooning woman's neck.

And this was but one of the more minor altercations, one involving only two people and no bared steel.

But all things—both the good and the bad—must end, and though it seemed to last for an interminable period, the long, difficult journey finally did come to an end. On a bright, sun-dappled morning, the vanguard passed from narrow mountain track onto the southernmost edge of a vast plateau of level fields and grassy leas crisscrossed with wide corduroy roads and strong stone-and-timber bridges over the watercourses. The column had at last arrived in the longer-settled, long-peaceful portion of the Kingdom of New Kuhmbuhluhn.

As the head of the main column commenced the gradual descent, Pah-Elmuh, mounted high on his huge Northorse, pointed to the northern horizon, mindspeaking to the young *thoheeks* and Rahksahnah, "Yonder is King's Rest Mountain. The city lies partway up its southern slope, on a smaller plateau, and is not visible to humans from this distance. The contested lands, those now held by the Skohshuns, lie north and northwest of mountain and city, being generally lower in elevation and sloping down toward the river called Ohyoh."

The remainder of the march was accomplished in easy stages, an initial encampment of several days allowing the squadron real rest, hot, plentiful, well-cooked food, and time to dry out blankets and clothing and perform much-needed maintenance on weapons and equipment that had remained damp for too long.

The free farmers and stockmen of the countryside through which the column passed proved friendly, generous to a fault and eagerly anticipatory of their needs. Locals were quick to point out the best areas for night camps, and, like as not, when the main column arrived at these sites, cordwood would be all neatly stacked and some cattle slaughtered, skinned, rough-dressed and hung on frames, ready for the butchering.

Bili, himself a landholder and fully cognizant of the costs of such lavish hospitality, protested to the petty nobleman of New Kuhmbuhluhn who stood waiting with the wood and meat on the occasion of the third halt, citing among other things his lack of funds to pay for the provender.

But the bandy-legged knight only smiled good-naturedly, saying, "If nothing else, it would be the least we could do fer you and yer squadron, my lord duke, especially when you come all the way up from Ganikland to help us drive the damn Skohshuns back where they come from. Even was all of the cost to come outen us, it would be but simple thanks, but"—here he grinned widely—"Prince Byruhn, he'll make up some of it all to us, sooner or later. So eat hearty and fret not. Come to that, me and my fellers, we'll even help yer folks to set up things, then help 'em to eat up them steers, too."

Sir Yoo Folsom—blond, blue-eyed, looking to be just approaching middle age and bearing enough scars to show that he had earned his title the hard way, even if the land was his by right of birth—and his men proved as good as his offer. All pitched to with a will in helping the squadron to do the multitudinous chores necessary to set up camp, lay and start the cookfires, then butcher the carcasses for quick, easy cooking.

Sir Yoo sent back one of the larger wagons with a double team, and before the beef was done, it and another laden wagon had arrived with beer for the bulk of the squadron and wine and brandy for the officers. Apparently sensing new protests from Bili, the knight made haste to justify these new and even more lavish gifts.

"Look at it this way, if you please, m'lord duke. The lives of you and yer fine force are going to be on the line right along with mine own soon enough. If we all live and win out o'er these Skohshuns, why then there'll doubtless be many another harvest to refill my cellars, while if we lose, then none of us will be around to quaff. So far better we do so now than leave such good fare for the damned invaders. Eh?''

So Bili gave over arguments and remonstrations, and soon the only wholly sober creatures in the camp—aside from the picket lines and the herd of remounts—were the Kleesahks and the prairiecat, Whitetip, all of whom took up the job of guarding the camp with their nonhuman keen senses, while carrying on a silent conversation concerning the hardly comprehensible foibles of the races of true-mankind.

The high-riding moon had been new when they had departed Sandee's Cot, far to the southeast; it was once more new when—all polished, burnished, brushed, currycombed and clad in their finest—they clattered through the main gate of New Kuhmbuhluhnburk and thence up High Street, bound for the citadel complex set above the city proper on its own much smaller plateau.

Bili of Morguhn had liked what he had seen in approaching this capital city of the monarch they all now were serving. There were but two approaches up the flanks of the mountain— one from due south and another from southeast and both converging a good quarter mile shy of the outer defenses, leaving but the single road up to the gates. The young commander also noted that although the underlying road had been hewn from the living stone of the mountain, it was overlaid with a corduroy of well-worn logs, and he doubted not that somewhere in or on the defenses above, there awaited vats or tuns of oil with which those very logs over which he and his column now rode might be drenched, then fired with an enemy upon them.

Sitting on the lap of the mountain, New Kuhmbuhluhnburk had scant need of defensive walls, so the arc of walls it did have were low—no more than about ten yards high, Bili guessed—but they looked every bit as solid as the living stone beneath them. Built by the Kleesahk and the even huger pure blood Teenéhdjook, the stones were the largest dressed masonry that Bili had ever before seen, and he doubted that the siege engine to breach them existed. Not even those made for him last summer by the Kleesahks themselves could have

106

damaged those walls in less than two or three years of steady pounding.

No, he thought, this New Kuhmbuhluhnburk would never fall to open attack, not with any decent sort of garrison. Did a reliable source of adequate water exist up there, along with ample provisions, the city could likely outlast the patience of any besiegers, too. That left only treachery from within, that or one of the deadly plagues that so often ran their course through garrisons and civil populations under siege.

On the ascending roadway, just beyond the outer works, Prince Byruhn and a score of peacock-bright noblemen had met Bili and, after requisite courtesies and a brief round of introductions, had joined with them to ride up to, into and through the city. Along broad, stone-paved streets they rode, between stone slate-roofed houses and lines of lustily cheering New Kuhmbuhluhnburkers.

Astride his big stallion, Mahvros—who gleamed like black onyx and proudly flaunted along in his high-stepping parade strut—beside the prince, with the silken banners of New Kuhmbuhluhn, Morguhn and the wolf device of Byruhn being borne just behind, Bili coolly wondered privately just how much of the noisy greetings of the populace was spontaneous and how much performed on orders from Byruhn or his royal sire.

Amid the tumult, conversation of any nature with the prince was an impossibility, but Bili, Rahksahnah and Pah-Elmuh the Kleesahk chatted via mindspeak.

"Pah-Elmuh," beamed the young *thoheeks*, "in the event that these Skohshuns prove too numerous or powerful for whatever field army the kingdom finally manages to scrape together, how well supplied is this city to withstand a lengthy siege? Are there existing stores of food and forage? And how reliable is the supply of water?"

The powerful beaming of the Kleesahk replied, "Since first this city was built, there have always been reserve stores of grain, dried or smoked meats, pickled vegetables and suchlike. The first king always feared that his hateful enemies from the north might pursue him and pen him and his folk up herein, and this precaution is now become habitual. But I have been long away from New Kuhmbuhluhnburk and I

107

therefore know not just what quantities lie available. For that information, you must confer with Prince Byruhn. As to forage, I know not, but few beasts have ever been lodged within the walls at any one time; most are kept on the plain, below, and brought up as needed.

"Within the bowels of the mountain is a huge lake fed by many small springs in its bed. Years agone, this lake's overflow ran out of the side of the mountain, across the smaller plateau whereon the citadel now stands, then down its nearer slope and partway around its base to pour down the northern flank of the mountain.

"Good King Mahrtuhn I, when first he chose this site for the city he envisioned, showed the Teenéhdjook and Kleesahk how to dam up this steady flow and then channel the resultant accumulation of water to supply the smaller and the larger plateaus with pure and plentiful water. Populous as that city he founded has become over the passing years, still is there no dearth of water for all purposes of those who here dwell."

"And this underground lake has never been dry?" Bili probed. "Its level never fluctuates?"

"Never, Lord Champion," the Kleesahk assured him. "Even in the very aridest of drought years has the flow stayed clear and cold and copious. I think, as did the good King Mahrtuhn, that some mighty river must flow far, far beneath King's Rest Mountain, so far down that it is unaffected by events upon the skin of earth and rock upon which we all dwell."

"The Hold of the Moon Maidens was watered by such spring-fed lakes and pools," put in Rahksahnah. "A few of them were of an icy coldness, but most were warm and some were boiling hot. It was these that kept the hold at an even temperature all of each year; even when snow and ice lay heavy upon the surrounding mountains and valleys, still did grain and other food crops and even bright flowers grow and ripen in the hold.

"The very ground and rocks themselves were warm to the touch, in our lost hold, so that the cold water falling from above rose up and often shrouded much of the land in a soft mist."

"The northern safe-glen, that one now squatted upon by the Skohshuns, has three hot springs," attested Pah-Elmuh.

"It is never so warm of winters as that one you describe, my lady, but even so it never is as cold as are the surrounding lands."

"I would much like to see this glen, Pah-Elmuh," beamed the *brahbehrnuh*. "Could such be arranged, perhaps it might serve as a new home for those of the Maidens of the Silver Lady who still hunger for the old ways, the ways of the hold. They would have to choose a new *brahbehrnuh*, of course, for my way now lies with my Bili and our little son, but I think that Kahndoot might fill that office far better than even I might have done, and she has yet to choose a man-mate."

But Bili, anxious to gain knowledge of this position he might one day soon have to defend or, at least, share in defending, abruptly returned to the subject he had chosen.

"I can discern but the two gates, Pah-Elmuh, the one into the lower city and that one up ahead, leading into the keep. Is there then no way to secretly sally out to prick a besieger? So meticulous a planner, so skilled a soldier as this King Mahrtuhn clearly was must surely have provided such a necessary convenience for those who might one day have to defend his city."

"There is assuredly such a way," beamed the Kleesahk. "It is tunneled through the mountain itself, and debouches into three branches, each leading to a well-concealed exit. Indeed, we passed close enough to one such to have touched the stones sealing it, today, on our approach to the city. Veteran as you are in the wars and ways of true-men, you did not note it, Lord Champion. Did you?"

"No, I did not," admitted Bili ruefully. "Despite the fact that I was examining, seeking, searching out any true or possible weakness to the city's approaches and defenses, I saw no trace of any tunnel mouth along the way we rode, Pah-Elmuh. Perhaps, had I dismounted, been afoot . . . ?"

"You still would not have found it, Lord Champion, even had you known the general area in which it lies. Nor can the mighty stones sealing it be shifted from without . . . certainly not by true-men. Nor are the other two egresses any less well concealed and inaccessible from without."

Up from the city streets, an inclined ramp led along the face of the elevation on which crouched the citadel. This way was broad for the most of its length—broad enough, thought Bili, for two large wains or wagons to pass abreast—with a balustrade of stone blocks along its outer edge to prevent mishaps and a bed corduroyed for better traction on the grade.

But at the top, where the roadway became almost level, the way narrowed considerably after taking a sharp turn to the right. Directly before them squatted a massive dressed-stone gatehouse, consisting of a brace of thirty-foot towers joined well above road level and housing strong-looking, double-valved gates between inner and outer portcullises of iron-sheathed, massy oaken timbers.

Beyond these outer works, a movable bridge spanned a chasm some twenty feet broad and as deep, seemingly, as the outer works were high. Bili decided that while the chasm might originally have been a natural feature, it had been deliberately broadened and deepened and rendered more regular in form, as was readily apparent to an experienced eye. Even the array of jagged boulders littering its bed seemed too evenly distributed to be entirely natural.

Like those of the city below, the citadel walls were massive but low—little higher than the gatehouse towers, in fact. No towers were built into the walls, and the mighty chains and thick cables for raising the bridge disappeared between merlons atop the walls. Another of the oak-and-iron grilles and another double-valved gate somewhat less thick than that in the outer works gave entry to the bailey of the citadel.

Due principally to the fact that most of the necessary outbuildings were built against or into the inner face of the protective wall, the bailey itself was relatively open and uncluttered. Aside from the palace—a rambling, two-story structure that reminded Bili of nothing so much as a vastly enlarged rendition of the hall at Sandee's Cot—the most notable features were the commodious stables and the countless stacks of cordwood, piles of charcoal, and covered mounds of baled hay or straw.

The keep itself, the place of final refuge if city, outer works and bailey all had fallen to a determined and overpowering foe, was a half tower, built against and into the very mountain which reared up behind the smaller plateau. Huge as were the worked stones of the walls of city and citadel, they were dwarfed by the mighty courses of the half tower. And high as had been the lakeside tower that dominated Sandee's Glen and Cot, this one seemed to rear to at least twice that height, soaring up to within bare rods of the summit of the very mountain.

Young Bili thought to himself that if all this—the city and its defenses, the citadel, with its outer and inner works and this patently invulnerable keep—had been the plannings of King Mahrtuhn I, the man had been nothing less than a military genius. Old Sir Ehd Gahthwahlt, High Lord Milo's siegemaster and senior fortress architect, would die shriveled with envy if ever he saw these masterpieces of defensive architecture and engineering.

Although of more than seventy years, King Mahrtuhn II of New Kuhmbuhluhn showed precious few signs of advanced age and none of senility. A few strands of dark red still were evident in his yellowish-white hair, and intelligence sparkled in his gray-green eyes under brows almost as shaggy as those of his son, Prince Byruhn.

For all that he was seated in a highbacked armchair, it was apparent that the elderly monarch was still both fit and muscular, his sinewy, callused hands resting easily upon his flat horseman's thighs. He lacked the height and massive breadth of Byruhn, but still, had he been standing, Bili thought that they two would easily have been able to stare eye to eye.

The man who lounged casually against the right side of the heavy carven and inlaid chair resembled the king far more than did Prince Byruhn, matching feature for craggy feature with the king Bili now was sworn to serve. So very close was the resemblance that the young *thoheeks* felt sure a glance at the lounger showed an accurate picture of the King Mahrtuhn of forty-odd years agone—thin, straight nose seeming to grow directly from the high forehead, shaggy brows and close-cropped hair of a dark red verging on auburn, protuberant cheekbones and broad chin, lips neither overthin nor overthick but hinting a ready smile, ears large and outjutting with pendulous lobes, hands large and square and the backs of them thickly furred with crinkly red hair.

The body shapes of the two were not the broad-shouldered and thin-waisted and almost hipless ideal so favored by the Ehleenee of Bili's homeland, but much closer in conformation to his own powerful young body. The shoulders were broad and thick enough, rolling with muscle even on the elder man, but there was none of the tapering so loved by the Ehleenee; rather were the waists almost as thick as the chests, sitting upon hips almost as wide as the shoulders. Bili reflected that if both the royal personages were not, by choice, axemen, they had missed their calling and wasted nature's gifts.

Although dutifully respectful of hereditary royalty, Bili was somewhat less than abashed, having been reared in the court of a far more powerful monarch than King Mahrtuhn, having swung steel tooth to jowl beside the very High Lord of the Eastern Confederation, not to mention having been for many months the well-loved lover of the High Lady Aldora Linszee Treeah-Pohtohmas Pahpahs who probably commanded more cavalrymen than the total numbers of every man, woman, child and Kleesahk in all of New Kuhmbuhluhn.

Therefore, as he came to a halt and followed Prince Byruhn's example by sinking onto one knee before the seated king and inclining his head in momentary deference, he sent his powerful mind questing forth at both the monarch and the younger companion . . . to run head on into a strong mental shield akin to Byruhn's own.

King Mahrtuhn showed surprisingly white, though crooked, teeth in an amused smile and said, in a pleasant, full-toned bass voice, "No, sir duke, we are not a telepath; few of our house ever have possessed that talent. But in protection against those who do and might pick our minds to wreak us ill, our good Kleesahks have schooled us in erecting a constant barrier against telepathic intrusion."

Bili answered grin for grin. "No trespass was intended, your majesty. With those of us who possess the ability, such becomes almost second nature, for mindspeak takes far less time than does verbal intercourse. Moreover"—his grin widened perceptibly—"it is most difficult for mindspeakers to delude those with whom they so communicate effectively."

King Mahrtuhn threw back his head and gusted forth his rumbling, basso laughter. "Our Byruhn had warned us of your tactful bluntness of speech, Cousin Bili. We think us that you are no stranger to courts and kings and their ways.

You go as far as is permissible and no farther, and with a long life during which we have endured far too many sycophants, we find a young man such as you seem most refreshing.

"Arise, cousin. Byruhn, have chairs and wine fetched. Your aged and doddering old sire would have words with this vital young nobleman."

CHAPTER VIII

Despite the singular oddities of their personal habits, Abner and Leeroy were as brave as any Ganik—just so long as they were faced with corporeal foemen—not to mention tough, resourceful, aggressive and utterly ruthless. These sterling qualities, coupled with the untarnished glamour of having been the personal bullies of the second leader of the main bunch of outlaw raiders, fitted them admirably as the leaders of the mob of stragglers from the bunches now based just beyond the southwest borders of Ahrmehnee lands.

When first they had arrived in company with some three-score other deserters from what had been the stronghold of the main bunch, nothing so mundane as physical cowardice had led them and their followers to desert the besieged camp, but rather the creeping, crawling, unnatural and unbearable dread of the unknown—ghosts, specters and maleficent demons.

Scores, possibly, hundreds, of the deserters had seen—with their own two bulging, horrified eyes—the huge ghost of their long-dead Kleesahk leader, Buhbuh, appear from out of a cloud of mist at various times and places to warn them that their Kuhmbuhluhner foes had enlisted the aid of a vast horde of the murderous specters of dead Ahrmehnee and Moon Maidens; had summoned up another horde of terrible demons to kill sleeping Ganiks in the very midst of tightly guarded camps or to bear them, living, away for an eternity of endless, hellish torture.

Therefore, when monstrous boulders and living fire began to rain down on the camps out of the empty skies of night, the former trickle of desertions became a torrent, with Abner and Leeroy and many another lesser bully riding in the lead, like as not.

114

With access to the western trails and the interior of New Kuhmbuhluhn blocked by the force of Kuhmbuhluhners and their supernatural minions, each group of deserters had, perforce, hied itself onto the easternmost, southbound trail and thence, naturally, into the Ahrmehnee lands where they had ridden on raids for long years.

At first, they had met with considerable success—loot, a few women, ponies and the like—the particular tribe they faced being weak, with few warriors to face their raiding hundreds. But then, quite suddenly, raiding party after large raiding party were butchered, routed and sent fleeing back across the ill-defined border as fast as their legs or those of their runty ponies would bear them, all swearing most forcefully and profanely that they had been attacked by a mixed agglomeration of Ahrmehnee warriors, Moon Maidens and *Kuhmbuhluhners!* Some of the smaller parties never came back at all.

Ganiks, both outlaw and farmer type, continued to trickle in from the north and west, and so the senior bully of this new, composite bunch, Crookedcock Calder, waited a few weeks until this trickle had once more filled out his ranks, then led a huge force of raiders in a fast-riding incursion ending in a dawn attack against the largest Ahrmehnee village. The assault should by all rights have succeeded. Instead, the Ganiks were thrown back after a savage encounter that left a good third of their number dead or dying in and around the partially palisaded village and saw nearly a third more of the defeated men slain during a furious pursuit that was pressed up to and even a bit beyond the border of the Ahrmehnee lands.

Due principally to the fact that they all forked real horses rather than ponies, Crookedcock, Abner, Leeroy and most of the bullies survived the disaster, but once again they had had to wait until more new-come Ganiks had straggled in to give them enough force to make another try. And this they did.

That time, they were careful to choose a smaller village, one with no palisades of any sort, and with only old men and striplings moving about amongst the toothsome women. After splitting off enough Ganiks to throw out strong guards along the several trails that converged on the village, they attacked at dawn—as was their wont—and then it seemed as if the

115

very ground suddenly vomited up armed and armored warriors, while the same toothsome women after whom the Ganiks had lusted as they reconnoitered the village threw off cloaks and outer coverings to reveal the gleaming armor and weapons of Moon Maidens and threw themselves into the fray.

And despite even more meticulous precautions and lengthy observance of another and smaller village, the same lethal subterfuge had been perpetrated only a few weeks later on yet another party of Ganik raiders.

Following the pursuit of the Ganiks after this second ambush of the raiders, the hard-riding and murderous force of harriers had come far enough over the border to attack the very bunch camp itself, panicking large numbers of the excitable Ganiks. In this surprise engagement, Crookedcock Calder, while trying to organize a defense, had his luck finally run out in the form of a spear that transfixed his unarmored chest and a blade that severed head from torso.

During the six weeks that followed the fresh disaster, the Ganiks had first spent considerable time and effort in rounding up the vast pony herd scattered by the attackers. Then had come a round of bully councils, each usually ending in one or more fights to the death between contenders for the vacant post of senior bully left by the violent demise of Crookedcock Calder. The hulking Abner had wisely refrained from voicing claims. Waiting until the preliminary battles were concluded and a single man remained, Abner challenged him, fought him and slew him, messily.

With the best parts of Abner's late opponent become a comfortable weight within their bellies, while the remainder of the butchered carcass simmered in stewpots about the camp, Abner chose several lieutenants, with his brother-cum-lover, Leeroy, as the chief one, then outlined to the bully council his plans for dealing with the Ahrmehnee and these strange eastern Kuhmbuhluhners.

Abner had both liked and admired Crookedcock Calder, and the plan he outlined was but a rehash of the plans of the deceased (and long since eaten) leader. They would mount no raids of a large enough size to invite any more of these calamitous attacks by the heavy-armed and well-mounted foe, not until they once more possessed numbers large enough to stand a chance of defeating the foe in open combat. They were to see that their small raiding parties left villages strictly alone, preying rather upon herders and charcoal burners and any isolated farms they could find still tenanted.

If they came across far-inferior forces of warriors, they might attack, but under no circumstances were they to do so if said forces were even half their numbers, and should more warriors come up after a fight had commenced, they were to break off, scatter and flee. Abner wanted live Ganiks, not dead ones, and he said so in no uncertain terms.

But the wait for reinforcements turned out to be a very long one, far longer than it ever had been when Crookedcock had still been alive and leading. It seemed that most of the farmer Ganiks who were coming east had already come and that the bulk of them had trekked south or southwest. And such few outlaw Ganiks as did ride in were mostly weary survivors of the final, bloody defeat of the old main bunch, back in New Kuhmbuhluhn; nor were there many of them.

It was full, frigid winter before a group of some two hundred Ganiks trotted their ponies into the environs of Abner's camp. The leader of this small bunch, one Gouger Haney, had been a bully appointed by Buhbuh the Kleesahk to head up one of the satellite bunches. When his bunch camp had been attacked and burned the preceding spring by the Kuhmbuhluhners, he had quickly recognized the futility of trying to stand and fight the large number of warriors with their superior arms and big horses, and so had led some three hundred of his followers in a breakout to the west.

Although they had won free of Kuhmbuhluhn, they had not ridden far into the completely unknown far west before they had found themselves being preyed upon by a very numerous and unremittingly savage race of people. After many vicissitudes, he and those who now followed him had won back into western Kuhmbuhluhn and headed for the camp of the main bunch, only to find it firmly in the hands of the very foemen who had burned their camp and massacred so many of them long months before.

And so, after a couple of near things which very nearly led to discovery by the superior Kuhmbuhluhner force, they had sought out the easternmost trail and proceeded southward until they encountered the Ganik markers showing the way to Abner's camp.

Abner freely and warmly accepted the newcomer bully as one of his principal lieutenants, second only to Leeroy, for he shied away from any set of circumstances that might lead to a leadership fight with the older man, some sixth sense assuring him that there could be but one sure outcome and that it would be Abner, not Gouger, who went to the stewpots.

But this arrangement seemed not to please Haney in any way. After hearing all that Abner and the others had to say of their unbroken string of reverses and bloody defeats, he still mocked and derided the cautious strategy and tactics of Abner and his predecessor, siding with every hothead already resident in the camp and casting so many aspersions upon the leadership ability (or lack, thereof) and personal courage of Abner, Leeroy and the rest that it soon became crystal-clear to Abner that he either must take his chances in a death match with this Gouger or include all the newcomers in a full-scale reinvasion of the Ahrmehnee lands, come what might.

Even with the addition of Gouger's Ganiks, there were still only a little over six hundred raiders. Abner had desired not to enter the Ahrmehnee lands again until he led a good ten hundred outlaws, nor did he particularly like the idea of having to force the stubby-legged ponies through the deep snows that now shrouded all the routes of access with the ever-present danger of being caught in the open by one of the fierce blizzards which had been so numerous this winter . . . but, faced with Gouger Haney, he felt he had no option.

Once across the nebulous border, the large party proceeded northeastward up a very familiar valley; many of them had fled several times down this very valley with the Ahrmehnee and the Moon Maidens and those strange, out-of-place Kuhmbuhluhners snapping at their heels. When last Abner had had a brief, running glimpse of the length of this valley, it had been littered with dead and dying Ganiks, all lying amid the scattered bones which were a well-gnawed testament to earlier Ganik defeats and flights; he wished that the deep snow might suddenly disappear long enough for the posturing Gouger Haney to see in advance the full extent of the folly into which he had forced Abner and his veterans.

A number of times during the ride up that valley, Abner's

well-developed senses had told him that they were all under the gaze of hostile eyes, but no move was made to attack them and the men and ponies were having enough trouble breaking trail through the relatively shallow depths of snow on the banks of the hard-frozen creek. Floundering in the deeper blanket of snow that waited on each flank, they would be virtually helpless, so he forbore even mentioning his firm suspicions that they and their slow progress were being constantly observed by those who could be naught save foemen.

But as that day lengthened, it became obvious to anyone that an irresistible and implacable foe would soon attack them head on. The increasingly keen winds and the ominousness of the northern skies gave certain promise of yet another of those murderous blizzards in the offing. Shelter of some sort was a dire necessity, for to be caught in the open would be the quick death of most of them; therefore, the blackened stone walls of a burned-out village near the head of the valley was a most heartwarming sight to the raiders, for all that many of the cottages were lacking all or most of the thatched roofs. Indeed, not even the Ganiks' usual fear of the spectral inhabitants which might be encountered in such a place served to deter them. Their justifiable terror of the fast-coming blizzard submerged even this primitive fear.

As the pitiless wind howled like a damned soul in torment about and through the enlarged and palisaded village of the *dehrehbeh* of the Behdrozyuhn Tribe of the Ahrmehnee *stahn*, Sir Geros Lahvoheetos sat comfortably in the warm, snug main room of the stone house that was his headquarters and personal quarters. Despite the freezing temperature outside, the combined efforts of the fire and the body heat of the half-score of men and women packed into the room to sip mulled wine and confer over how best to deal with this latest Ganik menace had served to so raise the inside temperature as to cause the young knight and many another to loosen the neck and front and sleeves of shirts and jerkins.

"Perhaps," mused Geros, occupying—at Pawl Raikuh's firm insistence—the only real chair in the room, "long and furious as this blizzard has proved to be, it will do all or a part of our fighting for us . . . ?"

"Not likely!" snorted Raikuh. "Those canny bastards have

lived all their lives at a primitive, savage level. They'll have found a place to hole up and wait out this howler, depend on it, Geros lad.''

"Yes, I too think so," agreed Tohla, one of the two leaders of the contingent of the Moon Maidens which rode and fought as a part of Geros' force against the mutual enemy. "These Muhkohee accustomed to hard living are, like the wild beasts they wear the raw skins of. But where? Close enough could the pigs be to under the cover of the storm attack us here?''

The *dehrehbeh* shrugged. "This all is hereabouts flat land— well, as flat as in these southern mountains likely you are to find. Only croplands or pastures or forest here nearby is, nor thick is the growth of the forest; the few tiny herder huts or dugout shelters scant help to a force so large would be, none at all, unless scatter widely they did. No caves there are for the ride of many days in any direction, and even these small are. Perhaps to be of rightness Sir Geros is, perhaps they even now are dying of cold and exposure. The Silver Lady grant that true it be!''

"*Ahem*! Your pardon, please, honored *Dehrehbeh* Ahrszin,'' said an elderly Ahrmehnee crouched near the hearth, speaking slowly and with deference.

Behdros Behdrozyuhn had been a mighty warrior in his long-ago day, adding many Muhkohee and lowlander heads to the impressive collection in the tribe lodge. Now, for all that he was aged, infirm and almost blind, he still was valued for his wisdom and had attended this meeting as the ears and the voice of the Council of Elders.

Now, at his utterance, all gazes turned onto the place where he squatted with his big-boned but withered body wrapped thoroughly in a thick woolen cloak lined with rabbit fur, his two eyes—one still dark and piercing, the other covered over with a thick film the color of thin milk—fixed on Ahrszin.

The *dehrehbeh* was, if anything, even more deferential in his reply to the old man. "Of what would my honored father speak?'' He spoke, however, in stilted, accented Mehrikan, as too had the old man, that all present might understand.

Straightening his body a bit under its wrappings, old Behdros said gently, "With so many weighty cares upon your shoulders, *Der* Ahrszin, I fear you have forgotten the one place the Muhkohee raiders were certain to find, did they come up that valley. It is of the village of the headman Mahrzbehd I speak; it lies at the very top of that valley, with enough buildings to shelter most of a force that size even if not all. True, the distance is too great for them to easily attack this village from there, but that is where they should be sought first, say I."

No less gently, the young *dehrehbeh* replied, "Honored father, that village was burned while still my honored uncle lived, along with the croplands surrounding it. All of its folk and most of their kine are now here, with us in this village. Of what protection are roofless walls even for the Muhkohee?"

The wrinkled lips of Behdros parted to reveal teeth worn down almost to the gum line. After the brief smile, he said, "*Der* Ahrszin, you have not fought over, raided in, alien lands earlier despoiled. I have. Even a roofless wall gives protection from most of the wind, and, with desperation and time, a roof of a sort can be fashioned from saplings, pine branches and hides, for that matter. Far better that than to try to backtrack, to run long miles before the storm back to the camp beyond the border; I doubt any Muhkohee would be so stupid . . . and I know that breed well; I fought them the most of my life."

Raikuh nodded, asking no leave to speak. "He's right, you know. In the Middle Kingdoms wars, I and my mates have seen ruined villages and hamlets with jerry-rigged roofs just like those he describes, have done some of it our own selves at various times. They ain't palaces, mind you, but they sure beat sleeping cold and wet. And that many Muhkohee working together for their common good could likely do a heap of work, fast."

"Yes, son Geros, I think that there village is a good bet for us to check out as soon as this weather lets up enough for patrols to ride again."

When once they had gotten fires going on the hearths of the ruined cottages and the few larger houses, the snow that the heat had melted on the makeshift roofs of interlaced conifer branches and long sapling-rafters had frozen to a film of ice and, when once more snow had accumulated on the surfaces, the rude coverings became almost windproof, though inclined to drip steadily in the warmer interiors.

Nonetheless, Abner and Gouger and their Ganiks were damned glad to be out of the deadly storm that surrounded the rude shelters wherein they crowded with their ponies. During the few, short spells of windlessness when there was a modicum of light, the hobbled and guarded ponies were allowed to forage under the snow blanket in the woods and burned-over fields, while as much of the accumulated dung—animal and human—as could be easily reached was tossed out the doors and other groups of Ganiks cut down and fetched in firewood from the nearest growth of woodland.

Food for the mob of Ganiks was, of course, no problem, not when there were so many other Ganiks about to be murdered and butchered and cooked and eaten. Abner hated to see this loss of fighting strength, but he knew that without food they would all be too weak to fight even did they survive. Besides, his stomach growled as loud as any man's when empty. So, as had ever been the Ganik way, the weaker and sickly went to feed the stronger and healthier.

There was no thought of killing and eating the ponies, of course. Not only did the little beasts constitute the only means of transportation, but Gouger and his crew and many another of the other lesser Ganiks were strict adherents of the old-time religion, and one of that creed's most powerful gods—Ndaindjerd—forbade the consumption of the flesh of any furred or feathered animal.

Abner, Leeroy and a minority of others were not so strict in observance of traditional Ganik dietary laws—or of any other aspects of the singular religion of the Ganiks, for that matter—but there was no denying that human flesh was tenderer, sweeter and more succulent than the stringy, tough and sinewy pony flesh would likely have been.

Aware that there existed a terrible need to keep the raiders busy at something in this crowded and enforced confinement, Abner, Gouger, Leeroy and the other bullies set the lesser Ganiks to scrounging, even digging up floors in a search for any bits and pieces of metal to be honed and made into dart points; any hard metal would do—steel, iron, brass, bronze, pewter, even hardened copper—the Ganiks were not and had never been picky in that regard. Because another of their ancient gods—Plooshuhn—forbade them the smelting or casting of metals, they always had had to take any worked metal

122

objects from their neighbors, cold-hammering and reshaping their acquisitions to their needs, where necessary, by any method that did not entail fire-heating of the metals, which would surely have called down upon them the awful wrath of the gods.

Pieces too large for dart tips were fashioned expertly into knife or dagger blades, for no Ganik outlaw ever felt himself to have enough knives, the bullies often carrying a dozen or more, large and small, scattered about their persons.

Not that the thrifty Ahrmehnee had actually left that much valuable metal when they hurriedly abandoned the site, but the search alone was an effective means of keeping the minds—far too many of which were, at best, ill balanced—of the lesser Ganiks occupied with something basically constructive.

The lesser Ganiks did not need to be actually driven to the hunt for and work upon metal. But they certainly did need to be so driven to and constantly supervised at other most necessary chores, such as the procurement of and the fetching back of food for the penned ponies.

For this was hard, cold work. It required digging beneath the icy snow with makeshift wooden spades to find grasses or herbaceous plants or even small bushes—mountain ponies were far less fastidious in their choices of food than were true horses—then hacking off armloads and bearing them back to the places wherein the snorting, stamping animals waited in ravenous impatience. And, like as not, the vicious winds or a loss of footing would see the hard-garnered loads torn from the grasps of the freezing Ganiks long before they reached their destinations.

But Abner and Gouger and the other bullies kept them at it as long as there was light enough every day, dealing a swift and brutal and very public corporal punishment to any shirker or laggard, trying hard to ensure that the lesser Ganiks would all be too exhausted through the long, dark, windy nights to do more than sip a few drafts of hot broth and then sleep.

But it did not always work out that way, of course. These outlaw Ganiks were hard, hardy, vital men, else they would never have survived long the savage, primitive life they had chosen to lead. In the cramped quarters, there were fights, many of them, night and day, for any reason or none. At last, alarmed at the number of fatal encounters, the bullies stripped

123

the lesser Ganiks of all their weapons, even their assortments of knives. They collected all of this vast agglomeration of hardware in the largest, most complete house—wherein dwelt Abner, Gouger and Leeroy, among others—issuing only what was needed for immediate foraging tasks, then taking it back before the Ganiks were allowed to return to their quarters for the night. There were still fights, of course, but fewer of them now ended in deaths or serious injuries. Nonetheless, some of the bullies and lesser Ganiks would live to rue and regret this universal disarmament.

At the first hint of a partial slackening of the ferocity of the ten-day-long blizzard, a strong patrol rode out of the palisaded village of Ahrszin Behdrozyuhn—four Freefighters under Captain Pawl Raikuh, Tohla and three other Moon Maidens, and a baker's dozen of Ahrmehnee led by Mahrzbehd Behdrozyuhn, the headman of the burned-out village they now thought the Muhkohee raiders to be occupying.

They set out in the gray light of false dawn, moving very slowly in the deep snows, exhalations of both humans and mounts smoking whitely out through the thick swaths of woolen cloth wrapping their faces against the sharp-toothed cold.

Observing just how slowly they advanced and with what difficulty, Geros did not expect them back soon. Nor was he wrong in his estimate. It was full dark before the near-frozen patrol, weaving and stumbling with utter exhaustion, plodded through the gate.

When once Pawl Raikuh had unwound enough of the frozen lengths of woolens to disclose his deep-sunken eyes and stubbly cheeks, he croaked, "They're there, Sir Geros. The Muhkohee and their ponies, all of the stinking bastards, I'd reckon. Been there since the start of the blizzard, from the looks of the place, with makeshift roofing on all the standing walls and every chimney smoking. They must be packed in like herring in a barrel, but they're all there.

"Now, by your leave, is there anything hot to drink abouts?"

But the blizzard had only been resting, marshaling its frigid resources for yet another fresh assault on the folk and beasts and lands it held in its pitiless grip. The winds howled their song of death through the most of that night and much of the following day, turning that day into a twilight of icy discomfort for those unfortunates who had to be out of doors for whatever reason.

At the hour that should have been sunset at this season of the year, but was now but a deepening of the darkness, yet another meeting was convened in the main room of the house in which Sir Geros resided.

Looking much less akin to walking, frozen corpses thanks to having eaten, thawed out in the sweat house, then slept for most of the night and a great part of the day, Pawl Raikuh, Tohla and Mahrzbehd Behdrozyuhn were there. So, too, were the other leader of the Moon Maidens, Klahra; *Dehrehbeh* Ahrszin and his cousin and sub-*dehrehbeh*, Hyk; the old man, Behdros; Lieutenant Bohreegahd Hohguhn; and, of course, Sir Geros.

In answer to a question, Pawl Raikuh was answering in his usual blunt way. "Lord Ahrszin, for all they was borned here and all, your men suffered just as much as the rest of us did out on that patrol yesterday, and if you don't believe me, just ask old Mahrzbehd here. So it won't be no attacking of them shaggies out yonder till the weather eases her up a mite.

"Sure, we could set the squadron on the march; we might even make it down there to that village by midday, was we to leave afore dawn. But I warrant that nobody—Ahrmehnee, Moon Maiden, Freefighter, horse or pony—would be in any fair shape to fight when they did get there. It was all we could do to just watch the shaggies for a while, then turn round and ride back here. That cold saps a man worse than a four-week drunk."

Absently rubbing at his great beak of a nose, the headman, Mahrzbehd, agreed. "It is true, *dehrehbeh*; all that Pawl says is fact. Almost forty winters have I lived through, and never have I seen the like of this terrible storm.

"But this there is, as well: The accursed Muhkohee are in no sense better off than we are; in many ways, they are worse. No game is about, so they must either be starving or, more likely, eating up each other. And each one that a cannibal dish becomes is one less that face we must when at last the time does arrive for fighting."

When the headman had fallen silent and applied himself to his jack of mulled wine, the woman, Klahra, her prickly

125

Moon Maiden pride surfacing, demanded, "The men have spoken, but what say you, Tohla? Could Maidens of the Silver Lady march down there and fight, think you?"

The young woman thus addressed gave off for the moment cracking nuts in her powerful callused hands, to reply no less bluntly than had Raikuh. "In a word, Klahra, no. A question of fighting skills or courage, it is not. Rather is it the true and pure fact that the flesh and the blood of woman or man or beast not equal is to such a task. It is as Pawl said; wait we all must until not so deep is the snow and clearer is the weather, with less wind. To attempt to now attack will death be for many even before is struck the first blow at the Muhkohee."

So Geros, Ahrszin and old Behdros decided to wait for better weather, and wait they did. They all knew that they had insufficient force as matters stood, and to rashly risk any of that force would have constituted rankest folly.

The last few days of the blizzard were the very worst, and the raiding party of Ganiks huddled in their crowded, inadequate shelters did not fare nearly so well as they had earlier. All of the Ganiks in one of the smaller cottages—some score and a half of them—froze to death one night when the gusting winds tore the roof off their sleeping place. Although the bullies saw the corpses dragged out and the cottage reroofed, none of the superstitious Ganiks would reoccupy it, so it was thenceforth used to stable some of the ponies, affording slightly more room in others of the packed shelters.

The only other good thing that the tragedy accomplished was to provide a ready source of food without the fuss and bother of clubbing down a living man. Now all that was necessary was to choose a stiff cadaver, drag it into one of the cottages and leave it near the fire until it thawed out enough to be skinned and butchered. There followed, of course, an ebbing of the deep distrust each man had felt of every other during their stay here, and there were, consequently, fewer fights. Had it been entirely up to Abner, he would then have given the men back their weapons, but Gouger, overcautious, disagreed and dissuaded him.

But no storm can last forever. One dawn, two weeks and two days after the first gusts of the blizzard had driven them to this place for shelter, the day arrived bright and clear and warmed sufficiently as it progressed to send showers of half-melted ice cascading down off the trunks and branches of the trees, while the ice-sheathed stone walls of the village began to drip and dribble water.

Naturally for the time of year, when the sun set, the temperature dropped and standing water or slushy snow froze. But the next day was just as warm if not actually warmer—opinions were mixed on this—and with all the ponies pawing through the wet snow covering the fields surrounding the village, the bullies began to think of moving on in a day or two, did the weather remain so warm.

As it developed, however, the usually canny Ganiks waited one day too long. Intermittent showers throughout the next two days persuaded them to delay while the water amplified the melting of the accumulated ice and snow, the process aided by the fact that on neither of those two nights did the temperature dip to the freezing mark.

But with the rising of the bright sun of the dawn following that second, warmer night, grim death came to call.

CHAPTER IX

The shaggy, filthy, verminous-looking man had woven leaves into his disheveled mop of dull, dirty hair and his scraggly beard. Streaks of a claylike mud now adorned the highlights of his already dusty, dirty face. Even while flies explored his ears and nostrils, even while tiny, maddening no-see-ums swarmed and whined about his head, he remained absolutely motionless, his gaze locked upon the firestick-armed man who stood alertly some few yards ahead of him.

The unkempt warrior had left his two ponies tethered a quarter mile back in the woods, most of his weapons and equipment with them, retaining only his dozen or so knives. The largest of these—both sides of its fourteen-inch single-edged blade liberally smeared with greasy soot and dust to prevent a telltale reflection of light along its length—was now grasped in his right hand, ready for slash or stab or throw, whatever the occasion might demand. This man had had years of experience at bushwhacking the unwary.

Almost imperceptibly, the shaggy man moved closer to his quarry. Not even a rustling leaf or the crackling of a single tiny fallen branchlet bespoke his passage, however. Soon, now. Very soon he would be close enough to arise for that last, lightning-quick and viper-deadly rush; then a knee in the small of the sentry's back, left hand clamped over the mouth and pulling the head back to bare the throat for its brief, sharp acquaintance with the edge of the blade, and it would all be over save the stripping of the victim of his weapons and any other desired loot, then a safe withdrawal to where the ponies waited, browsing the tender, green new growth of the springy underbrush.

Closer. The wind was right, blowing gently from the hunted

down to the hunter, bearing on it the mixed scents of man sweat, mule sweat, gun oil and tobacco, all registered by the flaring nostrils of the shaggy man. Closer. The shaggy man stopped in midmovement, froze like a statue, for the man with the firestick seemed to be staring directly at him.

But then the searching gaze wandered on and, ever so slowly, the shaggy man smoothly recommenced his interrupted stalking of his soon-to-be victim. Closer still. The keen eyes of the man with the long knife locked onto his quarry. He was come close enough; now he only need wait for the moment when the standing man turned his back.

That moment came at last, and, like a coiled spring suddenly released of tension, the shaggy man was on his booted feet and, in an eye-flickering rush of movement, behind the watcher. In a rhythm born of long practice, the left hand was clamped cruelly tight over the mouth and the body bent painfully backward over the knee sticking into its spine. The long, cruel knife blade came around for the throat-slash . . .

Old Johnny Kilgore waved the sooty knifeblade before the eyes of his "victim." "You daid meat, Jimmy Lewis. I done kilt yer ass, by naow."

"Not quite, Johnny, not quite." There came a sudden popping and crackling of brush and fallen branches from at least three points behind the shaggy man. Then the officer who had spoken and two troopers armed with rifles—scoped, sniper models—came from out the woods, their faces soot-darkened and the nets covering their helmets festooned with plant materials, the metal itself smeared with random patterns of mud.

The officer added, with a grin, "You've been under close observation almost from the time you left your ponies. Where did you get the smaller one, anyway? He looks like a real Ganik pony."

Kilgore released the sentry and sheathed his big knife. Shaking his head, he remarked, "Gump, you'n yore boys is a-gittin' good, dang good. Yawl won't be gittin' bushwhacked by no Ganiks, not if yawl stays thet sharp."

Smiling warmly, the officer nodded and holstered his big pistol. "We all had a good teacher, Johnny. Generations of Broomtown men will bless your name and memory, you know.

"But, back to that scrawny bag of bones you've acquired . . . ?"

Old Johnny shrugged. "I foun' 'im wand'rin' up yonder a ways, and he won't awl I foun', neethuh. Foun' whutawl 'uz lef' of a Ganik, too. A wild bunch Ganik looked fer to be, to me."

In a tight voice, the officer demanded, "Did he see you?"

"Not hardly!" The old cannibal chuckled. "Some critter, some dang big critter, had plumb chawed the life outen thet Ganik. An' whutawl the littler critters an' the birds an' awl had done lef' of 'im, won' much fer me to see 'cept his clo's an' boots an' knifes an' awl."

Johnny shoved aside the close-fitting cap stitched together from two well-matched human scalps and scratched at his bald pate with filthy, cracked fingernails. Then puzzled, he added, "But fer the life of me, I cain't figger haow one pore bunch Ganik got hisse'f this fer south by his lonesome to git chawed to death."

"You're certain he was alone then, Johnny?" probed Gumpner.

The old man shrugged again. "Had to be, Gump. Been any mo' boys with 'im, eethuh he wouldn' of got chawed a-tall, or they'd of took awl his knifes an' his boots afore they lef' 'im fer the critters. Ganiks, they lives hard an' they don' let nuthin jes' go to waste."

Gumpner tugged at his neat, iron-gray chin beard for a moment, then said, "Johnny, that bear we had to kill—could that bear have been the animal that killed this Ganik you found?"

Johnny bobbed his head once. "I thought 'bout thet, too, Gump. Could be, could sure be. It ain' thet much distance less'n you stick to the trail, 'long here, an' ain't no cawse fer no bar to. Bars don't eat folks often, but thet 'un, he might of come after the pony an' thet pore boy he darted him too fer back. So the dang pony, he got away, and the bar, he chawed thet pore dumb Ganik to death. Mighta happund, Gump."

"So, it was just the one man and his pony, then, Johnny?"

Kilgore gave another single, curt nod. "I backtrailed 'im, Gump. Foun' wher he camped up the trail the night afore he 'uz kilt. Won' nobody but him an' the one pony. An' thet ain't no particul of right in it, neethuh, Gump. Ganiks, they ain't nevuh liked bein' alone; the bigger the bunch they rides with, the better they likes it. Suthin' damned funny musta happund up nawth, elst thet pore boy, he woulda been with two, three othuh Ganiks, enyhaow.''

The officer turned to the two snipers. "Go fetch in those two ponies." Then, to Johnny, "There's a little brook between here and the camp. You can wash the worst of that stink off and then we'll go on in. I'm certain that the general will be relieved by your message."

Corbett was vastly relieved at the prospect of not having to fight Ganiks yet. Old Johnny, on the other hand, seemed aggrieved, attesting, as he squatted by the cookfire, "It jes' ain't no fun no mo', gin'rul. Thesehere boys is done got so sharp, I cain't hardly nevuh ketch 'em no mo'. I spent me a whole passel of time a-plannin' an' awl, lef' the ponies way, way back, then took up close to two hours fer to go the las' lil ways aftuh Jimmy Lewis, an' it awl looked perfic'. Then I come fer to fin' out it'd been rifuls awn me dang near the whole damn way. It jes ain' no fun no mo'!''

Corbett sipped at a metal cup of strong coffee and grinned. "It's your fault, then, Johnny. You're too good a teacher for your own good, apparently."

The old Ganik still looked and sounded hurt and offended, however. "But, gin'rul, it won't fair fer to tell Gump an' them I wuz gonna try to jump 'em today."

From where he squatted with his own coffee Gumpner said, "Johnny, neither the general nor anybody else told any of us that you planned to try the perimeter today, only that you would try to do it from time to time, as you've been doing periodically for months. It just happened that one of the outer line of sentries, a fellow up a tall tree, spotted you sneaking across that little ridge back there, and passed on the signal to the perimeter.

"He didn't recognize you—all he reported was a Ganik headed at us afoot. He had a scoped rifle and could likely have dropped you, then, but he was aware that the general wants live prisoners. It wasn't until I got up there that I saw you and realized you'd chosen this time and place for one of the general's impromptu problems. Still, you taught me and two snipers even more than you had in months past about camouflage and the fine art of bushwhacking. All I can say is, thank God you're on our side, Johnny."

The order of march for the next few days remained the same in all respects save that Johnny Kilgore rode with the point rather than ahead of it. They made good time in the week before any other singular events occurred, and Corbett was able to report the appreciable progress in the nightly conversations with Dr. David Sternheimer, via the big transceiver.

"Were we on the main trail, the big eastern one, David, we'd be making even better time than this. But I still agree that it will be better to stick to the one we came south on, this smaller, western one, for all its narrowness and twists and turns. Not only do Gumpner and I and some of the others who were with me last year know this trail well, there's the additional fact that the Ganiks themselves use it seldom, so it will be an unfortunate coincidence if we run onto any of the uncouth bastards."

During the conversation one night, Sternheimer had said, haltingly, "Now, Jay, you know that my belief in some of this parapsychological stuff is very limited. Nonetheless, I have this . . . how shall I say it? . . . this 'feeling' that Erica still is alive . . . somewhere. It's most likely simply a matter of pure and unadulterated wishful thinking, of course. But . . . but, Jay, please, as a personal favor to me, keep your eyes open. Any sign, anything . . . ? Since that vicious bastard Braun did what he did to her . . . she . . . I now know that she meant far more to me than I ever . . . than I ever allowed myself to consciously realize . . . admit.

"You see, Jay, we still are subconsciously bound by the strictures, the morals of the world in which we matured, even though that world hasn't existed for almost a millennium. In the beginning, when first Dr. Arenstein came down to work on the Project, she . . . just being near her, seeing her, hearing her voice, it . . . well, she aroused me . . . sexually, I mean.

"But back then, in our original bodies, there was a vast disparity in our ages. Dr. Arenstein . . . dammit! *Erica* . . . was no more than thirty-eight or -nine, while I was nearing seventy. I had my full share of enemies then, both outside

132

and inside the Project, and the last thing I wanted or felt I could afford was to have the label 'dirty old man' added to all the other canards; nor would that have then been all, of course. I then had a still-living wife, though we had not lived together for years.

"That frigid, feminist bitch! She would have loved nothing so much as to have had the ammunition to publicly humiliate me . . . us, Erica and me . . . had I been so rash as to give it to her. May she rot and suffer in whatever hell she's been in for these last thousand or so years!"

"And so, Jay, I was emotionally saddled with those same, senseless inhibitions for long centuries. Only when, last year, I . . . when I thought that Erica . . . dear, lovely woman . . . only then did I admit to myself just how stupid I had been for so long a time.

"Then, last winter, I began to have strange, disturbing dreams . . . dreams of Erica. I could see her in some low, smoky place . . . perhaps a cave . . . and there were other people there, too, men, I think, some of them, at least, armed with rifles. Laugh at me if you wish, but . . . but it all seemed so . . . so real that . . . that I thought, perhaps, if . . . ?"

"It's entirely possible, David. According to Morty Lilienthal, an intense emotional attachment when combined with enforced separation and longing can heighten, increase, latent psychic abilities."

Old frames of mind become often rock-hard and old habits are hard to break even in the face of suffering. "That fraud?" Sternheimer snorted scornfully. "That pompous ass of a Rhine-blinded idiot! I just wish I knew how that so-called psychometric, that lousy louse of a cheap fortune-teller, got assigned to the Project to begin with. I'm sorry to say so, Jay, but you have a very poor choice of associates."

"David," Corbett began, "now I know, along with everyone else at the Center, that you and Dr. Lilienthal don't particularly care for each other . . ."

Sternheimer snorted again. "That, General Corbett, is the unparalleled understatement of two millennia!"

Corbett pushed on, regardless. "No matter, David, you are just now caught between a rock and a hard place, and, like it or him or not, Morty Lilienthal just may be the only one down there who can help you.

"Now you have just gone through a protracted and obviously difficult admission to me about an affair of the heart that everyone save only you at the Center has known about or at least surmised for centuries. You once considered—and likely a part of you still considers—even admission of these feelings to yourself to be far beyond the pale, much less the thought of consummating them, but still you have found the strength within yourself to sufficiently reshuffle your mind enough to admit them not only to yourself but to me.

"Now you're going to have to do a bit more reshuffling, David. For all that mindspeak, as they call it, is a reality and has been a reality on this continent for centuries, and that this mindspeak is nothing more or less than what we once called telepathy, you have continued to regard it and all the other of the host of extrasensory abilities as, at the very best, pseudoscience and, as such, unworthy of your notice. Well, you've been wrong and you're just going to have to bite the bullet and admit that too.

"David, Morty Lilienthal respects you and admires you, has always admired you and fought very hard to get assigned to the original Project in hopes that his then-rare specialty might be of help to you and your Project. He has since been hurt and embittered by your often and loudly expressed scorn of him and his field, but still he never has ceased to admire you and your unimpeachable accomplishments.

"Go to him, David. Better yet, call him to your office and tell him all that you've just told me. He can teach you to mindspeak, if you possess the germ of the ability. He's already taught me in just the last few months to contact those capable of receiving at as much as several hundred meters distant.

"And David, there is another type of telepathy, one which non-Center people call farspeak. Certain unusual minds possessing this talent can communicate over vast distances, hundreds of kilometers; the outer ranges have never been determined. If you prove capable of this rarity, David, and if Erica *is* still alive somewhere, you might be able to actually contact her, converse with her or exchange thoughts and so make it easier for us to find her and bring her back to the

Center . . . to you. Would that be worth the consumption of a helping of crow to you, David?"

"Abase myself to that young charlatan? Never!" snarled Sternheimer, adding in a more normal tone, "You ask too much, Jay. You must remember, I am after all the Director."

"All right," agreed Corbett, trying to mask from his tone the exasperation and disgust he was beginning to feel for Sternheimer and his rigidly closed mind. "Look at the matter this way, David. If you *do* possess long-range telepathy and you can find a way to develop mastery of that ability, it just might prove of value—possibly, of inestimable value—against the mutants, all of whom do any important long-range discussion in just that way.

"And please understand, David, I'm not saying you should make a decision on it now; just think about it, weigh it in your mind. As of tonight, we're nowhere near where Erica was lost, and won't be for a week or more at our present rate of march. Besides, I want to see the job well underway up at the site of the landslide before I take any troops off on what well might well be a wild-goose chase and highly dangerous to me and my men, to boot."

A few hours after the end of that radio communication, it began to rain, nor did it ever stop for more than a few hours at a time, day or night, for weeks. Moreover, with the rain and mist came a drop of temperature to a level unseasonably low for the area they were traversing. The thin layers of soil covering the rocks on the higher elevations of the track became slick patches of mud, making these stretches even more hazardous than usual for the riders and heavy-laden pack animals. Corbett often found it necessary not only to dismount the column but to have men detailed to garner large quantities of weeds and brush to cover the slippery spots and provide some manner of traction for both men and beasts.

Consequently, the formerly good progress was slowed to a mere crawl, nor did all but sleepless nights of shivering under wet blankets add to the daytime efficiency of the troops and civilian packers. Tempers waxed short and the generally easy-going officers and noncoms found it necessary to exact and enforce strict, harsh discipline in order to maintain a unit rather than a mob.

Nor did the march on lower levels of the track provide any rest for the weary column. Streams that Corbett's mental map had recorded as hardly fetlock-deep were found, on this trip, to have metamorphosed into raging rivers, swirling, muddy, icy water between steep, slippery banks and belly-high for even a long-legged mule. Thicker layers of loam on the valley trails quickly developed countless and seemingly bottomless mudholes, from which cursing, mud-caked and thoroughly soaked men often had to extricate screaming, thrashing and terrified mules or ponies.

Due to these multitudinous difficulties, it was close to three weeks before the column wended its way between the high, rocky walls of that pass wherein Dr. Harry Braun had clubbed Dr. Erica Arenstein to earth and left her to the tender mercies of the cannibal Ganiks, while he galloped on after Gumpner and the wounded, leaving Corbett and the bulk of the force doggedly holding the northern mouth of the gap against hundreds of the savage Ganiks, and fully expecting to give their lives that their comrades and the two scientists might have a better chance at survival.

To their astonishment, all of the defenders had lived through the suicidal action, their well-used rifles having taken so heavy and ghastly a toll of the attacking Ganiks that the leaders of the savages had finally rounded up their own survivors and ridden back whence they came, apparently counting on a smaller contingent led by Johnny Skinhead Kilgore to chase down and slay Gumpner's party.

Instead, Corbett and his force had surprised Old Johnny and his Ganiks camping along the trail and shot or sabered all of them save Old Johnny himself. Then Corbett's group joined with Gumpner to continue on south, to Broomtown.

Now, arriving at the northern mouth of the pass, they confronted another difficulty, this one of their own making. What remained of the low breastwork of rocks they had had to erect so quickly before that long-ago battle was easy enough to shift aside with so many hands to join in the work, but the huge fallen tree that they had tumbled from one of the verges above proved another matter entirely.

There seemed to be no way that they could shove hard

enough against the thick mass of splintery roots or heave on ropes hitched around the trunk to do more than shift the tree a few bare centimeters. The spread of branches that had spanned the defile from wall to rocky wall and thus provided so excellent an abattis in last year's defensive battle now fought against their efforts to clear the gap. Those same branches that had forced the charging Ganiks to dismount and come slowly in afoot into the murderous fire of the rifles now sought out and wedged tightly into every crack and crevice and cranny of walls or floor and so added their resistance to the massive weight of hardwood against which the sweating, panting, cursing parties of men strained.

Nor, in the confined area, could enough mules to make a difference be hitched to either side of the stubby trunk of the mountain oak. Moreover, as the wood had had time to weather and season, efforts directed at the thick branches with axe or saber seemed endless and exhausting.

Finally, Old Johnny opined, "Gin'rul, I thanks the bestes' thang we kin do is to burn the bastid out."

Corbett shook his head. "I'd love nothing better, Johnny, and were we not now into Ganik country, I would. But on a clear, almost windless day like this, we'd be sending up a smoke you could see forty miles away. And since most fires are the work of men, just how long do you think it would be before we had a mob of your kinfolk on top of us?"

Kilgore shrugged. "Not lawng, gin'rul. Ganik's is awl curious. But thin why not jes' camp wher we is and do 'er t'night?"

Again, Corbett demurred. "Johnny, look up there." He pointed at the verges ten and more meters above. "Against anything more original or innovative than a direct frontal assault, this gap will be a deathtrap for anyone fool enough to get caught in it. I want to be clear of it well before dark. If only there were some way to get a dozen span of mules through the mess up there . . ."

Johnny scratched at his bald scalp and commented, "If it's jes' mules and riders you wawnts to git out yonder, gin'rul, ain' no trick to thet. R'member, me 'n' my boys, we rode raht roun' yawl, las' year?"

Corbett slammed clenched fist into palm. "Damn! What the hell was I thinking of? Of course you did. But those were

137

mountain ponies you rode, Johnny. Do you think these big mules could negotiate those trails?''

The old cannibal sniffed. ''Onlies' really rough part's gon' be gittin' 'em down the bluff inta the valley yonder. The rest of it's jes' a wide swing th'ough the woods, is awl.''

Corbett nodded briskly. ''All right, Johnny. Take any man you choose, trooper or civilian, and any animal. Gumpner, you go with him and see that he gets no lip from anyone, then report back to me when he's on his way. Once you and your party get into the valley, Johnny, we'll hook up the ropes and pass them through those damned branches to you.''

Johnny Kilgore proved as good as his word, and, with twelve pairs of brawny mules hitched to the tree and a clear expanse of valley before them, the heavy, unwieldy hulk soon was hauled clear of the gap, leaving in its wake only splinters and hunks of half-rotted bark. And the column moved on through.

Although there were several hours more of daylight, Corbett halted the bulk of the column in the meadow just to the north of it, along the banks of the wide, shallow brook that flowed southeast to northwest across it. They all waited there, setting up the night camp, until a strong patrol led by Lieutenant Vance and Old Johnny returned to report no sign of any nearby Ganiks or even of any recent movements of them along any of the network of smaller tracks.

At that juncture, Corbett announced that they would camp in their present location for two or three days. He thought that after the recent strenuous weeks of rain and cold, both the animals and the men needed a rest before they pushed on; it was a certainty that he, Jay Corbett, did.

On hearing this news, the indefatigable Johnny Kilgore found a fresh mount and a few kindred spirits and set out to fetch back fresh game. Corbett let the old man and his companions go with heartfelt wishes of hunter's luck, for he too was sick unto death of the monotonous rations on which they all had been subsisting these past wet weeks.

So quickly did the hunters return that Corbett at first suspected that they had run into Ganiks or some other trouble, but such was not the case. All were heavily laden with game, and the old man was ecstatic. ''Gin'rul Jay, long's I lived in theseheanh mountins, an' thet's a passul of years

138

too, I ain't nevuh come fer to see the critters be so thick an' easy to knock ovuh as they is, naow an' heanh. A body he'd thank they hadn' been huntid fer months. An' not one place could I fin' where nobody'd been a-diggin' no roots, neethuh, an' Ganiks is allus diggin roots, 'speshly in spring.''

As it developed, they stayed for six days, leaving the valley only when the mules and ponies had grazed it out. But they had mounted a strong, concentric perimeter guard twenty-four hours per day, while Corbett and Johnny or Gumpner and Johnny or Vance and Johnny led out large, far-ranging patrol and hunting parties to north and northeast and northwest, to find not one living Ganik of any sort, nor any trace of recent occupation of two deserted bunch camps and a handful of small farms.

One of the bunch camps was utterly abandoned and fast falling in upon itself, the new plants of spring quickly commencing overgrowth of the untenanted spot that had been some years before, or so Johnny assured them, the camp of his son, Long Willy Kilgore. But the other camp had been both slighted and burned, nor had the progress of seasons and weather and predators been able to entirely erase the traces of a large and hard-fought battle in and around the camp at some time prior to the conflagration. Nor could Old Johnny shed any light on the matter, confessing readily and with much scratching of his hairless scalp that he never before had seen the like.

The abandoned farms presented even more of a puzzle. No one of them seemed to have been subjected to any sort of violence, yet all looked to have been deserted well before harvesttime, for many of last year's uncollected crops had obviously reseeded themselves and were springing up afresh if a bit randomly. Aside from evidences of neglect and weather damage, all of the farm buildings were structurally sound and most still contained larger and bulkier items of furniture and household effects, only smaller, easily transportable items being missing.

With the sole exception of a few wild-looking chickens—most of which succulent fowl were downed with darts or sling stones and added to the day's bag—and a single, blatting billy goat which proved too elusive and chary for even Old Johnny to dart, no livestock remained anywhere. Nor did any wagon or cart remain on any of the farms, although quite a collection of larger agricultural implements were still in place.

Old Johnny Kilgore opined that "suthin' dang funny has done gone awn up heanh las' year," and Corbett and the rest could only agree. In all of the mountains and valleys there did not seem to be a single Ganik left resident. Nonetheless, the perimeter guards were maintained and the patrol-hunts went on, though the last three days were spent in ranging up the projected line-of-march, locating and marking favorable campsites and suchlike.

It began to rain again during the night before they broke camp and again marched northeast, but it was only a light drizzle and the winds that bore it were seasonally warm and gentle. By midday, it had ceased completely and the sun was beginning to dry up what little moisture had not soaked into the ground or run off into the little streams along the way.

At that time unaware of the network of smaller tracks connecting the three larger north-south traces, Corbett had led those of his last year's force who had survived the landslide on a grueling cross-country trek from the easternmost track to this one, but with Old Johnny as a guide, such a hellish journey was not necessary this time. A couple of hours into the second day's march after leaving the valley camp, the bald Ganik had set the column onto a narrow, overgrown track—little more than a game trail in the best of times, from the look of it—meandering eastward.

Due to the condition of the long-unused track and the bulk of some of the pack loads, some work with axe and saber was necessary on the part of the vanguard, but Corbett was quick to note that this clearance did not in any way approach the brutal labor of hacking out a passage where none had previously existed as he and his party had been compelled to do in last year's cross-country journey. Nor did this year's passage take the long days that that one had required. They were on the main, easternmost track before dark of the same day they had left the western one.

They camped that night at the junction of the smaller and larger tracks and resumed the march with the dawning of the new day. The midday halt was made just north of a place where a wide but shallow stream crossed the track. A small, brushy island flanked by deeper channels lay just downstream of the ford, and both Corbett and Gumpner were quick to recognize and remember the spot.

"It was here," Corbett informed Johnny and his officers, "on the island, yonder, that the bulk of what was left of the column found Sergeant Vance with the men and animals he'd led out of the forest fires and the Ganik he'd captured, one Jim-Beau Carter."

Old Johnny sniffed. "I knowed thet bastid, too. Won't none them Carters worth a moldy possum turd or a han'ful of rottun peanuts, not fer nuthin', they won't."

"Be that as it may," Corbett went on, "I know the trail now, from here on, and so does Gumpner. So, Johnny, you and Vance take a squad on ahead and find us a good, well-watered campsite, one near to plenty of graze, if you can. I want to be fairly close to the areas in which we'll be working, but not too close; there's no certain way to tell in advance which direction these explosives may throw rocks, and I'd prefer that said rocks not land in our camp.

"All right, then. As soon as the men have finished their coffee and whatall, let's get cracking. I'd like to excavate what's still worth it and get back down to Broomtown before autumn makes these mountains really miserable to travel through."

CHAPTER X

The lid of the simple stone sarcophagus was engraved with but five words: *MARTIN—KING OF NEW KUMBRLAND*. Behind the coffin, on stone pedestal, stood a lifesize figure that Bili at first took, in the dimness, to be a living man. Carved of well-seasoned hardwood by a past master, then enameled meticulously in fleshtones and finally clothed and equipped and bejeweled, the stunning effigy of King Mahrtuhn I stood in eternal vigil in the splendid crypt which now held his dust and that of his sons, and of his wives and theirs.

From where he stood beside Bili, the voice of King Mahrtuhn II of New Kuhmbuhluhn boomed softly. "Even whilst the Teenéhdjooks and Kleesahks were boring the passages and storerooms through the lower reaches of the mountain, using the blocks of stone thus quarried to build the city and walls, were certain of the most skillful of them all preparing this for the eventuality of my grandfather's death. Until die he did, no true-man knew of the existence of this crypt."

The king gestured upward, up into the dark vault above the wavery light of the lamps. "It is fifty feet from where our feet rest to the ceiling of this crypt, and only thirty feet above that is the windswept summit of King's Rest Mountain, yet so cunningly did those creatures who so loved my royal grandfather carve and handle the stones of this mountain that no earth tremor ever has had the force to damage this, their work. Even the terrible shocks of last year, though they sent boulders plunging down every flank of the mountain and tumbled some of the buildings within the city and even shifted a few of the massive stones of the walls, not a pebble or a grain fell in the crypt. Such was the invaluable skill of the Teenéhdjook."

The royal tomb was the first of the wonders Bili was shown within King's Rest Mountain, but far from the last. He saw the ebon sheet of water which was the spring-fed lake, and the catchments and holding basins and dams and copperlined aqueducts that provided citadel and city with abundant, clear, cold water.

He saw the storerooms and stables carved from the living rock within the mountain and reached by ramps wide enough for the largest wains or wagons to negotiate. Packed with dried, pickled, candied and otherwise preserved foods for man and beast, these siege larders were all protected from rodents by a resident colony of stoats. Semidomesticated, the long, slender, furry brown mustelids with their white, pointed, gleaming teeth showed no fear of either man or Kleesahk. A tentative mental probe told Bili that although they possessed at least marginal mindspeak abilities, they were none of them very interested in communicating with a two-leg creature.

Other huge rooms contained ceiling-high stacks of cordwood and sacks of charcoal or blue-black chunks of mountain coal. Nor were the armories less well stocked, although by modern, Middle Kingdoms standards, the armor in particular was all of archaic design and construction.

But the centuries had not seen so much innovation in weapons as in body defenses. The baskets of arrows and darts, the bundles of spears, the various sizes and powers of the crossbows, the racks of different-sized axes—from shorthandled franciscas to two-handed poleaxes—and the buckets of stone or leaden shot for sling or arbalest vastly impressed the young *thoheeks*.

With walls so stout, with such abundant provender and water, with such a quantity of arms, New Kuhmbuhluhnburk was in need of only a stout and determined garrison to be as close as might be to impregnable. A besieging force could break as many teeth as it cared to lose upon such a nut without even approaching the cracking of it; and the more prudent, patient course would likely prove but another form of futility.

With such a large, roomy bastion, Bili could see no reason at all to further risk the already decimated forces of the kingdom against a numerous foe armed with an apparently devastating new tactic, and he said so in council.

143

"Your majesty, my lords, as satisfying as is an open, honest combat to an experienced warrior, there be times when such enjoyments are not the best course from a strategical point of view. It would seem to me from all I have seen and heard that this is just such a time.

"You have here an admirably situated and designed burk, one which could be held passively by no larger or better-trained a force than those nobles and commoners presently resident within it. Moreover, you have enough room to bring in most if not all of the folk of the surrounding farming areas and much of their livestock and goods, as well. Few threatened cities are ever so fortunate in any respect as is New Kuhmbuhluhnburk, I can assure you . . . and I am not a tyro, not inexperienced in any phase of modern warfare.

"Therefore, in the light of your severe losses of heavy cavalry last year, I would advise that you and all other Kuhmbuhluhners withdraw into the city or the safe-glens and leave these Skohshuns to tramp at will around a burned, barren countryside until starvation brings them to the suicidal folly of attacking this burk. As for the safe-glens, if they are anywhere near as well fortified as Sandee's Cot, I see short shrift for the invaders at each of them, as well.

"Your majesty requested my thoughts and advice, and I have dutifully rendered it."

The king regarded Bili down the length of the polished table for a long, frowning moment, then he finally smiled with his lips and said, "And we thank you for your candor, young cousin. Perhaps what you advise is truly the wisest course, perhaps it is what an eastern monarch or prince would do in like case, perhaps it is even what our honored grandsire might have done, but it is not our way.

"We could not feel our honor served by burning our croplands and squatting behind walls of stone, whilst stopping our ears to the honorable challenges of our foemen. We deem it far better that our mortal flesh be deprived of life than that our souls be bereft of honor.

"No, we will gather all the folk of the plateau into the city, right enough, and the more distant folk will be urged to seek the safety of the fortified glens. But when once the foe comes into view, we shall assemble all our remaining host and ride out to meet him in honorable combat.

"Such is our royal will, gentlemen."

The brigadier's fierce mustachios bristled like a hedge of pikes and his eyes sparkled his righteous rage at the earl's patent stupidity and obstinacy in the light of this new intelligence, but long practice gave him control of his voice.

"Your grace, it was given to me to understand at our late-autumn conference last year that should it become obvious that these Kuhmbuhluhners had somehow made good their losses of heavy-armed horse, we'd not try again to fight them, but first offer to treat with them as equals. Another such 'victory' as we squeezed out and squeaked through at that last battle would spell our undoing."

As the earl remained silent, regarding his senior officer blandly over the tips of his steepled fingers, the old man drew a deep breath and went on. "Now we have heard no less than three experienced and trustworthy scouts attest that a large party—at least two hundred, possibly more—horsemen have ridden up from the south, braved both rain and unseasonal cold in the high mountains, to reach the plateau whereon sits the capital of New Kuhmbuhluhn. They—"

"They were none of them armored," interrupted the earl mildly. "The scouts saw no more than a helmet or two and a handful of scaleshirts among them all. We all honor you and your many achievements, brigadier, but I think—and I'd not say this were we two not alone—that that near thing last autumn has gone far to becloud your judgment so that you see fresh Kuhmbuhluhn heavy-armed horse where none exist. Belike, that column was but another train of supplies and remounts.

"No, our costly victory of last year has given us an undeniable edge, and we'd be fools not to use that edge for cutting, for further whittling down these Kuhmbuhluhners to a point at which they will treat on our terms.

"Thanks to that last long, hard freeze that made the river firm and solid enough for even wagons, we now have all of our people over here, and immediately the last regiments are refitted and in order, I mean to advance on the attack. And

145

I'll hear no more words at variance with that decision, Brigadier . . . even from you."

The old man did what he must do, having no option; he bowed his head in submission to his overlord. He still was not in agreement. He knew in his heart that the young earl's plan was wrong, ill advised, precipitate, but he was servant, not master, and he knew his place.

While ostensibly engaged in playing or watching the play of the game of battles, Bili, Rahksahnah, Captain Fil Tyluh and Lieutenant Kahndoot were actually engaged in a council of their own, a silent one, by mindspeak. The young war leader had first told them of all which had transpired in the king's council, then had awaited comments; nor were such long in coming.

"Typical male foolishness!" beamed the broad, solid axewoman, Kahndoot. "Your counsel was good, Duke Bili; this fool of a king would have been wise to follow it. What can he hope to accomplish by losing still more of the few fighters he yet has?"

"But foolish as it seems to us," put in Tyluh, "I am certain that it is anything but foolish to King Mahrtuhn. I have noticed that these Kuhmbuhluhners live by very old-fashioned precepts and principles, many of which have not been carried to such extreme lengths in the Middle Kingdoms in a hundred or two hundred years. To such archaic thinking, an honorable suicide is far preferable to a victory that smacks in any slightest way of cowardice or dishonor."

"If he wants to kill himself, let him fall on his sword," commented Rahksahnah coldly. "But why must he try to drag us, our squadron, down to his death with him?"

"He won't," Bili attested. "He and his fire-eaters can impale themselves and such of their horses as they can force to it on the Skohshun pike hedge if they must, but this unit will not be beside them.

"Fil, d'you recall the tale of how one of my maternal ancestors, a duke of Zunburk, devised a way to deal with the supposedly invincible Klahrksburk pikemen?"

The captain's face suddenly split in a broad grin. *"That's* it, lord duke! The dim recollection of that tactic has been nibbling at my memory since first we all heard of these

Skohshuns and their way of war. Such was always the inherent weakness of overlong polearms—they're worse than useless in a really close encounter with dismounted opponents, while they weigh so much that your average pikeman simply cannot bear the added weight of decent armor. Few of them will wear more than some kind of helmet, maybe some variety of metal reinforcement on the backs of their leather gauntlets and perhaps a skimpy breastplate.''

"Just so," agreed the young *thoheeks*. When he had explained the winning tactic of his ancestor to the two women, Kahndoot asked a question.

"But why our squadron alone, Duke Bili? Why not go to this king we now serve and tell him what you have just told the *Brahbehrnuh* and me? It makes good sense, if fight he must."

Bili sighed and beamed back, even while using his knight to bring Rahksahnah's king into check, "It is as Fil and I have said, Kahndoot—the king and all of his court are very old-fashioned in their outlook. They will allow us to do something new, innovative, but they would not do such themselves. In their blind, senseless pursuit of that which they deem to be honor, only riding out, *cap à pie*, to try to come breast to breast with this enemy whose leadership is obviously more modern and practical than archaically honorable is all that will apparently suit him and the court.

"My present position considered, I have said all that I can as regards the king's overall strategy. I like him and his heir—they are bluff, hearty warriors—and I will not like to watch them die, but I fear me much that that is just what I'll have to do, unless . . .''

He paused for a long moment, his mindshield erected as he thought hard. "Unless . . . ? Unless I can somehow persuade his majesty to allow us to charge first. Perhaps I can convince him that he owes us this ''signal honor'' as a boon for our service against those poor primitive farmers, last year.

"Can we go first, using the Zunburk attack, mayhap we can sufficiently roil the pike hedge to give the heavy horse an aiming point, a broken spot in the hedge through which they can ride and attack these Skohshuns at such close range that those overgrown pikes will prove a hindrance rather than a defense or a weapon.''

*   *   *

Erica and her Ganiks stayed in the area around the low cave in which they had wintered far longer than any of them would have preferred to do. As Ganiks had always done, they had not cared for or sheltered the horses through the long months of cold, but had simply left the mountain ponies to their own devices to live or die or stray far away. In the more southerly area from which she and the bullies had ridden, there were numerous large and small herds of semidomesticated ponies roaming hill and vale, and they were easily caught by even an unmounted man, were he good with a rawhide lariat—and few bunch-Ganiks but were proficient.

But such feral herds were obviously not a feature of these northern reaches, as they quickly discovered. The only ponies sighted and run down by the roving horsemen were easily recognized to be animals brought into the area by themselves last autumn. Wary of the large and murderous hunt that had driven them all out of the settled farming lands of their "relatives," the Kuhmbuhluhnized Ganiks, they were loath to raid there for the needed mounts.

However, it soon became obvious to all that if the entire party was to be mounted as they traveled on, such a raid was a necessity. But they took no chances on this raid. They set no fires, they murdered every man, woman and child quickly, then stole only small, valuable, easily transportable loot— foodstuffs, weapons, jewelry, clothing, blankets and the like— along with the horses, ponies, mules and few head of cattle the two neighboring farmsteads had afforded them. Reunited with those who had stayed behind for lack of a mount, the whole party immediately moved on westward, angling toward the north, traveling very fast for the first week or so.

Of course, they had no way of knowing that the bulk of the men of fighting age were not in the least likely to pursue them this time, being already on the march toward New Kuhmbuhluhnburk in obedience to the summons of King Mahrtuhn. Nor had they any means of being aware that their present course was leading them directly and inexorably into the very midst of a hot little war which would include another meeting with the very condotta that had destroyed the power of the Ganik outlaw bunches during the preceding year and thus set these few surviving leaders on the run.

148

Two weeks of travel brought the small party into a region profusely covered with huge-boled, high-thrusting oak trees, almost grassless for long stretches due to the acid quality of the tannin-laden leaf mulch underfoot. Scattered, overgrown stumps showed that once, long ago, someone had harvested oaks as large as or even larger than the biggest of the presently existing forest giants, but there was no recent sign of mankind. Not even when they chanced across a once-wide trail leading southwest did they espy any tracks but those of the beasts of the wildwood.

Therefore, since pursuit had not materialized this time, since game seemed abundant hereabouts and their plundered stores were almost expended, the Ganiks scattered to seek out a grassy area, if possible, near to a source of water. It was Horseface Charley's group that found an almost ideal spot.

Invisible from the disused trail, at some long-ago time the woodland glade had obviously been the abode of sentient beings. All that now remained of their shelters was the oval or circular pits—all eroded and fallen in, true, but too regular in outline to have been the work of nature—the rotted stumps of the posts and the deep beds of ancient charcoal between now-mossy stones. An icy-clear spring and the burbling brooklet it fed lay nearby.

The flatter portion of the glade grew thickly with what Horseface had reported to be grass. Erica, however, was quick to note that the growth was, rather, wild grain—oats, from the look of the still-green ears. And a partial excavation of one of the larger of the old dwelling sites in preparation for readying it for new occupancy brought to light a sickle wrought of decayed bone but still mounting a few teeth of flint and jasper, all sharp as the day they had been knapped.

There were a few other stone tools, mostly broken, and a vast quantity of chips near to one end of the former shelter, but not a single scrap of metal.

None of the Ganik bullies displayed even a smidgen of curiosity, simply accepting the partially prepared site and quickly adapting it to their uses, and in answer to Erica's deluge of questions about the previous occupants of this latter-day neolithic site, Bowley replied shortly.

"Hell, Ehrkah, I don' know! Could been Ganiks, mebbe. Lotsa real religious Ganiks won' use no metal of eny kin',

149

'count of Plooshun. But it don' matter none, enyhaow; whoevuh it wuz, they been done gone a lowng tahm.''

They stayed over for the best part of two more weeks, feasting on elk and deer and shaggy-bull, smoking more meat to take with them and rough-curing the hides to patch boots and jerkins and to fashion, according to Erica's instructions, bandoliers for loaded magazines and stripper clips of rounds for the rifles, as well as a belt and holster for her pistol.

Then they all set out again, riding the old trail, since it angled rather more south—the direction they wanted to go—than west at this point. After a couple of days of traveling, they began to flank a chain of high, tree-grown hills on their right, with the trail now leading almost due south but, disturbingly to them, showing signs of fairly recent use by men, beasts and wheeled conveyances. Visible signs of logging lined the trail, too, none of the stumps dating from any earlier than last autumn or early winter.

But they doggedly stuck to the trail, for all that most of the Ganiks loudly and often decried the folly of so small a bunch moving in the open in obviously settled Kuhmbuhluhner lands. Through Bowley, Horseface and Counter, Erica forced her will in this matter. While the Ganiks might consider a score of riders a small bunch, she realized the considerable edge given them by the four rifles and the pistol. She also knew that to take to the woods would be to cut their rate of speed down to a virtual crawl, and she was most anxious to get out of this provenly hostile land and on the road toward first Broomtown and then the Center . . . and a moment of reckoning with Dr. Harry Braun.

Nonetheless, they always took pains to camp well out of sight or sound of the trail, to maintain smokeless fires and to carefully scout out the trail in both directions before again setting out upon it of mornings. It was one of these scouts who first brought word of strange men on the trail, moving up from the south.

Ensign James Justis was given his orders for the morrow by his company commander, Lieutenant MacNeill. "Jimmy lad, a woodcutter party's to go out at dawn to fetch back some of the trees they girdled and left to cure last year. I doubt me there'll be any whiff of trouble, for we've seen not one of the Kuhmbuhluhn folk since the last battle, but you know the colonel—he insists on security, naetheless.

"So, put a couple dozen of our pikemen on ponies and you and them ride along out and back with the cutters and their wagons. Draw rations from regiment for you and ours. It's up to the cutters to bring their own. See how many boar spears you can ferret out—scarce as decent pikeshafts are become, I want none of ours broken or warped in those damp forests.

"You might choose a couple of good shots and give them a prod or two and maybe a crossbow. Some fresh game for the mess would warm my heart, I vow."

Ensign Justis had experienced scant difficulty in finding two dozen volunteers from the company of pikemen. The entire company would have come with him, so bored were they with the unceasing day-in, day-out pike drill, with the shouts and snarls and profane curses of glowering, red-faced sergeants and corporals, while the mounted officers watched critically from a distance.

The ensign had had only to choose men he knew to be good riders, plus a trio of keen-eyed and experienced hunters, plus a Corporal Gregory to convey his orders to the other ranks.

They rode out in the chill and damp of the dawning, all close-wrapped in thick, warm cloaks. The ponies moved out placidly, when once the ponderous gates of the captured safe-glen had been gaped, but Justis' horse showed his fine, hot blood and his joy to be out of the confines of the glen in an attempt or two at misconduct the curbing of which required a tight hand on the reins. Behind the ensign and the first dozen pikemen, the cutters and their rumbling wagons proceeded, they being followed by the corporal and the second dozen pony-mounted, spear-armed pikemen.

As the column issued out from the fortified gap that led into the glen-approach, the three hunters with their missile weapons peeled off from the column and set out at the best gallop the mountain ponies could muster under the weight of the big, solid humans. When they had gained something over a quarter mile on the van of the column, they reined up, spread across the width of the trail into the verges of the forest and so proceeded at a fast walk, their weapons cocked and ready for whatever game might pass near enough for a shot.

When the scouts came breathlessly back with the news of the strangers on the trail, both Bowley and Horseface Charley went back with them to see for themselves. Before long, Bowley returned to the night camp, having left Horseface with the scouts to mark the progress of the strangers.

"More Kuhmbuhluhners?" Erica was quick to ask.

Wrinkling his forehead, Bowley shook his shaggy head slowly. "Naw, Ehrkah, leas' wise I don' thank so. It's a whole passel of littul thangs makes me thank they ain' Kuhmbuhluhners. Boots, fer one thang. I ain' nevuh seed no Kuhmbuhluhner in no boot lahk thet. They belt knifes is made funny, too, 'n' so's they hats. The closes' one to me said some words, low-lahk, when his pony come to stumble; it 'uz Mehrikan, raht enuff, but it 'uz a kind Mehrikan I ain' nevuh heerd afore."

Erica's hopes leaped suddenly. *Broomtown troopers*? Could it be? Could it possibly be? But she kept her voice calm as she asked the necessary question.

"How are they armed, Merle?"

He shrugged. "Knifes, shortswords, crossbows—one of 'em a reg'lar one and two whut shoots rocks; prods, they cawls 'em, I thank. They looks lahk hunters, acks lahk it, too, but I done lef' Charley and them boys back ther fer to see if eny more is a-comin'."

Erica sighed softly. No, not Broomtown men. They'd have been armed with sabers and axes and rifles, not crossbows and shortswords. They were most probably Kuhmbuhluhners after all, despite Bowley's assurances to the contrary; likely they were just a northern type he had never before seen.

As for the oddly inflected language, she and others at the Center had never ceased to be amazed at how quickly so many, vastly differing, frequently all but incomprehensible dialects had sprung into being in various portions of what had once been the United States of America—all of them based on the one language of that vanished nation, Standard American English. The only people anywhere who still spoke the original language were occupants of the Center and its bases, plus that evil, murderous mutant, Milo Morai.

152

She went on to reflect that the present commercial tongue used by the traveling traders—most of them now hailing from the Aristocratic Republic of Eeree, though a hundred years ago, before a succession of long, bloody wars had completely disrupted formerly stable governments, the majority of the traders had been spawned by the various kingdoms of the Ohio River Valley—was about as close to the original language as any of the dialects came. But even this so-called Trade Mehrikan was tinged with numerous loan words, phrases, pronunciations and inflections from the disparate areas they touched in the years-long rounds of commerce.

Erica's reflections on language were violently interrupted by the sudden, crashing report of a rifle.

Out of the huge, hundreds-strong raiding party he had led into the Ahrmehnee lands, something less than thirty bullies rode out behind Abner. And those who did escape only did so because they were all horse-mounted and their fresh mounts' strength and longer legs allowed them to outdistance those grim pursuers who rode down and slew every one of the pony-mounted Ganiks, few of whom had been armed anyway.

Throughout the first leg of their flight, Gouger Haney had unceasingly and profanely railed at him for keeping the common Ganiks disarmed, although the decision had been as much his as it had been Abner's or Leeroy's. Abner had known with a cold chill of certainty that the older, deadlier man would force him into a death duel for full leadership immediately they were out of harm's way. It was far from pleasant to ride with the firm conviction that certain death lay both behind and ahead.

Fully aware of the sensitivity of Sir Geros, but also fully aware of what must now be done in the ruined village, Captain Pawl Raikuh slyly worked it so that it was the young knight who led out the pursuit of the knot of armed Ganiks who had broken through a weak point in the cordon of fighters that surrounded them. With the mixed force of Freefighters, Moon Maidens and Ahrmehnee well underway behind a sizable pack of the big, savage hunting hounds bred by the tribes of the *stahn*, Raikuh and *Dehrehbeh* Ahrszin set

153

the bulk of their force to the work which must be done were they to forever rid these lands of the Ganik threat.

It was incredibly brutal work. Into the open space between the wrecked buildings which once had been the village square, the Freefighters would drag screaming, pleading, sobbing, struggling Ganiks. When the scale-armored men had forced the victims to their knees, one would grasp a handful of matted, verminous hair to hold the head as still as was possible while one of the Ahrmehnee warriors hacked through the neck of the ancient and detested enemy with sword or axe.

Before very long, the spaces between the standing walls were fast filling with stiffening, headless bodies, stacked like so much cordwood, while the pile of grisly trophies at one end of the square was growing faster than the Ahrmehnee could pack them into the sacks brought for the purpose.

The entire square, it seemed to Pawl Raikuh, streamed and steamed and stank of spilled blood, and even with above thirty years of soldiering and hard fighting behind him, the veteran officer still felt more than a little queasy as his boots sank almost ankle-deep in bloody mud. But he swallowed his rising gorge and kept his face blank. Necessity must be served, duty must be done.

Moreover, that duty must be completed before Sir Geros returned from the pursuit. Pawl knew his young, ennobled commander well—fierce as a scalded treecat in battle, still did this knight of the Confederation deeply detest all which smacked of violence and bloodshed, and he would never have condoned this cold-blooded execution of hundreds of completely unarmed, helpless men, even cannibal shaggies.

That they had not enough strength to take and guard so many prisoners would not have mattered to Sir Geros. Nor would the fact that were the shaggies to be freed and escorted out of the *stahn*, they would assuredly have been back immediately they were rearmed. Not even the certainty that the Ahrmehnee would never have sat still in the face of such foolishness would have persuaded Sir Geros that what Raikuh had here ordered performed was necessary.

"Hohguhn," the tight-lipped captain called to one of his Freefighter lieutenants, "it took Ahdohm there three hacks to

154

do for that last shaggy. See he has a sharper sword, eh? Let's us git this butcher business over with.''

Well before the last shrieking Ganik had been shortened, the best of the captured ponies had been loaded with bulging bags of still-dripping, freshly severed heads, bundles of the rough, crude weapons the metal of which could be reworked by the skilled Ahrmehnee smiths and craftsmen, and such other usable items as the shelters and the piles of decapitated corpses had yielded to searching Ahrmehnee and Freefighters. The rest of the scrubby, thick-coated little equines were stripped of any gear and driven out of the environs of the blood-soaked village.

But disposal of the heaps of headless bodies was not so easily accomplished. Despite the recent thaw of the snow and ice which had for so many months blanketed the land, the earth below the top inch or so was still more or less frozen for some distance down. It was of dense, heavy consistency and studded with rocks of varying sizes at the best of times, winter frosts bringing them up from lower levels each year. Furthermore, the only shovels available were the few crude wooden ones of the now-dead shaggies, and while they had worked well enough in wet snow, they soon proved no match for hard ground.

At length, Pawl had all the corpses dragged to the nearest patch of thick woods and dumped in the heavy brush. Then he had his part of the force mount up and head back for the main village.

CHAPTER XI

General Jay Corbett stood beside Old Johnny Kilgore in the center of what had obviously been a temporary camp for some group of some nature. The layers of ash and charcoal from last year's horrendous forest fires had been removed down to bare earth and a half-dozen rude shelters had been constructed of saplings and brush brought in from less-damaged areas, and there was an arrangement of fire-blackened stones surrounding a shallow pit containing fresher charcoal.

But it was equally clear that this was not the site of a recent camp, for the green shoots of plants were now thrusting up from beneath the old, soggy coals in the firepit, and all of the shelters showed the effects of long disuse.

"It 'uz Ganiks, fer sure," averred Old Johnny baldly.

"How so?" inquired Corbett, though not doubting the oldster for a minute, having seen his judgments prove right too often during the last year or so. "What makes you think so, Johnny?"

"Way the lean-tos is scattered awl roun', fer one thang, gen'rul. The Kuhmbuhluhners, whin they sets them up a camp, they does it a lot lahk yawl Broomtowners does—straight 'n' purty 'n' awl. Ganiks, they puts they lean-tos up wherevuh it pleasures 'em, ushly the placet it's easies' fer to dig the posties in, mos'ly. Won' meny of 'em though, mebbe twenny, thutty fellas."

Corbett removed his helmet and scratched at his scalp. "But why, in God's name, would they have camped here, I wonder? There's no graze to speak of for a good mile, and the only reliable source of potable water is farther than that, I think. They'd have had to pack in their firewood, too, and

156

even the materials for their shelters and bough beds. It all makes no sense to me.''

"Simple, gen'rul.'' Johnny shrugged and spat. "They 'uz a-minin' loot fum unduh the edges of thet rockslide, is whut.''

"*Jesus H. Christ!*" Corbett softly swore. "I never thought of that, Johnny. Are you sure they were?''

The head of the bearded bald man jerked a brusque affirmative. "Shore they wuz. It's been a whole heap of them rocks a-shifted at places awn thet slide, and the raw poles they used fer to shift 'em is awl still up ther, too. Thang I can't figger is, if they'd come crost suthin' worth thet much hard work, how come they din't brang t' whole bunch with 'em? Two, three hunnert boys coulda done it quicker an' a damn sight easier.''

The officer whistled softly between his teeth. "David Sternheimer is not going to like tonight's report one damned bit. Let's just hope those Ganiks didn't get away from here with too much. Any idea just when they might have been here?''

The old cannibal walked over to one of the tumbledown shelters and poked around for a few moments, then answered, "Early las' fawl, gen'rul, enyhaow; mebbe evun afore thet, sumtahm inna summah.''

While speaking he arose and came back to the officer's side, adding, "But whin they did come fer to leave, they did 'er in a hellashus hurry, elst they'da took thisheanh with 'em, shore.''

He passed to Corbett a dagger in a scratched and battered gilt case. The finely balanced weapon had surely been a highly prized possession at one time, and even now, with its still-sharp acid-etched blade all discolored and pitted with rust, its crossguard bent and deeply nicked and most of the semiprecious stones missing from their settings, it still felt good in the hand. Clearly, no fighter, not even one of the savage Ganiks, would have left so fine a weapon behind by intent.

Tapping the scarred pommel of the dagger absently into the callused palm of his hand, the officer reflected that this latest find fitted neatly into the pattern they had been encountering since first they returned up here into Ganik—well, formerly Ganik—lands. The untenanted farms where someone had planted crops but had not been around to harvest them, the deserted bunch camps, and now this once lovely little weapon, left to deteriorate in a hurriedly evacuated temporary campsite.

Someone—some thing?—had either completely exterminated the Ganiks or driven them out of and far from their ancestral homelands within a space of less than a calendar year, that was all that could be assumed from the evidence. But who? What? No need to ask why, he thought. Take all of the most detested and heinous abominations of conduct despised and almost universally prohibited by races or communities of civilized man and you had the mundane, everyday practices of your average, run-of-the-mill Ganik, were Old Johnny and that earlier Ganik prisoner, Jim-Beau Carter, to be believed, and neither had had any reason to stretch the plain truth or to lie, especially in light of the fact that none of the Ganiks considered their rather outré customs and practices to be in any way wrong or even unusual.

They commonly practiced bestiality on both living and dead animals, nor was incest—of every possible form, both heterosexual and homosexual—unusual in Ganik families. Their singular religion forbade them to consume the flesh of any warm-blooded, furred or feathered creature save mankind, so they were all cannibalistic. They would eat captured or kidnapped neighbors of non-Ganiks or even members of their own immediate families, always subjecting their still-living entrees to bestial tortures and sometimes roasting and eating portions before they killed the whole. Jim-Beau Carter had chortled, in fact, over his own family's specialty—forcing maimed and tormented wretches to partake of broth made of their own flesh.

No, there was no need to wonder why any decent folk hated and feared and despised the race of Ganiks. One could only wonder that the stinking savages had not been dispersed or butchered years ago instead of last summer.

But that still left the question of who. Whoever they were, they must have been numerous, determined and well armed, and even with his large force with their advanced weapons technology, Corbett still would prefer to avoid any martial confrontation with whatever race or people had so recently purged these mountains of Ganiks. All he wanted to do was perform his assigned task and get the hell back to Broomtown with the same number of officers and men he had led up here.

Which was why, despite his veiled orders from David Sternheimer, he had no slightest intention of leading or sending any parties out to search for Dr. Erica Arenstein. Regardless of the Director's dreams, Corbett himself was almost certain that the woman was dead, long dead. She had probably become a Ganik feast, if those two-legged beasts had gotten to her body before the four-legged ones did.

No, he would send out security patrols, of course, once the permanent camp was established. But they would be small and fast-moving and with orders to try to avoid discovery or combat, especially by or with superior forces.

Although Old Johnny pooh-poohed the idea, Corbett felt that the nemesis of the Ganiks had most probably been that folk who were said to inhabit the mountains just to the north, the New Kuhmbuhluhners. From Johnny's descriptions of them, they sounded like burkers, from the Middle Kingdoms, and that there truly was a principality—once, long ago, a kingdom in its own right—up east there called Kuhmbuhluhn, he knew. He had been through it a few times over the centuries.

Recalling the fierce nobility and the Freefighter dragoons of the Middle Kingdoms, he could entertain little doubt that a few hundred such men on their big, war-trained horses would go through a mob of pony-mounted, unarmored, ill-armed and completely undisciplined Ganiks like the proverbial dose of salts.

It had been a great temptation to lay out the camp around the already partially cleared area on which the preceding Ganiks had camped, but Corbett had resisted that temptation. For one thing, the site was just too damned close to the tumbled rocks beneath which lay the remains of the pack train, and, when blast they finally did, who could say but what some portion or even all of that rockslide might start moving westward again; the low, crooked ridge which lay between the site he did choose and the area of operations would serve to protect the camp from accidents caused by the explosives. At least, Jay Corbett fervently prayed it would.

Another factor was that along the western slope of the ridge were no less than four spring-fed pools, all of which fed a streamlet that went angling southwestward through the desolate, burned-over landscape to probably eventually become a tributary of the larger stream some kilometers back to the south along the track. He immediately designated the pool farthest north for drinking and cooking water only; the three downstream ones could be used for watering stock, bathing or whatever else required water.

Once the site was chosen and paced out and stakes driven, the entire command—both troopers and civilians and only excluding sentries and a small, mounted patrol force—were set to the task of first clearing off the ash and old charcoal, then ditching and mounding the camp perimeter, adding the quantities of soggy ash and partially carbonized tree trunks to the earthen mound to increase its height and help in retarding erosion.

As soon as the perimeter was completed, latrines and offal pits and firepits dug and cookfires started in them with some of the better-quality charcoal, Corbett had Gumpner set every third man to pitching the two-man shelter tents. Most of the remainder rode off in details to the nearest stretches of unburned forest to fell and fetch back wood for fires and a multitude of other purposes, although the general was resolved to get as much use as was possible out of the charcoal so prevalent hereabouts in the wake of last year's horrendous conflagrations. When once dried out, it would burn slower and more evenly and with far less revealing smoke than even the best-seasoned hardwood, and he still was nagged with worry about the possible near proximity of whoever had driven out or slain the thousands of Ganiks who used to call the areas roundabout home.

Bili did not again approach the king directly, but went instead to seek out Prince Byruhn. He found that royal nobleman with some of his staff on the plateau-plain under the city walls engaged in overseeing the selection of replacement warhorses from the herds driven up from the lands of the civilized Ganiks and from several of the safe-glens.

Miscomprehending Bili's motives at first, the huge man said exasperatedly, "Look you, cousin, had the matter been allowed to come to a vote, you would've had mine and no mistake, for I've scant stomach for putting horses and gentlemen at those damnable rows of pikepoints again. But it did not and it will not and, although I strongly disagree with both him and my nephew, King Mahrtuhn is not only my sovran but my father, as well, and he commands both my loyalty and my obedience. I am like any other faithful subject.

"Now, tell me true, cousin, did ever you see so much ambulatory crowbait in one place in your life?" The prince waved a ham-sized hand at the herd of remounts, scathingly, contemptuously. "Our tame Ganiks own the best pasture-lands in the entire kingdom, and they therefore also own the responsibility for breeding and training and maintaining a herd of decent warhorses as the best part of their due to the king. Now, when that due is needed, this, this, this conglom-eration of equine abortions is what they provide! Half of the herd are too light of build or too clumsy to do more than draw a wagon or a plow, and less than one in five has had any modicum of war training. And I am expected to put gentle-men up on these dogs for imminent combat? *Pfaagh!*"

Bili did not think that most of the herd looked all that bad, though not one was a match for his own big destrier, Mahvros—but then, few horses anywhere were that. However, he thought it politic to say nothing if he could not just then agree with the angry prince, so he shook his shaven head—a noncommit-tal gesture that could have meant anything or nothing.

But the prince took the silence and gesture as he wished to take them, firmly gripping Bili's shoulder and nodding down at him. "Aye, no horseman of good sense but would have to agree with me, cousin, and I always knew you were a most sensible young man."

His hand still on the shoulder, he steered the *Thoheeks* of Morguhn a little away from the knot of New Kuhmbuhluhn noblemen and, when the distance was enough to suit him, halted and said in a lower tone, "Look you, Cousin Bili, *someone* has to command the city whilst the rest ride out—to our deaths, likely enough, but so be it, it's but our duty—behind the king. So why not you, eh? My power is enough here to work that much. Now, true, we have a hereditary castellan for the citadel, but the young fool who presently holds that sinecure is a frothing fire-eater, a hothead who would be much happier and fulfilled forking a horse in armor than carrying out his inherited functions.

"Of course, I'd have to take part of your squadron, the Confederation noblemen and the Middle Kingdoms dragoons, at least; but I could leave you the Moon Maidens and the Ahrmehnee, perhaps, plus the regular garrisons."

Bili chose his words carefully, his keen mind working apace. "If your grace truly believes that the city would be better served with or by replacement castellans during the coming field operations, then please hear the following recommendations."

He paused. When the prince raised his single, bushy eyebrow and nodded once, he went on. "Both Freefighter Captain Fil Tyluh and Freefighter Lieutenant Frehd Brakit are cadets of noble Middle Kingdoms families, as your grace surely knows."

Prince Byruhn nodded again. That he was slyly working at both of these Freefighter officers to either wed widows of his vassals slain at last autumn's costly battle or, if they wished not to set aside their Moon Maiden battlemates, to at least swear homage, accept lands in fief and settle down in New Kuhmbuhluhn was an ill-kept secret within the lowlander squadron.

Bili continued again. "But what your grace may not know is that both of these noblemen are skilled at certain aspects of siegecraft, Brakit in particular being a consummate and most innovative engineer, while Fil Tyluh's skills and his experience are so notable that he was personally chosen for staff work by the great Sir Ehd Gahtwahlt—perhaps the foremost living siegemaster in all of the eastern lands—and served under him for almost a year at the siege of the rebel-held city of Vawnpolis, in the Confederation."

Byruhn's white-flecked, red-roan eyebrow rose perceptibly over his blue-green eyes. "Say you so, young cousin? Now that is truly information of importance. I had known, of course, that both are valuable men, but I had not been aware of just how valuable they are.

"I take it then that you wish to ride out to war with your squadron and the rest of us, whether you agree with my father, the king, or not? Let me warn you, though, my father is a most hidebound and stubborn man, and my nephew no less. They both were cast of the same mold in all ways, and they will likely get themselves and the majority of the rest of us killed out there. The Skohshun herald who rode into the city a month or so after my disaster pricked at the king's pride, pricked deeply, and he and my nephew have been honing the blades of their axes and swords ever since the departure of that supercilious man.

"And if you think that your Freefighter archers and your Ahrmehnee dartmen might be used to soften up the pike hedge, don't so illusion yourself. The king is most contemptuous of missile warfare—save in conditions of siege—which is why we of New Kuhmbuhluhn own so few trained archers or slingers or dartmen. He means to keep charging that pike hedge until either it breaks or there are not enough of us left to throw upon it." The big prince paused and sighed deeply, his barrellike chest rising and falling. "And to be frank, young cousin, barring some last-minute miracle, it is my considered opinion that the latter will take place long before and rather than the former. But a man cannot but do what duty and honor and his love of king and country bid him."

Smiling, Bili said, "Your grace, I just may have a spare miracle in my quiver. A certain one of my maternal ancestors, a duke of Zunburk, developed and perfected a way to break a pike hedge in depth without the use of missiles. But I will need the overt support of your grace . . . ?"

The big man's grip increased to a painful intensity and his eyes sparkled. "Now, by Steel, I knew there was a good reason why I failed to have you . . . ahhh, eliminated, months ago at Sandee's Cot. Cousin mine, you show me an honorable way—honorable by the king's lights, that is—to get our heavy-armed horse through those goddam pikes and you'll have every scintilla of support I can muster!" Then he matched Bili's grin with one of his own. "Or does my young cousin want my sworn Sword Oath on this matter as well?"

"No, your grace, not this time," Bili said bluntly. "I think that you have as much regard for your life and well-being as I have for mine own."

Erica and Merle Bowley stood beside an abashed and rueful Horseface Charley and regarded the dead man sprawled on the roadway, part of his head blown away by one of the large explosive rifle bullets.

"I shot afore I knowed I'd done it," stated Horseface

baldly. "But one them fellers had jes' done shot his fuckin' prod in 'mongst us, heanh, fust thang."

Bowley sighed, shaking his head. "Hell, man, them fellers won't troopers, they 'uz hunters. They probly heerd ol' Snuffles thar an' took him fer a pot critter is awl. Wher'd them othuh two go to?"

"Back up the road, the way they awl come from, lickety-split, thet 'un's hoss, too," answered Horseface.

"Caint say I fawlts 'em none." Bowley nodded. "Theseheanh ryfuls does make a hellaishus racket. But, buddyboy, we is awl in the shit fer fair, naow!"

"How so, Merle?" asked Erica. "With four rifles, I hardly think we need fear any party of hunters."

Bowley shook his head. "It ain' hunters I'm afeared of, Ehrkah. Thisheanh is thick-settled country, jes' look at it—look at the shape the road is in and haow meny trees has done been chopped down, and not long ago, neethuh. Wher it's they many fowks, you bettuh bet it's gonna be troopers, too. It ain't lahk we wuz a-raiding in a real bunch, Ehrkah. Ryfuls 'r no ryfuls, it ain't thutty of us, awl tol!, and thisheanh ol' boy he don't lahk bein' hunted lahk we awl wuz las' fawl, back thar. 'Sides, haow many of 'em could we drop afore we dint have us no more bullits? And then who'd be big dawg?"

Erica frowned. "You've made your point, Merle. So what would you suggest we do? Go back the way we came?"

Again he shook his head. "Aw, naw, Ehrkah. Country mosta the way back is jest too flat; they'd run us daown, fer shore, 'fore lowng. Naw, I thank we best crowss the road and head up inta them hills, thar. It'll shore be rough ridin', but it'll be a lot rougher fer troopers, you bettuh b'lieve."

He turned to the other Ganiks. "Sumbody tek thet feller's prod and awl. Prod ain't nowher near good as a ryful, but it shore Lawd'll thow a rock futhuh nor enybody c'n heave a dart."

Immediately he was apprised of the killing of one of his hunters by the other two, young Ensign Justis dispatched a galloper to so inform Lieutenant MacNeill. After halting the column, he left it in charge of the corporal and himself rode forward with half his spear-armed pikemen and the two remaining hunters—one of them with a prod, one with a cross-

164

bow. Wounded game did not shoot back when loosed upon; the only things he could think of that did were men, likely Kuhmbuhluhners, scouts or spies. He led them at a slow walk, his barred visor still open, but his sword blade bared and sparkling with a silvery sheen for all of its well-honed length.

As they neared the site of the attack and slaying, the pink-cheeked officer spread his baker's dozen pikemen out in a crescent-shaped line that spanned the road and overlapped on both flanks into the roadside brush and saplings. Wisely, he kept his only two missilemen at the southward-bowed center of the line and rode just behind them.

The pikemen rode forward in grim silence, hefting and rehefting the short, broad-bladed hunting spears, feeling very vulnerable and wishing strongly that the familiar, comfortable formation was arrayed on either side and in front and behind, in place of so much dangerous emptiness. Approaching this someone or ones who had already slain one of their number, they all longed to be on their own two feet, supported by their sturdy legs instead of astride the small, shaggy, shedding ponies. They longed to be grasping their heavy pikes, three man lengths long, rather than these overshort, overlight spears which would not be, could not be at all effective until they were much closer to the unknown, not yet sighted enemy than they had the slightest wish to be. Even the sergeant's roared threats as he drilled and redrilled them and their mates would have sounded homey and comforting in their ears as they kneed their scrubby mounts forward toward the possibly deadly unknown.

The center of the line came atop a rise just in time to see a knot of riders—a score or more of them, mounted on full-sized horses, some ponies and a few mules and with a handful of led animals, as well—burst from the edge of the forest on the right-hand side of the road and, crossing near to where the dead hunter lay, urge their mounts up the sharply rising, wooded slope on the other side.

Justis halted his line just where they were. Leading a probing patrol was one thing, but attacking an armed force of at least twice his own numbers was another thing entirely. He would stay and observe the progress of the enemy as long as they remained visible, of course, but nothing was to be gained by moving closer and risking loss of more men. Let the armored horsemen take up the pursuit when and if they arrived.

They did, only an hour or so later, under the command of Major Sir Hugh Parkinson. He returned the ensign's stiff, formal, by-the-book salute with the casual gesture which passed for such amongst veteran cavalrymen.

"All right, youngster, what happened here worth the saddle-pounding of our poor backsides all the way out from the glen, not to mention taking us from a smashing good breakfast?"

"Sir," began Ensign Justis, sitting stiff as a pikestaff in the saddle of his horse, his head erect and his eyes set levelly ahead, for all that the major was a bit to his left, "last night, Captain MacNeill issued orders that—"

"Never mind your life history, young man!" the cavalry leader snapped brusquely. "Just tell me what occurred out here to cause you to send that galloper back into the glen, and please try to be brief about it. And for God's sake, *look* at me when you speak to me!"

When he had at length gotten the junior officer's report, the nobleman nodded. "Kuhmbuhluhners, no doubt, bound for the glen to wreak on us what damage they can before we march out for the season's campaign. Foolish ones, at that. They should never have let you see where they were headed, but God be thanked they did. Now we can see to it that they receive as warm a welcome as they deserve.

"As for the report your pikeman rendered, that a crack of thunder and lightning slew yon man"—he waved an armored arm up the road, toward where the body still lay—"I should hope that he's no dimwit who believes in fairies and wizards and witches. But sounds can be tricky amongst these hills and vales, ensign. Mayhap a clap of thunder or the echo of one did coincide with the dart or slingstone or prod pellet that downed that man, I'll not say that such couldn't happen."

He turned to one of his followers—a lieutenant, but a noble officer like himself, to judge by the equipage—and said, "Percy, ride you back and tell the colonel all of what you have here heard. Assure him that I shall maintain some slight pressure on this group of Kuhmbuhluhners. Perhaps I can speed them on their way into the glen, wherein I should hope that the colonel and the earl will have a suitable reception awaiting them. Understood?

"Oh, and as you pass by that sorry agglomeration back there, tell that corporal to turn them all about and head them back into the glen. There'll be no timber cutting today."

Then, back to Ensign Justis. "Young man, you and your force will ride with me and mine; that will help to even out the numbers. We're going up into the hills after those scum."

"Sir, I'll certainly accompany you, if you wish," said Justis, then protested, "But my men are just common pikemen, not dragoons. Their ponies are small and will never be able to keep up with the horses. Besides, none of them are armored and they're armed only with shortswords and hunting spears."

The major threw back his helmeted head and laughed gustily. "Never you mind about those ponies' size, ensign. Up in those hills, these little buggers can easily outstrip any horse. Your men will most likely have to hold them back, see if I'm not right. As for the armament, or rather lack of it, don't worry. I have no intention of running this lot to ground, only of driving them out of the hills and into the glen where they can be more easily dealt with.

"Now let's be at it, eh? You and that crossbowman will ride with me. The rest of yours can fall in at the rear of my force."

Ensign James Justis had no available option. With many misgivings, he issued orders to his men, then joined the major. As matters developed, his misgivings were well founded.

They had been at it for hours, up and down the steep wooded or brushy slopes of the increasingly high and precipitous ridges and hills that walled in the glen, and the supercilious major had proved right about the ponies, at least. Despite their size and the solid bulk of their riders, they had easily kept up with the bigger, longer-legged horses and, being far more nimble-footed, could be safely ridden in places where horses had to be led by dismounted riders.

The brace of hunter-pikemen had had scant difficulty in following the track of the band of marauders, who apparently were exerting little if any effort to conceal signs of their passage. At one point, Sir Hugh crowed exultantly that they were gaining on the quarry. He shortly was proved to be far more correct in his assumption that he would have preferred to be . . . had he lived to prefer anything, one way or the other.

They had just successfully descended a steep, shaly hillside and were proceeding at a fast walk along a more or less flat, more or less level stretch of slightly marshy ground so narrow that no more than two horsemen abreast could easily negotiate it. Suddenly, from within the concealment afforded by the dense brush covering the flanking hillsides, a sleet of deadly missiles inundated the leading elements of the column—darts, a few prod pellets and twenty rounds of rifle bullets!

Never having been in real combat with them, Ensign James Justis had been completely unaware of just what fine, stolid, dependable men he commanded, not until then and there in that narrow defile suddenly filled with chaos and death.

While cavalrymen fought to control wounded or panic-stricken horses, the beasts driven into temporary madness by the succession of earsplitting explosions, the shrieks of man and animal and the reek of fresh-spilled blood, Ensign Justis—providentially neither he nor his horse had been so much as scratched—forced his mount through the press back toward his own command.

At last he made it, to find that the veteran infantrymen had dismounted, leaving the nervous mountain ponies to their own devices, and were formed into two neat ranks. Handling the boar spears like pikes, they stood staunch against the unseen menace, presenting a double row of broad, knife-edged spearheads.

The pikeman who had obviously taken command in his absence—to his sudden shame, James realized that he did not know the name of that man or any of the others—saluted briskly and said, "Sir, beg to report the unit formed for attack or defense. Do we go up there after them, sir?"

Ensign Justis was no fire-eater. There had been no missiles for the length of time it had taken him to get back here from the head of the shattered column, and he was strongly in favor of letting well enough alone, guessing more accurately than he realized that the primary purpose of the ambush had been to slow or to halt the pursuit, not to exterminate them all.

He shook his head vehemently, started to speak, then

remembered to gape the visor he had automatically closed in the first moments of the attack. "I commend your nerve, corporal, but no, we'll not attack them and, were they going to attack us, they'd have certainly done so by now. I doubt me not that having so well accomplished their purpose, they've gone from up there, anyhow. So have your men see what they can do for the wounded cavalrymen and collect all the sound mounts. We're going back down to the road and then into the glen. What's your name, anyway, corporal?"

"If it please the ensign, sir, I be no corporal, only a common pikeman, Phillip Simpson."

Justis just nodded. "Well, so far as I'm concerned, you're a corporal as of this minute, and you'll be so in fact as soon as I speak to Lieutenant MacNeill and the captain. *I* didn't form up those men so quickly and neatly, *you* did, and a man possessing such quick wits and proven qualities of leadership not only deserves promotion within the ranks but will do the army far more good in a position of authority.

"Now, let's to it, Corporal Simpson. The sooner we're out of these accursed hills, the better."

CHAPTER XII

Captain Pawl Raikuh walked on invisible eggs when duty took him into the company of Sir Geros for almost a week after the affair at the Ganik-occupied village. But he was a blunt, honest man, and finally it all became just too much to bear.

"Sir Geros . . . son," he began one night at table, "what Chief Ahrszin and I did, had done, up in that shell of a village, whilst you and the Maidens were chasing down the bastards what got away . . ."

Sighing, the young knight shoved back his dish of braised raccoon meat and interrupted in a regretful tone. "Had to be done, Pawl, I know, not that that knowledge makes it all sit any better in my craw. I deeply appreciate what you did for me, taking the decision and the onus off my conscience. It's damned hard to be a savage, bloodthirsty warrior when you just weren't cast in that mold. I'm just glad that the horrible business is all over. Perhaps now, if the weather stays good, we can get back to looking for *Thoheeks* Bili and the Moon Maidens' *brahbehrnuh*."

Raikuh squirmed uncomfortably. "I fear me it's not quite done, yet awhile, Sir Geros, nor will it be until we have put paid to the very last of those damned shaggies. And that means taking the fight to them, attacking their camp in full force and killing every one of the buggers we can get steel into."

Geros looked pained. "But why, Pawl? I doubt if more than a bare score got out of the *stahn* alive. How dangerous could so few be to the Behdrozyuhns?"

The spare captain ticked off his points on his fingers, one by one. "First off, Sir Geros, many of them as rode into here

170

to start, I doubt me if it was all of them; they'd've surely left a couple hundred or so to guard their camp, I figger. Second, the reason those what got away did get away was 'cause they was the leaders and the onliest ones armed.''

At Geros' incredulous look, he nodded. "That's right, Sir Geros. Every weapon in that village, even the knives, was all stacked up in the shelter the leaders had been in. I reckon those crazy bugtits had took to killing each other off at such a lick that the top dogs was afeared they'd weaken the force too bad to fight us.''

The captain made a moue of disgust, then corrected himself. "*Were afraid* they'd weaken their force too badly to fight us, dammit. If I keep living under the same roof with Bohreegahd, I'm going to ride out of here speaking like, hell, probably thinking like a damned hillman myself!

"Anyhow, Sir Geros, I feel it to be imperative that we strike, strike hard, as soon as possible, and Ahrszin agrees with me completely.''

It was on the tip of Geros' tongue to point out that that particular Ahrmehnee headhunter never failed to be completely in favor of any stratagem or tactic that would see a few new skulls added to the gruesome display that adorned the rafters of the warriors' cult house. But he thought it might be better to be a bit diplomatic and keep such thoughts to himself, for the two Ahrmehnee girls who looked after this house and his needs understood, he suspected, more Trade Mehrikan than they let on, and he still hoped to persuade some of the fierce Ahrmehnee of the Behdrozyuhn Tribe to ride with him when finally he was able to get back to the real reason he and Raikuh and the rest were here—to search for *Thoheeks* Bili and his lost command. So he simply held his peace and allowed Raikuh to continue.

And the captain did go on at some length, advising from his vast experience in strategy, tactics and logistics, oblivious of course of the fact that there was no longer an enemy resident in that camp just beyond the *stahn* border.

Somewhere in the confused few moments it had taken them all to dash out through the weak point of the tightening lines of the Ahrmehnee and the Freefighters they had thought were Kuhmbuhluhners, an Ahrmehnee wardart had thunked into the high cantle of Abner's saddle. Thrown with all the force of a brawny arm, the missile was still there when, several hours later, Abner reined in his lathered, steaming horse just long enough to doff some of the heavier portions of his armor to ease the animal's burden and perhaps increase its speed.

Leeroy halted beside his brother/lover and commenced to follow his example in shedding helm, plates and mail. The rest of the small knot of bullies had not halted, casting off what they could while still pushing on, for the border was not far ahead now and the relative freshness of their mounts had, they hoped, given them enough of a lead on their pursuers to get them out of the Ahrmehnee lands alive.

It was Leeroy who noticed the waggling butt of the dart, but Abner who half turned in his saddle and worked the point free. He was on the verge of tossing it, too, away when he noted how finely balanced it was, so he dropped it into his dart quiver, which hung on the offside withers of his mount.

Brutal use of spur and whip got their almost foundered horses moving again, and they both were almost at the unmarked border when they suddenly came into a little glade wherein another rider had halted. Plates and helm lay in the slushy snow on either side of the trembling gray horse as it stood with its fine head hung low, panting, its chest working like a smithy bellows.

The head of the rider was hidden in the oily steel folds of the hauberk he was working up over his head, but the horse and the bits of discarded plate identified him immediately to Abner and Leeroy. It was the fearsome Gouger Haney.

Almost without conscious thought, Abner's hand went to his dart quiver, sought out the Ahrmehnee dart, and sent it winging to sink its sharp, needle-tipped steel point and a good half of its length of shaft into the helpless bully's back, just a bit below the left shoulder blade.

Then, in dire fear that some one of their victim's own bullies might have witnessed the treacherous act, the two rode on, not sparing Gouger Haney so much as a backward glance.

As earlier agreed in their shouted, in-saddle, in-flight council, the first bullies to arrive in the camp had set those lucky enough to have not, for varying reasons, taken part in the disastrous raid to preparing to repel imminently arriving

172

foemen—foemen who, as matters developed, never appeared, since Sir Geros halted his pursuit just shy of the border.

A few, a very few, other Ganiks trickled in after Abner and Leeroy, their journeys slowed by the thickness of the forest to which they had taken. But it was not until almost midnight that a weary horse plodded in, a gray horse, baring on its back a stiffening corpse with a hauberk bunched up around its shoulders and an Ahrmehnee wardart jutting out of its back.

The next day—with the best parts of the late Gouger Haney in various stewpots about the camp and his late rival's fine hauberk now weighting his own shoulders—Abner gave orders to the remaining bullies to strike camp.

"It jes' ain' uhnuff of us lef' fer to faht them Ahrm'nees and Kuhmbuhluhners and awl, and they shore fer to hit us, heanh, raht soon. So we'll move awn south a ways and wait till we gits mo' fellers in."

Accustomed to obedience to a senior bully, not even the Gouger's onetime bullies stopped to wonder why the Ahrmehnee whose dart had slain their leader had not, as Ahrmehnee always tried to do, taken his head, horse and weapons.

Once he had cleaned it, Abner put the Ahrmehnee dart back in his dart quiver. It had brought him luck, he felt.

Rahksahnah looked up into the oval-pupiled orange eyes of the bulky, hairy Kleesahk who knelt before her. "You are certain, then, Pah-Elmuh? Two of them?" she mindspoke.

"Yes, Lady of the Champion," came back his powerful beam. "There are two little living ones forming within your body. Their birthing should be before the first autumn snows, does some tragic mishap not occur, so it might be wise of my lady to not go a-warring, this year."

Wavy, blue-black hair swirled about her square shoulders as she shook her head forcefully. "But I must, babes within me or no, Pah-Elmuh. I must fight at my Bili's side, must be with him every moment that I can . . . while still I can."

"What means my lady?" asked the Kleesahk.

"Only this," she replied. "I have . . . have had and still have a presentiment. Such is neither rare nor even unusual to women of my race and stock—my mother foresaw and foretold the exact circumstances and almost the exact day of her

173

death. So too did her grandmother and many another brave woman of revered memory amongst the Maidens of the Silver Lady.

"I know that I must stay by Bili, for my time of living with him is short now, and growing ever shorter. So, yes, I will fight beside him for as long as the Goddess allows it."

The huge being's not quite human facial features twisted in what Rahksahnah had learned to recognize as a frown. "It could well be, my lady, that ill-advised, strenuous activity carried on for too long could result in a miscarriage. And such might well kill you were I or another skilled Kleesahk not near to prevent what nearly happened to you last winter, at Sandee's Cot."

But she shook her head again. "No, Pah-Elmuh, I know how I will die—it will be of the bite of steel. It is in most ways very cloudy, this scene I presense. Bili is there, but I do not think it happens in a battle, though there are . . . will be . . . three deaths, in all—me, another woman and a man, but not Bili. My Bili will live on and on, a very long life for a human man."

"Yes," the Kleesahk agreed, "I have seen this, too, in the Lord Champion. He will live nearly eighty more summers—long and long for you short-lived true-men—and fully many will be the high and the mighty who will mourn his passing."

"That last, that is more than I could scry out." Her sloe-black eyes narrowed. "If you could read so much of Bili, then how much have you read of me, Pah-Elmuh? How much time is now left to me? Tell me!"

The massive, furry shoulders rose and fell once, a thoroughly human gesture of the hybrid humanoid. "Not even I can be certain of exact times, my lady," he hedged, breaking off eye contact with her.

"Please tell me, Pah-Elmuh." There was no mistaking the sincerity and firm resolve in her silent beaming. "I've *got to know*—can't you see?—for . . . for my Bili."

Still he kept his eyes averted, shaking his craggy head and beaming, "No, my lady, please, some things it . . . it is not good for true-men to know, it . . . it does things, terrible things sometimes, to their minds."

Mindspeaking still was a new way of communicating to Rahksahnah and now, in her rage, she forgot it completely.

174

"Tell me!" she hissed aloud from between clenched teeth. *"Damn you, tell me!"* The knuckles of her right hand shone out white as snow, so fiercely did she grip the wire-wound hilt of the dirk that hung from her belt.

Once more the Kleesahk looked into her blazing, angry eyes with his own infinitely sad ones. "Very well, my lady. No more than another year from today . . . perhaps not even that long. There are . . . reasons? things? . . . which prevent me from being more certain. Does my lady understand?"

Rahksahnah shuddered strongly and was very glad that she had learned to mindspeak, for she did not think that she could just then have forced cooperation from her lips and tongue.

She beamed, "Yes, yes, I think so, Pah-Elmuh. It . . . I think it—the whatever that beclouds your ability to see exactness and detail—must be akin to the . . . to this thick, misty, smoky something that hinders my own foreseeing of my death. Surely it is all but the mysterious Will of Her, the Lady, and who among us is fit to question the ways of the Goddess?

"Yes, I understand, Pah-Elmuh, and I thank you for that which you were able to reveal to me. The sum of your scrying and mine own will guide me in the scant time I have remaining.

"And Pah-Elmuh . . . please." She stepped closer and laid her hard, callused palm on his enormous, furry arm, tilting her head far, far back to maintain eye contact with the humanoid. "Bili, the Lord Champion, is to know none of this—not of the two babes within me, but especially not of . . . of this other. Please."

His massive chest expanded and contracted in a last, deep sigh. "Very well, my lady, it shall be as you wish. For my part, I shall reveal naught of these matters here discussed to the Lord Champion."

"It's because I know of your interest in odd animals that I mention this, David. We've run into two specimens of the oddest I've ever seen or heard of."

The transceiver crackled briefly, then Sternheimer's voice was asking, "Do they seem to be mutations of some pre-existing species, Jay?"

"It's possible," Corbett agreed. "I just don't know all that much about reptiles and the lower orders to tell with anything approaching certainty. What we really need is Mike Schiepficker or one of your other zoology types up here. If you could have him coptered up from Broomtown Base, I could have a party there waiting for him at prearranged coordinates in a few days."

"Is it worth the expense and the difficulties, Jay?" the Director asked. "Do you, in your considered judgment, think so?" The doctor paused, then added, "At least give me some idea what these things look like, eh?"

There was a wondering tone in Corbett's answer. "As best I can describe them, David, like a cross between a snake and some humongous earthworm. The biggest of the two we've thus far had to kill—and damned devilish hard they are to kill, too, even with the best part of their bodies blown away or apart with explosive bullets; the only sure way you can be certain the bastards won't take a sizable plug out of you is to cut off their heads—was around three and a half meters long and about sixteen or seventeen centimeters thick.

"There was very little tapering at either end, although there was a definite point on the tail. The head—I have one on the table before me right now—is broad and flattish with a rounded snout; *it* looks fairly reptilian, David, separated from the body, except that it has two rows of teeth.

"What about its skin?" asked Sternheimer. "How are the scales arranged?"

"It had no scales, David," was Corbett's reply. "As I said, it looked like a huge earthworm. Except for the head, the epidermis consisted of rings, just like a worm, but it was no worm. It had a bony spine, ribs, the works, including what looked like vestigial legs front and back. Another thing, David, every millimeter of the thing apparently secreted a sticky, viscous, mucuslike substance. Everywhere the damned thing crawled, it left a trail of slime like some gigantic garden slug or a snail. So, do you want to send me up an expert or not? Does this beastie sound worth it?"

"I'll let you know by tomorrow night, Jay, after I've had a chance to get together with O'Hare and Schiepficker. Do you need any additional supplies or personnel up there, for the primary mission? Arms, munitions, explosives or whatnot?"

"Not really, David," replied Corbett. "If anything, we have an overabundance of ammo just now, since the only use we've made of our weapons is killing animals for food . . . plus, of course, one bear and those two whatchamacallits we had to kill in self-defense. There've been no contacts of any sort with living humans, Ganiks or otherwise, since Johnny found that dead one back down the track.

"He and I took a patrol over as far west as what used to be—or so he avers—the camp of the overall leader of the Ganik raiders, and the only living things we found up there were a herd of scrubby ponies.

"However . . . look, David, if you do decide to send Mike up here, why not have the copter bring as much extra fuel as it can and still get decent range? I'll have the party I send down there pack spades and picks and dig a hole big enough to cache the fuel. I have a feeling that if we do suddenly need resupply or reinforcement, we're going to need it in one hell of a hurry and may not be able to spare the men to send down to pack them back up here. Okay?"

Erica's party of Ganik bullies worked northward into the range of steep, forested hills from the site of the successful ambush of the pursuing cavalrymen. They moved as fast as the terrain and the animals would allow, bearing a little westward and essaying to traverse the roughest and most thickly grown areas until, at last, they came down into a tiny, grassy vale watered by a burbling, icy-cold little streamlet barely a foot in width. There they made a cold camp, dining on their packed rations while the horses and other mounts grazed the new, tender shoots of grass. No fires were built, and after eating, all but the guards rolled up in their blankets and plunged into deep, exhausted sleep.

When they awoke out of that deep, deep slumber, in the dawning light of the new day, it was to find themselves completely surrounded by hundreds or thousands of big, burly men armed with immensely long pikes, shortswords and dirks.

"B'god, but you're a scruffy-looking lot!" remarked the brigadier, with the bare trace of a sneer. "Are you and your detachment the best that King Mahrtuhn can do? If he's scraped the barrel so deeply, perhaps we can march at once."

Erica could not place the mustachioed old man's accent, it or the less precise version spoken by the pikemen and most of their officers. Some of the pronunciations and usages of certain words reminded her a bit of the speech still affected by a fellow member of the Board of Science—Dr. Bertram Underwood Deverell Crawley, called Bud Crawley by his few friends, Creepy Crawley by the majority at the Center. The doctor had never—not in nearly a thousand years, despite the scores of different bodies his consciousness and intellect had inhabited in that amount of time—forgotten or allowed anyone else to forget his "Hahvahd" education or the additional bits of ersatz British speech patterns he had acquired during a two-year stint at Cambridge University.

Nonetheless, the language of the old man was far closer to educated twentieth-century English than anything she had heard at any place not controlled by the Center in a long, long while, and that ancient tongue that his so resembled was the one in which she answered him.

"You mean you think *we* are Kuhmbuhluhners, troops of King Mahrtuhn of Kuhmbuhluhn? Sir, we had thought that you were Kuhmbuhluhners. If you're not, then what are you?"

"Hummph!" snorted the brigadier. "No irregular or spy ever admits to his or her true status, of course. But I could almost believe you, woman, for you certainly don't talk like any other Kuhmbuhluhners I've ever heard. So I'll give you your question back: If you and your riders are not Kuhmbuhluhners, then what, pray tell, are you, and why did you find it necessary to murder so many of my cavalrymen?"

Erica shrugged. "As to what we are, we're all that's left of the Southern Ganiks. The rest were all, in their thousands, driven out of Kuhmbuhluhn or butchered by King Mahrtuhn's heavy cavalry, last summer. So we are no friends of that red-handed king or his people, needless to say.

"As regards your own troops: The first one, the hunter on the road, was killed because he loosed at one of us first, with a stone from his prod; as regards our ambuscade of the cavalry, well, they were hard on our trail with bared steel and the obvious intention of using it when they caught up to us, so we could hardly be expected not to try to turn the tables on them. What would you have done in our position, sir?"

178

"Probably just what you did, woman," said the brigadier bluntly, shrugging. "It was sound tactics, that, and you'd like to have gotten away from us clean, had you stayed up in those hills and not come down into the glen, as you did. But we were expecting you to do just that, you see. It is just what a party of Kuhmbuhluhners out to foment a guerrilla movement amongst the conquered Kuhmbuhluhners still living here, in the glen, would do."

She shook her tousled head ruefully. "The joke's on us, sir, grim joke that it is. We had no idea where we were, as we had no knowledge of this area, having but just come down from the northwest where we wintered. We thought that that little vale was just what it seemed to be—a good place to camp and rest and breathe the beasts before pushing on on the morrow."

"Then why," the brigadier snapped, "did you build not one fire? Were you as innocent as you'd have me to believe, you'd at least have set a watchfire to burning."

"And be spotted by the surviving pursuers?" replied Erica. "We're not fools . . . and we've been hunted before, by Kuhmbuhluhners, last autumn. Furthermore, we knew that we had not gotten all of that cavalry; yes, we dropped most of the heavy-armed, horse-mounted forward elements, but there were close to a score of spearmen on ponies coming up behind them when we withdrew. In our place, under such circumstances, would you have built a fire and slept sound beside such a beacon?"

He shrugged again, sipped at his flagon of beer, belched loudly twice, then said, "Probably I would have done just as you did, woman. You make sense. All right, let us imagine for the nonce that I truly believe your cover story. Just what are you Ganiks? I've heard the term from some of our enemies, along with some very disgusting supposed habits and practices allegedly common to Ganiks, but I've discounted the most of said stories, for similar garbage and slander has been attributed to us Skohshuns at various times and in varying places by *our* enemies, too.

"Now, tell me, woman, just why did King Mahrtuhn set his army against your people? Were you, perhaps, in rebellion against established authority?"

179

Erica thought hard before she framed an answer. In all truth, the Ganiks had been in rebellion against the Kuhmbuhluhners—an ongoing rebellion of scores of years' standing. That was all that the outlaw bunches could have been called, for all that the bunch Ganiks had preyed as much upon their own people, the farmer Ganiks, and the Ahrmehnee as they had upon the Kuhmbuhluhners. Furthermore, she was certain that most if not all of the "disgusting" facts that this old man had heard of the Ganiks were probably pure, unvarnished truth, but it would do no one any good just now to tell him so. But she also sensed him to be a shrewd, intuitive man, who would quickly sense a fabrication if she spread it on too thickly, gave more than a bare outline. The more closely the lie skirted the actual truth, the better, she felt, in this case.

"Not rebellion, sir, not really," she replied. "Ganiks, you see, were settled here for years before the Kuhmbuhluhners arrived. King Mahrtuhn's ancestors took over the north, here, where there had never been very many Ganiks, but they grew in numbers and aggressiveness and, over the years, encroached steadily upon Ganik lands. Most of the Ganiks were a peaceable folk to begin, but the dispossessed joined with the naturally warlike and as the resultant bands grew in size they began to openly resist further Kuhmbuhluhner encroachments. If you choose to call the defense of one's ancestral lands rebellion, then, yes, the Ganiks were indeed rebels."

The brigadier nodded. "Yes, land, that is always at the bottom of most wars. That's the reason we Skohshuns find ourselves in Kuhmbuhluhn, you know. Donkey's years back, we fought our way through the northern reaches of the Ohyoh country and settled in the southerly parts, then fought as much as two or three times a year to hold what we'd won at such a bloody price. But to the natives there we always were strangers, interlopers. Finally, three years or so back, the various principalities settled their differences and united to push us out or exterminate us. We fought for a while, resisted until it became obvious that we could not win against so many determined foemen.

"We sent scouts in various directions, seeking a land to which we could withdraw. Those who came into Kuhmbuhluhn brought back reports that it was sparsely settled in its northwestern parts, but held promise of richness when once put under the plow. So we developed one of our small river ports into a large, strong embarkation point and began a gradual, fighting withdrawal from our Ohyoh lands. We ferried over a small but powerful force, first, then began to send noncombatants a few at the time.

"The Kuhmbuhluhners began to attack us savagely, and when we determined that they were using this glen as a base of operations against us, we brought over enough pikemen to take it from them. Not that that was an easy task, mind you, not in any way. Many a brave man lost his life in that undertaking, you may be sure. But it was done! We Skohshuns are nothing if not a stubborn lot.

"We have fought the Kuhmbuhluhners often since then, even before we had all of our folk over the river as we now do, thanks in no small part to that fortuitous hard freeze of last winter which allowed us to cross the river without the use of boats or barges. We came very close to utterly routing their heavy-armed cavalry last autumn, for all that a good third of our forces still were engaged across the river, holding off the allied army of the Ohyohers. Now that we have all of our host here, I see no reason why we cannot conquer the best part of Kuhmbuhluhn this summer."

The old man paused for another draft of beer, then regarded Erica and Bowley for a moment before saying, "Despite the near certain triumph of our arms, native auxiliaries who know the country better than do we could likely be most helpful to us in this final year of our conquest. I feel entirely confident that the earl would be most generous to willing allies against these Kuhmbuhluhners.

"Now if I decided to free one or two of you to ride south, how many Ganiks do you think could be brought back here to join us, fight with us against the common enemy?"

Erica felt like pinching herself to be certain that she was not dreaming it all. It sounded just too good to be true. The two of them alone, well mounted, with Bowley's proven skills at keeping out of sight in hostile country, should have little if any difficulty in passing through the thinly settled Kuhmbuhluhn lands, and thence down one of the tracks to Broomtown Base, and so to the Center.

But then Merle Bowley proceeded to blow it!

"Ganiks, you wawnts?" he snorted. "Wal, you jes' too late, mistuh! It ain't no Ganiks lef' in awl Kuhmbuhluhn, 'ceptin' of us'uns, it ain't. Them whut din' run awf is daid, an' by Plooshun, thet be the trufe!"

Had she still had her pistol, Erica would likely have shot him, so coldly furious was she.

Banners and pennons snapping in a fresh mountain breeze, armor and weapons flashing in a warming sun, King Mahrtuhn, his son and his grandson, his personal staff and his officers filed out of the citadel and rode through the brightly bedecked streets of the lower city, between rows of cheering citizens.

Thoheeks Bili of Morguhn sat his glossy-black warhorse in the procession beside one of the other officers. While Mahvros—his mount and faithful horse brother—joyously flexed his pasterns in his own parade strut, Bili mindspoke Rahksahnah, who rode farther back in the procession.

"I sense no good in this insanity, my dear. I wonder how loudly these poor fools would cheer and applaud could they sense what Pah-Elmuh and I can in the king. Mahrtuhn and his grandson, too, seem walking, talking, breathing corpses to me and have for weeks, increasingly. The look, the feel, even the sweet-sick smell of death is in them, about them, and I know that Pah-Elmuh has sensed it too, else he'd not have tried to persuade Mahrtuhn not to ride out himself or at least to leave his grandson here, if go to fight he must."

"Do you think, Bili," she beamed, "that he will actually allow us, give us the time, to try your ancestor's tactic against the pike hedge before he and his gentry charge? And, even if he does, how many of us do you think will survive it?"

"Yes," he silently replied, "if our Byruhn has anything to say on the matter, we'll get our chance to soften up the formation, chop an opening for the heavy-armed horse to aim for. And if everyone remembers the drill, it *will* work, Rahksahnah; I'm not the first to copy my many-times-great-grandsire, you know—it's worked for others too, over the years."

Slowly, the mounted column passed through the city, filed out of the gates and down the path flanking the massive walls, to finally join the bulk of the army massed upon the plain.

As he took his place at the head of his squadron, Bili looked back at the city and its fluttering decorations. He hoped that he and Rahksahnah and all of the other men and women who rode behind his Red Eagle Banner would see that city again.

EPILOGUE

Crushed blossoms and herbs littered the carpeted floor of the high-ceilinged, dim chamber, while scented resins and other varieties of incense glowed atop the coals in the many braziers. But despite these, the stench of suppurating flesh was easily detected. Three persons occupied the room—old Bili of Morguhn, Prince of Karaleenos, lay upon the massive bed, slowly dying of his infected wounds, while his overlords, the Undying High Lords Milo of Morai and Tim of Sanderz-Vawn, stood in a far corner talking in hushed tones.

The two High Lords thought old Bili completely comatose, but he was not. He had, for some hours now, been mentally reliving his tempestuous days of youth and love and war, now almost four score years in the past. The combination of drugs and posthypnotic suggestion by use of which the Zahrtohgahn physicians were easing his pain made such journeyings down the dim corridors of memory often far more real than the smoky, stinking chamber and the sweat-soaked bed upon which his old, torn, broken body now lay.

While the two low voices droned on—the baritone of Lord Milo, the tenor of Bili's half-brother, Lord Tim—the dying prince thought, "New Kuhmbuhluhnburk. Well, we did see it again, the most of my squadron, but by then the king was dead along with his heir, and poor, brave, cursed Prince Byruhn gravely wounded. Sun and Wind be praised that that city was as good as invulnerable to attack, for King Mahrtuhn's death-dealing stupidity left precious few of the New Kuhmbuhluhn heavy-armed fighters alive or unwounded to defend it from the Skohshuns.

"Of course, as well-victualed and -watered as that city was, we could easily have sat up there until the Skohshuns

184

starved or grew long, white beards in their siege-camps and lines. But with crawling, nameless horror stalking the streets of the city by night . . .''

"*Aaarrgh!*" The burning flash of agony struck the old man with such unexpected suddenness that he cried out before he could clamp down his worn teeth to stifle the cry. His wasted body involuntarily flexed, and this gave birth to more pain.

Abruptly, the speakers broke off their low-voiced conversation, and after a second, one hurried out, to return with a brace of dark-skinned men clad in flowing, white garments, the younger of them bearing a small, brass-bound leathern chest.

Dimly, seemingly floating above him, Bili recognized the wrinkled face of Master Ahkmehd, concern, pity and sorrow mingling in his brown eyes.

"Well, old friend," rasped Bili hoarsely, from between his clenched teeth, "we've not many more rods to ride in company, you and I."

The Zahrtohgahn nodded, sadly. "If only my lord had seen fit to allow me to remove the smashed, poisoned limbs . . ."

A fresh wave of pain caused old Bili to tighten his jaws until the knots of muscle stood out at the corners and beads of sweat popped from his forehead. When he again spoke, his voice was noticeably weaker. "I'd have died anyway and you well know it, Master Ahkmehd. Since Sacred Sun granted me the choice, I simply chose to die whole. Now, if it please you, I'll have a bit more of that vile concoction you brew . . . that, and a sharp-pointed dagger, for I feel that it is about time that I commence another journey, one long-deferred. And, please, have your apprentice take my axe off yonder wall and lay it here, beside me. Who truly knows but what I may not need it on this new road I'll so shortly ride?"